AN UNDERWATER MYSTERY.
AND A MAGIC MOMENT OF DISCOVERY . . .

It was there. Not an object of fear, but of awe. Sarah stepped backwards, one foot behind the other. Her sketchbook trembled in her hands. "Mark," she called hoarsely. "Mark, come down here, please."

The creature lay still, back arching in the water, wavelets licking at its skin. Its head and neck curled from side to side, slowly seeking food.

"What?" Mark called, plunging down the embankment to her side. He hadn't brought a camera.

"There," she said, with a grand wave at the loch, the wake, the fish, the basking creature. It seized another salmon, tilted its neck upwards, splashed about as if playing with its prey.

Mark collapsed onto a rock, swearing slowly, reverently, under his breath. Sarah plucked a pencil from her pocket and began to sketch.

"No camera," Mark mourned. "Strobe's blown a fuse. No sonar, no hydrophone."

"You can see it, can't you?" Sarah flipped to the next page. Magic flowed through her eyes, through her fingertips; the image leaped from the paper.

"I see it," said Mark. "Whether it's really there is another matter."

The creature slipped beneath the waves and disappeared. The water smoothed itself and lay still. The sunsheen reflected from the surface of the loch like from a burnished shield . . .

—From "Out of Darkness"
by Lillian Stewart Carl

Magic Tales Anthology Series From Ace Books

SEASERPENTS!

EDITED BY
JACK DANN & GARDNER DOZOIS

ACE BOOKS, NEW YORK

SEASERPENTS!

An Ace Book/published by arrangement with
the editors

PRINTING HISTORY
Ace edition / December 1989

ISBN: 0-441-75682-4

Ace Books are published by The Berkley Publishing Group,
200 Madison Avenue, New York, New York 10016.
The name ''ACE'' and the ''A'' logo are
trademarks belonging to Charter Communications, Inc.

PRINTED IN THE UNITED STATES OF AMERICA

10 9 8 7 6 5 4 3 2 1

The editors would like to thank the following people for their help and support:

Susan Casper, Jeanne Van Buren Dann, Patrick Delahunt, Edward Ferman, Virginia Kidd, Trina King, Brian Perry and Tawna Lewis of *Fat Cat Books* (263 Main St., Johnson City, New York 13790), Stuart Schiff, Jody Scobie, the staffs of the Vestal Public Library and the Binghamton Public Library, Tom Whitehead of the Special Collections Department of the Paley Library at Temple University (and his staff, especially John Betancourt and Connie King), Sheila Williams, and special thanks to our editors, Susan Allison and Ginjer Buchanan.

CONTENTS

Preface

by

Gardner Dozois and Jack Dann

Of all the fabulous creatures who populate the worlds of fantasy—dragons, unicorns, griffins, trolls, mermaids—the sea serpent is the only one who may actually *exist* in the corporeal world as well as in the world of the imagination. At the very least, it is the one fabulous beast whose existence is still widely *believed* in by a significant percentage of the contemporary population. For instance, there are probably very few (if any) citizens of the modern world who still believe in the actual physical existence of, say, griffins or sphinxes or centaurs—but every year there are dozens of eyewitness reports of sea serpents (or USOs—Unidentified Swimming Objects—as they are sometimes called), as there have been year after year for centuries.

There have been literally thousands of reports of sea serpents, many of them by trained observers: naturalists, oceanographers, experienced seamen, naval officers, submarine crews. Sometimes they have been seen by hundreds of people at once, as in the nineteenth-century sighting by the crew of HMS *Daedalus*, or in the sightings of the famous Gloucester Sea Serpent, who for a decade from 1817 on appeared every summer off the New England coast, where it was often observed by crowds of monster-watchers. Nor are sea serpents restricted to the open ocean. Similar creatures known as "lake monsters" have been spotted for hundreds of years in lakes all over the world. The Loch Ness Monster—familiarly known as "Nessie"—is the most famous of these elusive creatures, but there is also "Issie," the monster of Japan's Lake Ikeda, "Champ," the monster of Lake Champlain, "Ogopogo," the monster of western Canada's Lake Okanagan, "Manipogo," the monster of Manitoba's Lake Winnipegosis, Sweden's Storsjön Animal, the Black Beast of Quebec's Lake Ponenegamook, and Iceland's Lágarfljótsormur, among many others.

Even after hundreds of sightings, though, no irrefutable *physical* evidence of the existence of sea serpents has ever been found—barring a few blurry and indistinct photographs that are not only inconclusive, but often fiercely contested by people who are convinced that they are the work of hoaxers. None of these creatures have ever been captured or killed, no authenticated remains or carcasses have ever been found; even the fossil record is empty of their traces.

So then, if we say, for the sake of argument, that sea serpents do *not* exist—then just what is it that all of these people have been *seeing*?

There are as many theories as there are theorists. Discounting deliberate hoaxes, delusions, and hallucinations, the candidates include: illusions caused by winds or currents, floating trees, the wash from passing vessels, sea weed, motorboats, upwelling gas bubbles, masses of floating birds, gaseous rubbish floating up from the bottom, whales, schools of porpoises, watersnakes, leaping salmon, sturgeons, elephant seals, walruses, giant sea turtles (which do exist), giant long-necked seals (whose existence is conjectural), giant otters of an unknown species (the largest known otter *was* eight feet long—but sea serpents are often reported to be forty feet long or more), conger eels, ribbonfish, manta rays, basking sharks, sunfish, sea-going crocodiles, sea slugs (of an unknown giant variety), worms (ditto), alligator gars, giant squids, giant octopuses, the supposedly extinct Steller's Sea Cow (the last living specimen of which was seen in 1768), manatees, zeuglodons (primitive ancestral whales, the skeletons of which *do* look quite a bit like eyewitness descriptions of sea serpents), and, of course, the ever-popular Plesiosaurs (the image of the sea serpent as a long-necked, flippered, dinosaurlike swimming prehistoric survivor has probably established itself as the most common idea of what sea serpents would look like—if we could ever find one).

And yet there *is* some circumstantial physical evidence: a very detailed and sober description in a wartime report of a dead monster that washed ashore in Scotland in 1942; the sonar gear of the USS *Stein*, which, when hauled out in drydock for examination, proved to have been gouged and battered by a creature of "a species still unknown to science"—who had left hundreds of pointed teeth embedded in the rubber covering of the sonar dome; inconclusive but suggestive sonar tracings of vast swimming objects of unknown types that have been recorded from time to time; and the aforementioned photographs, some of which, in spite of their blurriness, *do* seem to show a large physical object of *some* sort out in the middle of the water where no such object should be.

So who knows. One thing is sure—if they caught Nessie tomorrow, all the other candidates (however reasonable they might now seem) for what Unidentified Swimming Objects really are would be at once dismissed, and all the reasons why there *couldn't* be such a creature would be instantly and easily forgotten.

In the meantime, whether sea serpents exist in fact or not, they have been alive and swimming for years in the imaginations of fantasy writers, and swim there still, mysterious and huge, elusive and powerful and vast . . . as the stories you are about to read will vividly and evocatively demonstrate.

Algy

by

L. Sprague de Camp

L. Sprague de Camp is a seminal figure, one whose career spans almost the entire development of modern fantasy and SF. For the fantasy magazine Unknown *in the late 1930s, he helped create a whole new modern style of fantasy writing—funny, whimsical, and irreverent—of which he is still the most prominent practitioner. His most famous books include* Lest Darkness Fall, The Incomplete Enchanter *(with Fletcher Pratt), and* Rogue Queen. *His most recent book is* Bones of Zora, *a novel written in collaboration with his wife Catherine Crook de Camp.*

Here he takes us to the sunny, sylvan, deceptively sleepy shores of peaceful Lake Algonquin for a traditional lake monster sighting that is not quite what it seems—in more ways than one!

* * *

When I parked behind my aunt's camp on Lake Algonquin, the first face I saw was Mike Devlin's wrinkled brown one. Mike said:

"Hello, Mr. Newbury! Sure, it's good to see you again. Have ye been hearin' about *it*?"

"About what?"

"The monster—the Lake Algonquin monster."

"Good lord, no! I've been in France, getting married. Darling, this is my old friend Mike Devlin. Mike, my wife Denise."

"Me, I am enchanted, Monsieur," said Denise, whose English was still a little uncertain.

"You got yourself a good man, Mrs. Newbury," said Mike. "I'm after knowing him since he was no bigger'n a chipmunk. Gimme them bags."

"I'll take this one," I said. "Now, what's this about a monster?"

Mike scratched his crisp gray curls. "They do be saying that, on dark nights, something comes up in the lake and shticks its head out to look around. But nobody's after getting a good look

1

at it. There's newspaper fellies, and a whole gang of Scotchmen are watching for it, out on Indian Point.''

''You mean we have a home-grown version of the Loch Ness monster?''

''I do that.''

''How come the Scots came over here? I thought they had their own lake monster. Casing the competition, maybe?''

''It could be that, Mr. Newbury. They're members of some society that tracks down the shtories of sea serpents and all them things.''

''Where's my aunt?''

''Mrs. Colton and Miss Colton are out in the rowboat, looking for the monster. If they find it, I'm thinking they'll wish they hadn't.''

Mike took us into the camp—a comfortable, three-story house of spruce logs, shaded by huge old pines—and showed us our room. He pointed at the north window. ''If you look sharp, you can see the Scotchmen out there on the point.''

I got out the binoculars that I had brought for wild-life watching. Near the end of Indian Point was a cluster of figures around some instruments. I handed the glasses to Denise.

The year before, Mike had been left without a job when my old schoolmate, Alfred Ten Eyck, had been drowned in the quake that sank Ten Eyck Island. I recommended Mike to my aunt, whose camp on Lake Algonquin was twenty miles from Gahato. Since my aunt was a widow with children grown and flown, she could not keep up the place without a handy man. Mike—an ex-lumberjack, of Canadian birth despite his brogue—filled the bill. My aunt had invited Denise and me to spend our honeymoon at the camp. Her daughter Linda was also vacationing there.

Settled, we went down to the dock to look for my aunt and my cousin. Several boats were out on the lake, but too far away to recognize. We waved without result.

''Let's go call on the Scots,'' I said. ''Are you up to a three-quarter-mile hike?''

''That is about one kilometer, no? *Allons!*''

The trail wanders along the shore from the camp to Indian Point. When I was a kid there in summer, I used to clear the brush out of this trail. It had been neglected, so we had to push through in places or climb over deadfalls. At one point, we passed a little shed, almost hidden among the spruces, standing between us and the water.

"What is that, Willy?" asked Denise.

"There used to be a little hot-air engine there, to pump water up to the attic tank in the camp. When I was a kid, I collected wood and fired up that engine. It was a marvelous little gadget— not efficient, but simple, and it always worked. Now they have an electric pump."

Near the end of Indian Point, the timber thins. There were the Scots around their instruments. As we came closer, I saw four men in tweeds and a battery of cameras and telescopes. They looked around as we approached. I said: "Hello!"

Their first response was reserved. When I identified myself as Mrs. Colton's nephew and guest, however, they became friendly.

"My name's Kintyre," said one of them, thrusting out a hand. He was a big, powerful-looking, weather-beaten man with graying blond hair, a bushy mustache, a monocle screwed into one eye, and the baggiest tweeds of the lot. The only other genuine monocle-wearer I had ever known was a German colonel, captured in the last month of the war.

"And I'm Ian Selkirk," said another, with a beautiful red beard. (This was before anybody but artists wore them.) He continued: "Lord Kintyre pays the siller on this safari, so he's the laird. We have to kneel before him and put our hands in his and swear fealty every morning."

Lord Kintyre guffawed and introduced the remaining two: Wallace Farg and James MacLachlan. Kintyre spoke British public-school English; Farg, such strong "braid Scots" that I could hardly understand him. The speech of the other two lay somewhere in between. At their invitation, we peered through the telescopes.

"What about this monster?" I said. "I've been out of the country."

They all started talking at once until Lord Kintyre shouted them down. He told me essentially what Mike Devlin had, adding:

"The bloody thing only comes up at night. Can't say I blame it, with all those damned motorboats buzzing around. Enough to scare any right-thinking monster. I've been trying to get your town fathers to forbid 'em, but no luck. The younger set dotes on 'em. So we may never get a good look at Algy."

"Algae?" I said, thinking he meant the seaweed.

"Surely. You Americans call our monster 'Nessie,' so why shouldn't we call the Lake Algonquin monster 'Algy'? But I'm afraid one of these damned stinkpots will run into the poor creature and injure it. I say, are you and your lovely bride coming to the ball tomorrow at the Lodge?"

"Why, my lordship—I mean your lord—"

"Call me Alec," roared his lordship. "Everyone else does. Short for Alexander Mull, second Baron Kintyre. My old man sold so much scotch whiskey abroad, after you chaps got rid of the weird Prohibition law, that Baldwin figgered he had to do something for him. Now, laddie, how about the dance? I'm footing the bill."

"Sure," I said, "if Denise can put up with my two left feet."

Back at the camp, we met my aunt and her daughter coming back from their row. The sky was clouding over. Linda Colton was a tall, willowy blonde, highly nubile if you didn't mind her washed-out look. Nice girl, but not exactly brilliant. After the introductions, my Aunt Frances said:

"George Vreeland's coming over for dinner tonight. Briggs gave him the time off. Do you know him?"

"I've met him," I said. "He was a cousin of my late friend, Alfred Ten Eyck. I thought Vreeland had gone to California?"

"He's back and working as a desk clerk for Briggs," said Aunt Frances.

Joe Briggs was proprietor of the Algonquin Lodge, a couple of miles around the shore from the Colton camp, the other way from Indian Point. Linda Colton said:

"George says he's going to get one of those frogman's diving suits to go after the monster."

"I doubt if he'll get very far," I said. "The water's so full of vegetable matter, you can't see your hand before your face when you're more than a couple of feet down. When they put in the dam to raise the lake level, they didn't bother to clear all the timber out of the flooded land first."

I could have added that what I had heard about George Vreeland was not good. Alfred Ten Eyck claimed that, when Alfred was away, George had rented the camp on Ten Eyck Island from him. While there, he had sold most of Alfred's big collection of guns in the camp to various locals. He pocketed the money and skipped out before Alfred returned. I wouldn't call Vreeland wicked or vicious—just one of those old unreliables, unable to resist the least temptation.

Instead, I told about our meeting the Scots. Linda said: "Didn't you think Ian Selkirk just the handsomest thing you ever saw?"

"I'm no judge of male beauty," I said. "He looked like a well-set-up-man, with the usual number of everything. I don't know that I'd go for that beard, but that's his business."

"He grew it in the war, when he was on a submarine," said Linda.

Denise said: "If you will excuse me, I looked at Mr. Selkirk, too. But yes, he is handsome. And he knows it—maybe a little too well, *hein*?"

My cousin Linda changed the subject.

At dinner time, George Vreeland came roaring over from the Lodge in an outboard. He did not remember me at first, since I had met the little man only casually, and that back in the thirties when we were mere striplings.

It was plain that Vreeland was sweet on Linda Colton, for all that she was an inch taller than he. He talked in grandiose terms of his plans for diving in pursuit of Algy. I said:

"It seems to me that, if there is no monster, you're wasting your time. If there is a monster, and you disturb it, you'll probably end up in its stomach."

"Oh, Willy!" said Linda. "That's the way he always was, George, even as a boy. Whenever we'd get some beautiful, romantic, adventurous idea, he'd come out with some commonsense remark, like a cynical old gentleman, and shoot down our lovely plan in flames."

"Oh, I'll have something to protect myself with," said Vreeland. "A spear-gun or something—that is, if the goddamned Scotchmen don't harpoon the thing first."

"They told me they had no intention of hurting it," I said.

"Don't trust those treacherous Celts. Trying to stop our motorboats, ha! They'd ruin the whole summer-visitor season, just to get a strip of movie film of the monster."

Soon after dinner, my Aunt Frances called our attention to distant lightning. It flared lavender against the clouds, which hung low above the forested Adirondack ridges.

"George," she said, "since you came by water, you'd better be starting back, unless you want Linda to drive you to the Lodge and come back tomorrow for your boat."

"No, I'll be going," said Vreeland. "I have the night duty tonight."

After he had gone, we talked family matters for an hour or so. Then an outburst of yells brought us out on the porch.

The noise came from the direction of Indian Point. I could see little flickers of light from the Scottish observation post. Evidently the Scots thought they had seen something.

Between flashes of lightning, the lake was too dark to make out anything. "Wait till I get my glasses," I said.

The glasses proved of no help so long as the lake remained dark. Then a bright flash showed me something—a dark lump—out on the lake. It was perhaps a hundred yards away, although it is hard to estimate such distances.

I kept straining my vision, while the three women buzzed with questions. I picked up the thing in several more lightning flashes. It seemed to be moving across my field of vision. It also seemed to rise and fall. At least, it looked different in successive glimpses. I handed the glasses to my aunt, so that the women could have a look.

Then thunder roared and the rain came down. Soon we could see nothing at all. Even the hardy Scots gave up and went back to the Lodge.

When we awoke next morning, it was still raining. We came late to breakfast. When I started to apologize, Linda Colton said:

"Oh, that's all right, Willy. We know that honeymooners like any excuse to stay in bed."

I grinned sheepishly. Denise, who comes from a somewhat straitlaced French Protestant family, stared hard at her orange juice.

That morning, I studied economics for my trust company job. By noon, the rain had stopped and the skies had begun to clear. When the afternoon turned warm, I suggested a swim. Denise said:

"But, Willy, *mon cher*, if there is a monster there, what if it eats us?"

"Listen, darling, my friends and kinsmen and I have been

swimming in these lakes for most of my thirty-two years, and Algy has never bitten any of us. If there is a monster here, it's had plenty of chances.

"Besides, I used to argue with the geology prof at M.I.T. about such monsters. He explained that such a critter needs an area big enough to support the food, such as fish, that it feeds on. Lake Algonquin couldn't support anything much bigger than a snapping turtle. *Il n'y a rien a craindre.*"

"Well then, how about the alligators and crocodiles that you have in the Florida? They do not need a whole sea to live in," she said.

"In the first place," I explained, "they live in interconnected bodies of water, so they can move around from one to another. You need, not just enough area for one, but fifty or a hundred times that much, to support a breeding population. Otherwise, the species dies out. So don't look for a *Plesiosaurus* or a *Mosasaurus* in these lakes. Besides, no alligator—or any reptile of that size—could survive the winters here, where the lakes freeze over."

Denise looked doubtful, but she went swimming. I fear, however, that I do not have enough masochist in me really to enjoy that icy Adirondack water.

When we were dried and changed, we hiked out to Indian Point, partly to warm up and partly to see how the Scots were doing. Present were Farg, MacLachlan, and another man introduced to us as Professor Ballardie. Him I understood to be the big brain of the expedition. They were setting up a searchlight along with their other gear.

"There may be nought to it at all," said Ballardie, a cheerful little gray-haired man. "But this is the only way to find out."

"Aye," said Farg. "If we dinna try, we sanna learn."

I brought up the arguments of the M.I.T. professor of geology. As I expected, for every argument of mine they had ten counter-arguments. I thought it best to pipe down and listen; after all, I was not selling securities in their enterprise. When Ballardie ran out of breath, I asked:

"Where's Mr. Selkirk?"

"He's off this afternoon," said MacLachlan.

Farg added: "Forbye, he'll be makin' hissel braw for the ba'."
At least that is what I think he said.

* * *

My aunt decided not to go to the "ba'." George Vreeland came across the lake in his motorboat and carried Denise, Linda, and me back to the Lodge. Since this all happened before the era of youthful scruffiness in the sixties, both George and I had donned coat and tie. While we were trudging up the path from the Lodge dock, I could hear Lord Kintyre's booming laugh.

Inside, there was Joe Briggs, fat and red-faced, playing the genial host. I saw what Wallace Farg had meant by Selkirk's making himself "braw for the ba'." Selkirk had on a kilt, complete with sporran, dirk in the stocking, and one of those short little jackets with angular silver buttons—the works. Lord Kintyre was similarly clad, although the rest of the Scots made do with their weathered tweeds. We met Lady Kintyre, a mousey little gray-haired woman, and a couple more Scots whom I had not yet seen.

I was struggling through a rumba with Denise when Vreeland and Linda went by. Selkirk stepped up and tapped Vreeland on the arm. "May I cut in?" he said pleasantly.

I doubt if Vreeland even knew about the custom of cutting. While he gaped, Selkirk whisked Linda neatly out of his arms and danced off with her. When we passed them again, he had turned on the charm, whispering in Linda's ear and making her laugh.

After more dances and drinks, Lord Kintyre roared: "Now we'll show you a couple of Scottish dances. Ian, bring the young lady out here to demonstrate."

Selkirk led out Linda Colton. Having enough trouble with dances that I have practiced in advance, I was happy to steer Denise back to the bar. Since Lord Kintyre was paying, and since my Aunt Frances served nothing stronger than sherry, I was glad to wrap myself around some real booze.

There was George Vreeland, sopping up the sauce. His face was flushed, his speech was thick, and his manner was offensive. We avoided him.

We watched the Scottish dances from the sidelines. When it came time to go, Vreeland was not to be found. In the end, Selkirk drove us back to my aunt's camp in one of the expedition's cars. Linda had stars in her eyes when she bid us goodnight.

About three in the morning came another outburst of sound from Indian Point. From our windows, I saw nothing except the wavering beam of the searchlight. I was not fascinated enough by lake monsters to get up and go out, but the racket kept up for over an hour. We never did get back to sleep, although I would not say that the time till morning was wasted.

The Scots later said that they had seen Algy again and that he hung around so long that they launched a boat to get a closer look at him. Then, however, he dived.

Sunday was one of those rare fine days. Denise and I took a hike in the morning and in the afternoon went out on the lake. We had been rowing for maybe half an hour when Denise said:

"There is a canoe, Willy, which comes from your aunt's dock. I think I see the red beard of the Mr. Selkirk."

Sure enough, there came Ian Selkirk and Linda Colton out in one of Joe Briggs's rentable canoes. I waved, but they must have been so absorbed in each other that they never saw us.

When they got closer, I saw that they were in bathing suits. This is not a bad idea, if you want to paddle a canoe without previous experience. Linda, in the stern, was paddling and calling out instructions to Selkirk in the bow.

I rested on my oars, watching. After a while, they stopped paddling. I noticed something odd about their position. They had slid off their thwarts and were sitting on the bottom, so only their heads and shoulders showed. They were inching closer to each other, all the while talking and laughing at a great rate.

Denise said: "I think they are about to try *un petit peu de l'amour*."

"It's an idea," I said, "if you remember to keep the weight well down in the boat." I wondered if I ought to try to save my cousin's virtue. This was before the sexual revolution, when many families still took their girls' virtue seriously. But then, I did not even know whether Linda had any virtue to save.

"Well," said Denise, misreading the look on my face, "don't you get any such ideas, my old. Me, I could not enjoy it in a boat for fear of tipping over."

The two were now so close together that Selkirk was embracing Linda. I do not know what would have happened if Algy had not interfered.

Out of the water, on the lakeward side of the canoe and not ten feet from that craft, a reptilian head, as big as that of a horse, arose on a long, thick neck. The head had staring white eyeballs and long white fangs. It rose six feet out of the water and glared down upon the occupants of the canoe.

It took several seconds for the canoeists to realize that they were under observation. Then Linda shrieked.

Ian Selkirk looked around, jumped up, dove overboard, and struck out for shore at an Olympic speed. He left the rocking canoe and Linda behind.

"The dastard!" I said. "I'm going closer."

"Willy!" cried Denise. "It will devour us!"

"No it won't. Take a second look. It's just some sort of amusement-park dragon."

Disregarding Denise's plaints, I rowed towards the apparition. Algy proved a gaudily painted structure of sponge rubber. I poked it with an oar to make sure and then rowed to the canoe.

Linda was in hysterics, but she calmed down when she saw me. Soon she was paddling the canoe back towards our dock. We followed in the rowboat.

Ashore, we met Mike Devlin. He said: "Mr. Newbury, what's all this about the monster? The young Scotchman is after asking—"

Then the two figures appeared running on the trail from Indian Point. First came George Vreeland with a bloody nose. After him pounded Ian Selkirk, in swimming trunks and sneakers, howling imprecations in some tongue I did not recognize. It may have been very braid Scots, or it may have been Gaelic. They vanished along the road to the Lodge.

"It's the pump shed," said Mike. "The Scotchman was asking me if there was any such place. I told him yes, and off he went like the banshee was after him."

"Let's go see," I said.

We had to push through heavy brush and second growth to get to the pump shed, for nobody had gone there in years. A canoe was moored at the edge of the water below the shed.

Inside the shed, dust and drifted pine needles lay thick. The old hot-air engine and pump were covered with rust. But something new had been added.

"Mother of God, look at that!" said Mike. "So that's how the young felly had us fooled!"

On the inside wall of the shed were mounted a pair of wind-lasses. Each consisted of a drum, around which a number of turns of clothesline had been wrapped, and a crank handle for turning the drum. The ropes led out through holes in the wall. They extended to the water's edge and disappeared into the lake on divergent paths.

It was clear what Vreeland had done. He had laid a couple of stanchions—concrete blocks or the like—on the lake bottom, with pulleys or rings stapled to them. The ropes, attached to Algy, led through these stanchions and back to the shed. By turning the cranks, one could make Algy, who was buoyant, rise or sink or, within limits, move horizontally along the surface.

Mike explained: "I heard the racket, and I seen the monster out in the water and the young Scotchman swimming for shore like the Devil was ahint of him. When he climbed out and got his breath, he says: 'It's after me!'

" 'Look, man,' I says. 'Anybody can see 'tis not a real monster at all, with the boats paddling all around it, and shtanding shtill in the water.'

"So he looks. 'By God, you're right!' he says. Now this is a smart young Scotchman, and it don't take him ten seconds to figure out what's happened. 'Quick!' he says. 'Is there any sort of hut or cabin along the shore near here?' So I tell him about the old pump house. 'I'll show you,' I says. 'No, thanks,' he says. 'Just tell me where it is. I don't want any witnesses.' And off he goes. He must have caught Mr. Vreeland just coming out."

Denise went into a fit of giggles until I had to pound her back. *"Comme c'est rigolo donc!"*

Every boat on Lake Algonquin soon put out for a look at the monster. Selkirk did not succeed in annihilating Vreeland. The latter ducked into the woods and, knowing the terrain, soon lost his pursuer. Hours later, Selkirk, scratched and mosquito-bitten, staggered back to the Lodge. I suppose he felt his loss of face too keenly to show himself, for none of us saw him again.

My cousin Linda accepted neither of these dubious suitors. A year later, she married a rising-young-businessman type.

Next morning I got a telephone call. "Mr. Wilson Newbury, please . . . Oh, is that you, Willy? Alec Kintyre here. I say, Willy, could you do me a favor? My lads have packed up all our gear to leave, but I want to go over the ground once more with someone who knows it. Could you . . ."

Half an hour later, I was showing Lord Kintyre the shed in which Vreeland had set up his control mechanism.

"You know," said Lord Kintyre, "it was all Briggs's doing."

"How so?"

"When Vreeland came in this morning, he and Briggs got into a blazing quarrel, and Vreeland blew the gaff. Seems Briggs hired him last spring to set up this hoax, to draw more summer trade. It did, too.

"They might have got away with it, since Vreeland was supposed to surface the bloody monster only at night. He'd paddle over in that canoe so the noise of his motorboat wouldn't give him away. Everybody knew he was a damned stinkpot fanatic, so nobody suspected him of being a canoeist.

"Ian Selkirk spoilt the scheme. Vreeland was so eager to do Ian one in the eye that he brought up Algy in broad daylight. Then it took only a good second look to show it was a fake. The lads on the point realized that when they got their telescopes on it.

"Rum thing about Ian. He's not really a coward—he was in submarines with me during the war—but just this once he panicked. He didn't even wait to help with the packing but left last night. Trouble with Ian is, all he thinks of is dipping his wick. Now could we go out for a look at Algy?"

I took Lord Kintyre out in the Colton rowboat. We circled Algy, who was still sitting in the water as he had been left.

Algy consisted of head, six feet of neck, and an egg-shaped body without limbs, save for a kind of rudder aft. This fin made the monster face forward when towed through the water, so that Vreeland could parade the thing back and forth, as far as his rope tackle allowed.

The last Scots had left Indian Point with their apparatus. We moved up close to Algy, and Lord Kintyre took out a pocket knife. "I'll cut a little piece off as a souvenir, if you don't mind," he said.

He got his piece of sponge rubber, and we started back. Then I said: "Hey, Alec! Look around!"

Something was happening to Algy. He was moving back and forth by jerks, stirring the water to foam. The jerks became wider and more violent. Have you ever seen a dog shake a squirrel or similar small prey to death? Algy was moving as if he had been seized from below and was being thus shaken. The boat rocked in the waves. Lord Kintyre's monocle fell out and dangled on its string. Algy was drawn down until he almost disappeared.

Then the water quieted. Algy bobbed up again—but in pieces. We sat quietly, afraid (at least I was) to move or speak, lest whatever had mangled Algy come for us.

When nothing more happened, I took a few cautious strokes towards the scene of the disturbance, backing water so that I could pull for shore in a hurry. I fished out a piece of blue-green sponge rubber, the size of my foot. I think it came from Algy's neck.

Lord Kintyre replaced his eyeglass and sighed. "Just my damned luck," he said, "to be without camera or other equipment."

"Are you going to call your boys back, to start watching again?"

"No. Some have already left for home, and the rest are all packed up. We've spent enough money and got enough material for our report to the Society. Someone else will have to chase the real Algy."

In the years since then, I have heard of no further mysterious phenomena on Lake Algonquin. But, although I have been back there several times, I have always found some excuse for not going swimming.

Out of Darkness
by
Lillian Stewart Carl

In the story that follows, a contrasting study of faith and technology, new writer Lillian Stewart Carl suggests that how you look at something is as important as what you see . . .

Lillian Stewart Carl has been a newspaper columnist, librarian, engineering aide, and college history teacher. She has published stories in Isaac Asimov's Science Fiction Magazine, Amazing, Amazons II, *and elsewhere. Her novels include* Sabazel, The Winter King, Shadow Dancers *and, most recently,* Wings of Power. *She lives with her family in Carroliton, Texas.*

* * *

Sarah laid her cheek against the cold glass of the porthole, extinguishing her own reflection. The water outside was only swirling darkness. No; there was light, an infinity of tiny gleams, suspended peat particles both refracting and swallowing the halogen searchlights of the submersible.

Sarah wondered once again why she had let Mark talk her into joining him on this run. The water was dark and cold and deep. Loch Ness, it was said, never gave up its dead.

She turned away from the window, inhaling deeply to reassure herself. But the air was stale. Sweat ran in tickling streams down her back.

Mark sat at the controls, humming delightedly to himself. Hydrophone, speakers cleared of static and echoing with the hollowness of deep water. Sonar transponder, steady lines on the oscilloscope, registering only fixed objects—the camera rig at the end of the pier and a couple of sunken logs.

He loved this, Sarah thought with exasperated affection. Electronic senses extended, circuits opening and closing at his command. No wonder he'd given up his summer vacation to take this job with the Expedition. It was his summer vacation. His yearly fix of marine biology spiking his day-to-day expertise in electronics. And I can work anywhere, in my mind or out of it.

Of course, the doctor said she was fully recovered, ready for

14

a change of scene. Therapy for a nervous breakdown, or nervous hyper-excitement, or however coolly they defined that shadow lurking among her thoughts. They had defined the horror that had sucked Julie's life as cancer.

Sarah realized that her damp palms had left grey smudges along the edge of her sketch pad. The first page, mountains. The second page, cottages along the road to Inverness. The third page—nothing. Nothing here but darkness.

In the ravaged husk of Julie's body only her eyes remembered youth, staring in a dumb, anguished betrayal from the thicket of plastic tubes and leads and hoses that tied her down like a technological sacrifice.

The speaker clicked. Mark leaped to his dials, adjusting them as delicately as he had been touching Sarah since her sister's death. The speaker clicked twice more. "Listen," he said over his shoulder. "There it is again, just like yesterday. No known reason for those clicks. Don thinks that it might be some kind of sonar signal emitted by the animal."

The animal. The mythic monster. Estimated to be twenty feet long. Coasting silently through the darkness, through the cold darkness, attracted to the dim yellow shape and the muted lights of the submersible.

The submersible was about the same size as one of the beasts. Sarah's fingers tightened on her pencil and it broke. Sixty feet of thick water lay between her and the surface; this was the animal's element. Something hovered just beyond the circle of light, sensing their passage. She inhaled again, but her breath stuck in her throat and she choked. The sweat was cold now, flowing in streams down her face and body. Perhaps the sub was leaking, perhaps the seams had broken open.

"There!" Mark cried. Several small slashes startled the oscilloscope, moving fast across the field. Following them was a thick, heavy line, something big. Something very big. "It's chasing those salmon," said Mark. And, into his headset, "Don, we've got it! We're following!" He jerked the submersible around and accelerated.

No! Sarah screamed, but her voice was glue in her mouth. No, leave it alone, don't follow it into the dark!

The line on the oscilloscope wavered, thickened, thinned again. A barrage of chirps reverberated from the speaker. Sarah crouched, her hands over her ears. Mark, please, she moaned silently, let it go.

It was gone. The speaker hummed, the oscilloscope steadied. "Wow," Mark said, "it sure can move. It dived, Don, and it dived fast. Straight to the bottom, six hundred feet. Did you get anything?"

Sarah sat up and tried to quell her shivering. Come on, it was childish to be afraid of the dark.

"Yeah," continued Mark, "it does seem to be shy of the camera rig. Some kind of electrical field, do you think?"

"Can we go up now?" Sarah asked. Her voice was thin and faint.

"Hell," Mark said, and for a moment she thought he was speaking to her. Then, "Yeah, we're on our way. Blowing ballast."

"Mark?" she asked.

He glanced around at her, grinning in both exhilaration and frustration. "Almost had it, honey. Sub just can't move fast enough. Talk about a critter perfectly adapted to its environment. Straight down to the bottom!" He turned back to the controls.

The bottom of the loch. Centuries of silt, icy mud, dark like a grave. She shook herself, grasped at her sanity and steadied. Adults were too afraid of the dark, she told herself. The oscilloscopes around Julie's bed had registered not life but inexorable death.

The water outside the porthole lightened, became the color of thick tea. Then waves, and daylight. Glorious daylight. Sarah gathered up book and shattered pencil, her limbs as limp and loose as floating seaweed. But her head was clear. Transparent, she thought. Mark should be able to look right inside her, analyzing each curving track of thought.

"What's the matter?" he said. He stood to release the hatch.

"A touch of claustrophobia," she replied shamefacedly. "Too much water out there."

"Scuba diving along the Barrier Reef didn't scare you."

"This is different."

"Nessie has you spooked? You have too much imagination."

"I wouldn't be an artist if I didn't have imagination."

"You can say that again." His expression wavered between

concern and annoyance and settled on a noncommittal shrug. He clambered topside and reached back to help her out.

She inhaled eagerly of the cool breeze and scanned the blessedly open horizon, hillsides quilted in shades of green, the stone houses of Lewiston, blue sky blotted with wisps of cloud. Don and a couple more Expedition people rowing out to the sub.

Sarah sat down on the wet coping of the hatch, folded her hands, and waited for rescue.

Sarah glanced with distaste at her breakfast plate. Every morning the same meal, eggs and a bland link sausage and broiled tomato, cold toast in a rack and oatmeal that tasted of vinegar. The waitress brought pots of boiling hot water and tea, and then handed around the plates one by one by one, making a labored trip back to the kitchen each time.

Mark and Don were deep in discussion, electronics, cameras, anguilloform eels, *Nessiteras rhombopteryx*. The long, intense face of the Expedition leader shimmered in the steam from the teapot, as if he spoke through a barrier of water. "Popular superstition has that it's an elasmosaur, left over from the Age of the Dinosaurs. But no reptile could survive in water that cold."

Mark nodded savagely. "You can't tell from the fossil record whether the dinosaurs were cold-blooded. There's a good case for warm-bloodedness."

Sarah cradled a warm cup in her hands and gazed out the window. Science sought to disprove superstition. But if superstition hadn't recorded a creature in the loch, science wouldn't be looking for one.

Myth, which wrests meaning from the unknown, is hard-wired in the circuits of the human brain. The terminology might be Mark's but the thought seemed to be Sarah's alone. How could these men deny the fear of the unknown?

A ship moved slowly down the loch, leaving a V-shaped wake. The wake would be reflected from the nearly vertical banks, meeting again in the middle of the water long after the boat had passed. Some tourist would take a picture of it and declare it the tracks of a monster.

But the loch was deceptive. Waves, wakes, glassy spots and sudden outbreaks of bubbles—most of it could be explained by wind, by temperature gradients, by rotting vegetation. Loch Ness was the deepest loch in Scotland; perhaps the water guarded the

secret of its depths by casting illusion across its surface. The
Buddhist philosophers might be right, that life itself was just an
illusion.

"I didn't believe in Nessie," Don was saying, "until I saw
Rines' pictures during the seventies. And his videotape! I mean,
there it was; a moving and therefore living animal, its size tri-
angulated by the strobe, its passage recorded and measured."

"I have measured out my life in coffee spoons," Sarah muttered.

"Huh?" said Mark.

"Rage, rage against the dying of the light!" she declaimed.

"Ah. Poetry. Thomas Eliot or somebody." Fondly thinking
he had responded, he turned back to Don.

"Lousy picture, though," Don sighed. "This year we'll do
better. Get it all down. Irrefutable evidence."

Evidence, Sarah thought. Exhibit A in the murder of a legend.
She turned back to the window.

Patterns of light and shadow played across the loch. Beneath
its surface was another world, where sight was useless, where
hearing was a primitive sonar receiver, where touch—what of
touch? Did Nessie touch with pleasure the rough, scaly skin of
her mate? Did she fear the dazzling sun-blast beyond the water's
surface membrane?

Imagination, Sarah told herself. What matters is not the
threads of data, but what our imagination weaves from it. What
we believe.

"And if you get that irrefutable evidence?" Mark asked.

Don's eyes gleamed. "A new species unknown to science.
Think of the fallout! Biology, medicine, genetics; environmental
ecology . . ."

"Admit it," teased Sarah. "You simply want to be the little
boy who slays the dragon."

Don turned to her. "No one ever said anything about killing
it," he remonstrated soberly.

Mark rolled his eyes upwards, whether at Don or at Sarah was
hard to tell. Sarah allowed herself a dry laugh and picked up
her sketchbook. "I'll leave you with your evidence. I'm supposed to be illustrating a book about intangibles, after all." And
not distracting you from your quest for certainty, she added to
herself.

"Yeah," said Mark, as he blew her a conciliatory kiss. "The

elves' quest for the dragon's magic sword, or whatever it is. Fantasy.''

"Fantasy is good for the soul," she retorted. "Even though you'll never find irrefutable evidence of the soul's existence.'' Her smile was equally conciliatory, even indulgent, if somewhat strained at the edges.

They had already dismissed her. "Now," Don was saying, "if we take the submersible beyond Foyers this afternoon . . .''

Sarah hiked down the road toward Urquhart Bay. The castle, poised on its promontory beside the lake, was picturesque enough. But passive, somehow. Not like the water itself. Or like the stream of tourists heading for Drumnadrochit and the Official Loch Ness Monster Exhibition. It might be the twentieth century, the age of the antibiotic and the integrated circuit, but mankind still craved myth. Created it, if necessary, now that genuine gut-wrenching, nape-crawling, awe-inspiring Mystery had been enlightened into a few shadowy corners.

The local Scots profited from the religious impulse just as had innkeepers on the great medieval pilgrims' routes. They even offered good quality woollens, ceramics, and jewelry among the plastic Nessies and the children's tee-shirts reading "I'm a wee monster from Scotland.''

Sarah found a low stone wall, sat down, opened her sketch-book. A few strokes and the castle rose against the mountains opposite, no more substantial than its reflection, only a dream. Elf lords danced on the battlements, and the skirling of their pipers summoned narrow heads and necks from the water. The necks swayed to the music. The stones in the castle trembled beneath the dancing feet, left the bounds of earth and sailed across the water.

A groundskeeper worked on the steep grassy slope leading to the castle, his scythe swishing back and forth like yet another image from the dark ages. Suddenly, despite herself, Sarah wondered if the man's battered hat concealed a death's head.

She ripped the page from the book and tore it into dirty shreds. Mark, she thought, I'm sorry. I'm not a computer or a submarine; my nerves are not neat columns of facts and figures on a CRT. It would be a lot easier if they were.

But then, even those facts and figures had to have a programmer.

It must have been the reflected wake of a ship that moved at a stately pace down the center of the loch. A brilliant illusion, as if something swam just beneath the surface, at the boundary of two worlds.

The afternoon was shrouded with hazy cloud. The breeze that stirred the valley of the loch was fresh from the Highlands, Sarah told herself, scented with heather and gorse. Presumably heather and gorse had scents.

The launch crested another wave. Not good Nessie weather, this; the loch surface was chopped and broken. So was Sarah's stomach. Again she gulped, and again she wished she hadn't had that broiled tomato.

But her resolve was as sharp as her pencils. Everything would be all right, no more fear, no more resentment. She was just jealous, that's all, of the attention Mark paid to the Expedition.

"Steep sides," Mark called out. His eyes were not focused on the steep boulder-strewn banks slipping by, a mile distant on either side; he watched the readout, sensing the invisible land beneath the surface, sheer cliffs, caverns, cold bottomless silt.

All right now, Sarah said sternly to herself. Calmly, calmly.

Don leaned over the stern of the launch, calling directions over his shoulder to the person steering. "Nice even speed, slow gradually. Wide curve toward Invermoriston."

If the boat swung around too fast it would foul the leads of the sonar towfish. Damned expensive towfish, thought Sarah. You could endow an art scholarship or build a library with what it had cost. But then, the elusive beastie was probably worth it. Not to prove its existence—a myth, by definition, did not require proof. It was the search that mattered.

Near Invermoriston, soon after the disastrous battle at Culloden in 1746, a certain Roderick MacKenzie sacrificed his life by acting as a decoy for Bonnie Prince Charlie, wearing the prince's jacket and drawing the English fire upon himself. Romantic, even quixotic, gesture, but it had bought him an immortal name.

"Carefully!" Don bellowed.

Sarah's pencil danced. Don's aquiline profile appeared on the paper, shadowed by the peaked hat of an eighteenth-century British admiral. Nelson, cloaked in his own mythic certainty, strolling the quarterdeck until a French sharpshooter could immortalize him, too. Sarah bit deep into her lower lip. A paradox, that dying could win deathlessness, but the bereaved would embrace any paradox if it promised meaning.

"Signal's breaking up," Mark called.

Don boomed, "Slowly!"

"No, no, probably just a thermal layer."

Sarah laid down her book and pencil, reached for the thermos, then rejected the idea of hot tea. The chill of the afternoon was only accentuated by the gradual carbonation of her stomach. Maybe if she changed her position. She stood, gingerly, and stretched.

"Don't rock the boat," Mark growled from the corner of his mouth.

"Rocking boats is my specialty," she responded.

The waves smacked rhythmically against the side of the launch. The wake was barely discernible. Ahead was dark corrugated water, flecked with foam—Irish coffee, grumbled Sarah's stomach, and again she quelled it.

There was a smooth place between the waves, a dim shape moving dimly beneath the surface just at the bow of the boat. A trace of a wake, overwhelmed by backwash. Sarah, bemused, leaned over the side. Through a glass darkly. . . .

Then she realized what she was seeing. A creature from another world, a dream at arm's length, toying with its pursuers. She inhaled, opened her mouth to speak.

The shape veered to the side, cutting across the bow. The launch ran up onto it and stopped with an abrupt clatter of equipment.

Sarah was catapulted over the side. For a fleeting second she thought something had seized her, jerking her from the boat. No, she was falling, loose-limbed and helpless as a doll, downwards into darkness. The water rose up, slapped her, swallowed her.

Cold, bone-chilling cold. *Loch Ness never gives up its dead.* Her open mouth filled with water, her throat clogged with it. Her blood clotted with horror. The sensation drained from her hands, her limbs. Then, with some desperate flash of rationality she told herself, Dammit, you can swim! She thrust herself upwards, breaking the surface, spitting and coughing. The boat, where was the boat!

Her waterlogged sweater dragged her back under. Into the

element of the creature, borne downwards into impenetrable night. She fought, screaming silently, for the surface.

A searing breath of air. Shouts in the distance, a motor. And something touched her leg. Her numbed nerve endings thrilled with it, a rough, flexible appendage. She wrenched away, floundering, and the water pulled her down again. Crushing cold, and darkness watching, waiting . . .

Something grabbed her and dragged her gasping into the air. She struck out, but she was moving in slow motion, hands like lead weights.

It was Mark. "Hey," he shouted, "calm down."

Easy for you to say. This isn't your nightmare. Hands pulled her from the water and hauled her like a sack of dead fish over the gunwale of the boat; she noted the metal ridge but felt no pain. Mark splashed down beside her and she clutched at him, shivering with more than cold.

"Are you all right?" Don asked. And to the others, "Get the towfish in, quick. We have to get her back to camp." He peeled off his jacket and wrapped it around her.

Her hair leaked runnels of water down her face. She was crying, she realized, hot salt tears mingling with the peat-dark drops of chill.

"Towfish is fouled," someone called.

Don turned. "That sudden stop; could've been a log, I guess."

"Yeah. Sure. I just hope we didn't hurt it."

They hauled in the torpedo-like bundle of equipment, clucking solicitously. The motor roared and the boat slapped against the waves. The banks of the loch heaved and shuddered, tumbling from the sky in waves of varied green.

"What got into you?" Mark asked. "You were flailing around out there as if you'd never swum before."

"S-scared," she stammered.

"Of what? Of Nessie?"

"Of the dark. Of getting lost in the dark. Of never coming back."

"Sarah," he sighed, shaking his head, but even so he pulled her closer to him.

Don sat beside them and opened the thermos. The sketch lay water-stained at his knee. "I like that," he said. "Always admired old Horatio."

His courage? Or his ego? Sarah's teeth chattered on the cup Don offered. "Thank you."

The boat sped up the loch, riding the crest of superstition, suspended between daylight and shadow.

Sarah stood on the narrow curve of beach beside Urquhart Bay. Behind her were the trailers—the caravans, she corrected herself—of the Expedition. The rhythmic chug of a motor, a door slamming, voices; the evening stillness caught it all and held it suspended, swirling particles of sound. Shadows lay long across the glassy surface of the loch.

Hands touched her shoulders and she started. Mark's voice intoned, "From ghoulies and ghosties and long-legged beasties and things that go bump in the night . . ."

"Good Lord deliver us," Sarah finished. How appropriate.

He stood beside her, contemplating translucent sky and translucent water separated by the black horizontal slash of the opposite shore. "Sarah," he said, "surely you didn't mean to imply this morning that Don is only hunting sensation."

"I'd like to see him turn down a guest spot on the Carson show."

Mark snorted. "All right; we all want a shot at immortality. But give him some credit as a scientist."

"And what he's doing is cool, dispassionate scientific research? Cheap rhetoric." She scuffed at the gravel. The water lapped questioningly at her toe. "It's like those people who say they've seen a UFO. They have an emotional stake in the answer. They want to believe there's more to existence than death and taxes."

"So?" He stared at her, brows tight, as he would stare at some unidentifiable marine creature.

"Irrefutable evidence? Tapes, pictures, whatever, it all comes in through the senses and is evaluated by that brain which causes emotions, too. The local superstitions are evidence. One of my drawings is as valid as a photograph."

"But not in the same way. Superstitions, art—they can't be quantified."

"Why should everything be quantified? Because your particular fear of the dark finds comfort in quantification?"

A boat beat up the loch, sending shock waves through the twilight. After a long time Mark laid his arm across Sarah's shoulders and said quietly, "Julie's death was—pretty ghoulish, wasn't it? Respirators, plastic tubing, all the technological paraphernalia that only prolonged her agony and left us to wonder why."

She stood stock still in the circle of his arm. She had thought him insensitive, but what he was, it seemed, was sensible. "Yes," she whispered, "if we didn't wonder why we'd be vegetables."

A faint gleam diffused into the sky above the dark ridge of the distant shore. A thin pale gold circlet swelled up and out. The moon rose over Loch Ness and laid a shining path across the water.

"Beautiful," said Sarah. She could step onto the light, follow the path up and across the dark water and into the sky. She could dance among the Pleiades, as light as one of her pencil-and-paper fairies, unencumbered by mortal flesh.

Mark's face was burnished by the light. How handsome he was, how sturdy. She warmed in his glow.

"Just think," he said, "how much equipment the Apollo astronauts had to leave up there. Perfectly good cameras."

Sarah's image cracked, shattering into crystalline shards that cut deep. . . . No. They did not cut. She would not let them cut. They tickled instead, and she clung to his arm wreathed in helpless giggles.

"Now what?" he asked warily.

"You. You're so refreshingly honest, straightforward, unimaginative."

"That's a compliment?"

"Yes. Yes, actually it is."

"Okay," Mark said, baffled but obliging.

Sarah could see him plunging fearlessly into the dark, eager to see what lay on the other side. Foolish bravado, to court the silent shapes in the depths, to risk oblivion. Wasn't it?

They turned toward their own tiny trailer, pausing just outside for one glance back at the gleaming celestial disc. "Luna," Sarah conjugated, "lunacy, lunar tides, lunar rover." Light, perhaps, an imperative beyond darkness.

Arm in arm they went inside and shut the door on the night.

Sarah stood on the threshold of the Expedition hut. It was morning of a clear day. Brilliant sunshine danced on the waters of the loch before her, and the waters heaved, slowly, stretching toward the light.

Beneath the surface sheen, in the darkness where the light could not penetrate, an earlier expedition had found ancient stone rings. Relics of an earlier time when the water level had been lower, Sarah told herself. Man's ancient impulse toward ritual, to propitiate the dark even as it swallowed him. To defy it.

No one was in camp; Don and the rest of the Expedition staff had left early to haul the submersible up to Lochend. Mark had promised to follow later that afternoon. Right now he was working over the monitors in the hut, creating a minestrone of wire, capacitors, transformers, trying to line their 110-volt equipment to the 220-volt power source.

Rather like us, Sarah thought. Two different voltages, the neurasthenic nut mated to the scientist, together forming something unique and vital.

Mark was humming something under his breath that could have been anything from a Beatles tune to a Beethoven symphony. With a grimace Sarah tucked her sketchbook under her arm and strolled down to the beach. There was another anomalous wake pleating the water, probably an echo of the Expedition launch.

One of the videotape camera leads was snagged on a rock, and she bent to retrieve and straighten it. The sinuous shape of the wire piqued her imagination. She sat down beside it and drew a pencil from her pocket. The wires became living appendages reaching into the water, reaching into another element, defining shapes in a shadowy world, human eyes and ears and voices, human senses cleaving the darkness. If truth is beauty, she thought, perhaps science was indeed art. What did scientists want, after all, but to believe in the quark or the quasar or the validity of the human observer who named them both?

Mark stopped humming, encountering some problem that absorbed his entire attention. Sarah began humming, stilling a quaver of fear with melody. The twin wave of the wake crimped the surface of the loch.

She remembered the peat-dark water closing over her head. She remembered the touch of something—not unearthly, because it was from Earth.

Without darkness, light would be meaningless; without light, darkness would be impenetrable. Human perception was sketched in shades of gray. The quest for understanding, whether pursued by scientist or artist or tabloid myth-monger, was its own ritual of propitiation.

She grinned; here I go again, purple prose and all. Julie used to call me a real vapor-head, and she was probably right.

Sarah's pencil danced. An animal, long neck, flippers, strong rhomboidal tail sending it with swift, sure strokes through the darkness. An animal questing, warily, fearfully, toward the mystery of light.

Several salmon leaped from the loch and fell back, spattering themselves across the water. The wake followed, the twin wave curling white and thick. Iridescent bubbles skimmed upwards, neither light nor dark, joining world to world.

A long dark neck, eyes and nostrils like slits, thin protuberances like horns. A mouth gaping open, seizing a salmon. A thrashing in the water, spray cast upwards like tiny prisms into the sun.

The fish disappeared. Sarah's pencil fell from nerveless hands. The illusions of the loch, the surface concealing the depths—she could not trust her senses. She had called it, surely, from the fevered depths of her need to believe.

The creature flopped over, flippers beating the air, rounded belly facing the sky. Its thick tail beat the water, sending droplets high into the air. The droplets, cold ice flakes, fell on Sarah's face and she started.

It was there. Not an object of fear, but of awe. An affirmation. She stepped backwards, one foot behind the other. Her sketchbook trembled in her hands. "Mark," she called hoarsely. "Mark, come down here, please."

The creature lay still, back arching from the water, wavelets licking at its skin. Its head and neck curled from side to side, slowly, seeking food.

"Mark!" Sarah croaked.

Distracted, he called, "Huh? What?"

"Forget the monitors. Get your camera, if your own eyes aren't good enough." And a moment later, softly, "Thank you, Julie."

"What?" Mark called again, plunging down the embankment to her side. He hadn't brought a camera.

"There," she said, with a grand wave at the loch, the wake,

the fish, the basking creature. It seized another salmon, tilted its neck upwards, splashed about as if playing with its prey.

Mark collapsed onto a rock, swearing slowly, reverently, under his breath.

Sarah plucked another pencil from her pocket and began to sketch. Head, neck, back—even the fish leaping from the water.

"No camera," Mark mourned. "Strobe's blown a fuse. No sonar, no hydrophone."

"You can see it, can't you?" Sarah flipped to the next page in her book, beginning again. Magic flowed through her eyes, through her fingertips; the image leaped from the paper.

"I see it," said Mark. "Whether it's really there is another matter."

"Yes, Mr. Spock," she returned with a smile.

The creature slipped beneath the waves and disappeared. The water smoothed itself and lay still. The sunsheen reflected from the surface of the loch like from a burnished shield.

Sarah's fingers slowed and stopped. She was weak with effort. Her knees buckled and she sat beside Mark.

"God!" he wailed. "No camera!" His eye fell upon her drawings and lightened. "Hey, those are good. Now if we can only get Don to believe it."

"Do you believe it?" she asked quietly.

"Yes. I saw something. And I'd sure like to see it again, even if it takes a lot of looking."

"That's all that matters."

"Is it? Is it really?" He laughed. "It's that easy, then?"

"No, it's never easy," Sarah replied. "But the wanting to search; that's enough." They sat close together by the deep water. The darkness ebbed.

Leviathan!

by
Larry Niven

Larry Niven made his first sale to Worlds of If *magazine in 1964, and soon established himself as one of the best new writers of "hard" science fiction since Heinlein. By the end of the seventies, Niven had won several Hugo and Nebula awards, published* Ringworld, *one of the most acclaimed technological novels of the decade, and had written several best-selling novels in collaboration with Jerry Pournelle. Niven's books include the novels* Protector, World of Ptavvs, A Gift from Earth, Ringworld Engineers, *and* Smoke Ring, *and the collections* Tales of Known Space, Inconstant Moon, *and* Neutron Star. *His most recent book is the novel* The Barsoom Project, *written in collaboration with Steven Barnes.*

Here Svetz—the hapless, harried, and overworked Time Retrieval Expert who has coped with one disastrous assignment after another in a number of Niven stories (collected in The Flight of the Horse)—*may finally have bitten off an assignment that's more than he can chew—one, in fact, that may chew him . . . and swallow* him, *too!*

* * *

Two men stood on one side of a thick glass wall.

"You'll be airborne," Svetz's beefy red-faced boss was saying. "We made some improvements in the small extension cage while you were in the hospital. You can hover in it, or fly it at up to fifty miles per hour, or let it fly itself; there's a constant-altitude setting. Your field of vision is total. We've made the shell of the extension cage completely transparent."

On the other side of the thick glass, something was trying to kill them. It was forty feet long from nose to tail and was equipped with vestigial batlike wings. Otherwise it was built something like a slender lizard. It screamed and scratched at the glass with murderous claws.

The sign on the glass read:

GILA MONSTER
Retrieved from the year 1230 AnteAtomic, approximately,
from the region of China, Earth. EXTINCT.

"You'll be well out of his reach," said Ra Chen.

"Yes, sir." Svetz stood with his arms folded about him, as if he had a chill. He was being sent after the biggest animal that had ever lived; and Svetz was afraid of animals.

"For Science's sake! What are you worried about, Svetz? It's only a big fish!"

"Yes, sir. You said that about the Gila monster. It's just an extinct lizard, you said."

"We only had a drawing in a children's book to go by. How could we know it would be so big?"

The Gila monster drew back from the glass. It inhaled hugely, took aim—yellow and orange flame spewed from its nostrils and played across the glass. Svetz squeaked and jumped for cover.

"He can't get through," said Ra Chen.

Svetz picked himself up. He was a slender, small-boned man with pale skin, light blue eyes, and very fine ash-blond hair. "How could we know it would breathe fire?" he mimicked. "That lizard almost *cremated* me. I spent four months in the hospital as it was. And what really burns me is, he looks less like the drawing every time I see him. Sometimes I wonder if I didn't get the wrong animal."

"What's the difference, Svetz? The Secretary-General loved him. That's what counts."

"Yes, sir. Speaking of the Secretary-General, what does he want with a sperm whale? He's got a horse, he's got a Gila monster—"

"That's a little complicated." Ra Chen grimaced. "Palace politics! It's *always* complicated. Right now, Svetz, somewhere in the United Nations Palace, a hundred plots are in various stages of development. And every last one of them involves getting the attention of the Secretary-General, and *holding* it. Keeping his attention isn't easy."

Svetz nodded. Everybody knew about the Secretary-General.

The family that had ruled the United Nations for seven hundred years was somewhat inbred.

The Secretary-General was twenty-eight years old. He was a happy person; he loved animals and flowers and pictures and people. Pictures of planets and multiple star systems made him clap his hands and coo with delight; and so the Institute for Space Research was mighty in the United Nations government. But he liked extinct animals too.

"Someone managed to convince the Secretary-General that he wants the largest animal on Earth. The idea may have been to take us down a peg or two," said Ra Chen. "Someone may think we're getting too big a share of the budget.

"By the time I got onto it, the Secretary-General wanted a brontosaur. We'd never have gotten him that. No extension cage will reach that far."

"Was it your idea to get him a sperm whale, sir?"

"Yah. It wasn't easy to persuade him. Sperm whales have been extinct for so long that we don't even have pictures. All I had to show him was a crystal sculpture from Archeology—dug out of the Steuben Glass Building—and a Bible and a dictionary. I managed to convince him that Leviathan and the sperm whale were one and the same."

"That's not strictly true." Svetz had read a computer-produced condensation of the Bible. The condensation had ruined the plot, in Svetz's opinion. "Leviathan could be anything big and destructive, even a horde of locusts."

"Thank Science you weren't there to help, Svetz! The issue was confused enough. Anyway, I promised the Secretary-General the largest animal that ever lived on Earth. All the literature says that that animal was a sperm whale. There were sperm whale herds all over the oceans as recently as the first century Ante Atomic. You shouldn't have any trouble finding one."

"In twenty minutes?"

Ra Chen looked startled. "What?"

"If I try to keep the big extension cage in the past for more than twenty minutes, I'll never be able to bring it home. The—"

"I know that."

"—uncertainty factor in the energy constants—"

"Svetz—"

"—blow the Institute right off the map."

"We thought of that, Svetz. You'll go back in the small extension cage. When you find a whale, you'll signal the big extension cage."

"Signal it how?"

"We've found a way to send a simple on-off pulse through time. Let's go back to the Institute and I'll show you."

Malevolent golden eyes watched them through the glass as they walked away.

The extension cage was the part of the time machine that did the moving. Within its transparent shell, Svetz seemed to ride a flying armchair equipped with an airplane passenger's lunch tray; except that the lunch tray was covered with lights and buttons and knobs and crawling green lines. He was somewhere off the east coast of North America, in or around the year 100 Ante Atomic or 1845 Anno Domini. The inertial calendar was not particularly accurate.

Svetz skimmed low over water the color of lead, beneath a sky the color of slate. But for the rise and fall of the sea, he might almost have been suspended in an enormous sphere painted half light, half dark. He let the extension cage fly itself twenty meters above the water, while he watched the needle on the NAI, the Nervous Activities Indicator.

Hunting Leviathan.

His stomach was uneasy. Svetz had thought he was adjusting to the peculiar gravitational side effects of time travel. But apparently not.

At least he would not be here long.

On this trip he was not looking for a mere forty-foot Gila monster. Now he hunted the largest animal that had ever lived. A most conspicuous beast. And now he had a life-seeking instrument, the NAI . . .

The needle jerked hard over, and trembled.

Was it a whale? But the needle was trembling in apparent indecision. A cluster of sources, then. Svetz looked in the direction indicated.

A clipper ship, winged with white sail, long and slender and graceful as hell. Crowded, too, Svetz guessed. Many humans, closely packed, would affect the NAI in just that manner. A sperm whale—a single center of complex nervous activity—would attract the needle as violently, without making it jerk about like that.

The ship would interfere with reception. Svetz turned east and away; but not without regret. The ship was beautiful.

The uneasiness in Svetz's belly was getting worse, not better.

Endless grey-green water, rising and falling beneath Svetz's flying armchair.

Enlightenment came like something clicking in his head. *Seasick*. On automatic, the extension cage matched its motion to the surface over which it flew; and that surface was heaving in great dark swells.

No wonder his stomach was uneasy! Svetz grinned and reached for the manual controls.

The NAI needle suddenly jerked hard over. A bite! thought Svetz, and he looked off to the right. No sign of a ship. And submarines hadn't been invented yet. Had they? No, of course they hadn't.

The needle was rock-steady.

Svetz flipped the call button.

The source of the tremendous NAI signal was off to his right, and moving. Svetz turned to follow it. It would be minutes before the call signal reached the Institute for Temporal Research and brought the big extension cage with its weaponry for hooking Leviathan.

Many years ago, Ra Chen had dreamed of rescuing the Library at Alexandria from Caesar's fire. For this purpose he had built the big extension cage. Its door was a gaping iris, big enough to be loaded while the Library was actually burning. Its hold, at a guess, was at least twice large enough to hold all the scrolls in that ancient Library.

The big cage had cost a fortune in government money. It had failed to go back beyond 400 AA, or 1550 AD. The books burned at Alexandria were still lost to history, or at least to historians.

Such a boondoggle would have broken other men. Somehow Ra Chen had survived the blow to his reputation.

He had pointed out the changes to Svetz after they returned from the Zoo. "We've fitted the cage out with heavy duty stunners and antigravity beams. You'll operate them by remote control. Be careful not to let the stun beam touch you. It would kill even a sperm whale if you held it on him for more than a few seconds, and it'd kill a man instantly. Other than that you should have no problems."

It was at that moment that Svetz's stomach began to hurt.

"Our major change is the call button. It will actually send us a signal through time, so that we can send the big extension cage back to you. We can land it right beside you, no more than a few minutes off. That took considerable research, Svetz. The Treasury raised our budget for this year so that we could get that whale.''

Svetz nodded.

''Just be sure you've got a whale before you call for the big extension cage.''

Now, twelve hundred years earlier, Svetz followed an underwater source of nervous impulse. The signal was intensely powerful. It could not be anything smaller than an adult bull sperm whale.

A shadow formed in the air to his right. Svetz watched it take shape: a great grey-blue sphere floating beside him. Around the rim of the door were antigravity beamers and heavy duty stun guns. The opposite side of the sphere wasn't there; it simply faded away.

To Svetz that was the most frightening thing about any time machine: the way it seemed to turn a corner that wasn't there.

Svetz was almost over the signal. Now he used the remote controls to swing the antigravity beamers around and down.

He had them locked on the source. He switched them on, and dials surged.

Leviathan was *heavy*. More massive than Svetz had expected. Svetz upped the power, and watched the NAI needle swing as Leviathan rose invisibly through the water.

Where the surface of the water bulged upward under the attack of the antigravity beams, a shadow formed. Leviathan rising . . .

Was there something wrong with the shape?

Then a trembling spherical bubble of water rose shivering from the ocean, and Leviathan was within it.

Partly within it. He was too big to fit, though he should not have been.

He was four times as massive as a sperm whale should have been, and a dozen times as long. He looked nothing like the crystal Steuben sculpture. Leviathan was a kind of serpent armored with red-bronze scales as big as a Viking's shield, armed with teeth like ivory spears. His triangular jaws gaped wide. As he floated toward Svetz he writhed, seeking with his bulging yellow eyes for whatever strange enemy had subjected him to this indignity.

Svetz was paralyzed with fear and indecision. Neither then nor later did he doubt that what he saw was the Biblical Leviathan. This had to be the largest beast that had ever roamed the sea; a beast large enough and fierce enough to be synonymous with anything big and destructive. Yet—if the crystal sculpture was anything like representational, this was not a sperm whale at all.

In any case, he was far too big for the extension cage.

Indecision stayed his hand—and then Svetz stopped thinking entirely, as the great slitted irises found him.

The beast was floating past him. Around its waist was a sphere of weightless water, that shrank steadily as gobbets dripped away and rained back to the sea. The beast's nostrils flared—it was obviously an air-breather, though not a cetacean.

It stretched, reaching for Svetz with gaping jaws.

Teeth like scores of elephant's tusks all in a row. Polished and needle sharp. Svetz saw them close about him from above and below, while he sat frozen in fear.

At the last moment he shut his eyes tight.

When death did not come, Svetz opened his eyes.

The jaws had not entirely closed on Svetz and his armchair. Svetz heard them grinding faintly against—against the invisible surface of the extension cage, whose existence Svetz had forgotten entirely.

Svetz resumed breathing. He would return home with an empty extension cage, to face the wrath of Ra Chen . . . a fate better than death. Svetz moved his fingers to cut the antigravity beams from the big extension cage.

Metal whined against metal. Svetz whiffed hot oil, while red lights bloomed all over his lunch-tray control board. He hastily turned the beams on again.

The red lights blinked out one by reluctant one.

Through the transparent shell Svetz could hear the grinding of teeth. Leviathan was trying to chew his way into the extension cage.

His released weight had nearly torn the cage loose from the rest of the time machine. Svetz would have been stranded in the past, a hundred miles out to sea, in a broken extension cage that probably wouldn't float, with an angry sea monster waiting to snap him up. No, he couldn't turn off the antigravity beamers.

But the beamers were on the big extension cage, and he couldn't keep the big extension cage more than about fifteen minutes longer. When the big extension cage was gone, what would prevent Leviathan from pulling him to his doom?

"I'll stun him off," said Svetz.

There was dark red palate above him, and red gums and forking tongue beneath, and the long curved fangs all around. But between the two rows of teeth Svetz could see the big extension cage, and the battery of stunners around the door. By eye he rotated the stunners until they pointed straight toward Leviathan.

"I must be out of my mind," said Svetz, and he spun the stunners away from him. He couldn't fire the stunners at Leviathan without hitting himself.

And Leviathan wouldn't let go.

Trapped.

No, he thought with a burst of relief. He could escape with his life. The go-home lever would send his small extension cage out from between the jaws of Leviathan, back into the time stream, back to the Institute. His mission had failed, but that was hardly his fault. Why had Ra Chen been unable to uncover mention of a sea serpent bigger than a sperm whale?

"It's all his fault," said Svetz. And he reached for the go-home lever. But he stayed his hand.

"I can't just tell him so," he said. For Ra Chen terrified him.

The grinding of teeth came itchingly through the extension cage.

"Hate to just quit," said Svetz. "Think I'll try something . . ."

He could see the antigravity beamers by looking between the teeth. He could feel their influence, so nearly were they focused on the extension cage itself. If he focused them just on himself . . .

He felt the change; he felt both strong and light-headed, like a drunken ballet master. And if he now narrowed the focus . . .

The monster's teeth seemed to grind harder. Svetz looked between them, as best he could.

Leviathan was no longer floating. He was hanging straight down from the extension cage, hanging by his teeth. The antigravity beamers still balanced the pull of his mass; but now they did so by pulling straight up on the extension cage.

The monster was in obvious distress. Naturally. A water beast, he was supporting his own mass for the first time in his life. And by his teeth! His yellow eyes rolled frantically. His tail twitched slightly at the very tip. And still he clung . . .

"Let go," said Svetz. "Let go, you . . . monster."

The monster's teeth slid screeching down the transparent surface, and he fell.

Svetz cut the antigravity a fraction of a second late. He smelled burnt oil, and there were tiny red lights blinking off one by one on his lunch-tray control board.

Leviathan hit the water with a sound of thunder. His long, sinuous body rolled over and floated to the surface and lay as if dead. But his tail flicked once, and Svetz knew that he was alive.

"I could kill you," said Svetz. "Hold the stunners on you until you're dead. There's time enough . . ."

But he still had ten minutes to search for a sperm whale. It wasn't time enough. It didn't begin to be time enough, but if he used it all . . .

The sea serpent flicked its tail and began to swim away. Once he rolled to look at Svetz, and his jaws opened wide in fury. He finished his roll and was fleeing again.

"Just a minute," Svetz said thickly. "Just a science-perverting minute there . . ." And he swung the stunners to focus.

Gravity behaved strangely inside an extension cage. While the cage was moving forward in time, *down* was all directions outward from the center of the cage. Svetz was plastered against the curved wall. He waited for the trip to end.

Seasickness was nothing compared to the motion sickness of time travel.

Free fall, then normal gravity. Svetz moved unsteadily to the door.

Ra Chen was waiting to help him out. "Did you get it?"

"Leviathan? No, sir." Svetz looked past his boss. "Where's the big extension cage?"

"We're bringing it back slowly, to minimize the gravitational side effects. But if you don't have the whale—"

"I said I don't have Leviathan."

"Well, just what *do* you have?" Ra Chen demanded.

Somewhat later he said, "It wasn't?"

Later yet he said, "You killed him? Why, Svetz? Pure spite?"

"No, sir. It was the most intelligent thing I did during the entire trip."

"But *why*? Never mind, Svetz, here's the big extension cage." A grey-blue shadow congealed in the hollow cradle of the time machine. "And there does seem to be something in it. Hi, you idiots, throw an antigravity beam inside the cage! Do you want the beast crushed?"

The cage had arrived. Ra Chen waved an arm in signal. The door opened.

Something tremendous hovered within the big extension cage. It looked like a malevolent white mountain in there, peering back at its captors with a single tiny, angry eye. It was trying to get at Ra Chen, but it couldn't swim in air.

Its other eye was only a torn socket. One of its flippers was ripped along the trailing edge. Rips and ridges and puckers of scar tissue, and a forest of broken wood and broken steel, marked its tremendous expanse of albino skin. Lines trailed from many of the broken harpoons. High up on one flank, bound to the beast by broken and tangled lines, was the corpse of a bearded man with one leg.

"Hardly in mint condition, is he?" Ra Chen observed.

"Be careful, sir. He's a killer. I saw him ram a sailing ship and sink it clean before I could focus the stunners on him."

"What amazes me is that you found him at all in the time you had left. Svetz, I do not understand your luck. Or am I missing something?"

"It wasn't luck, sir. It was the most intelligent thing I did the entire trip."

"You said that before. About killing Leviathan."

Svetz hurried to explain. "The sea serpent was just leaving the vicinity. I wanted to kill him, but I knew I didn't have the time. I was about to leave myself, when he turned back and bared his teeth.

"He was an obvious carnivore. Those teeth were built strictly for killing, sir. I should have noticed earlier. And I could think of only one animal big enough to feed a carnivore that size."

"Ah-h-h. Brilliant, Svetz."

"There was corroborative evidence. Our research never found any mention of giant sea serpents. The great geological surveys of the first century Post Atomic should have turned up something. Why didn't they?''

''Because the sea serpent quietly died out two centuries earlier, after whalers killed off his food supply.''

Svetz colored. ''Exactly. So I turned the stunners on Leviathan before he could swim away, and I kept the stunners on him until the NAI said he was dead. I reasoned that if Leviathan was here, there must be whales in the vicinity.''

''And Leviathan's nervous output was masking the signal.''

''Sure enough, it was. The moment he was dead the NAI registered another signal. I followed it to—'' Svetz jerked his head. They were floating the whale out of the extension cage. ''To him.''

Days later, two men stood on one side of a thick glass wall.

''We took some clones from him, then passed him on to the Secretary-General's vivarium,'' said Ra Chen. ''Pity you had to settle for an albino.'' He waved aside Svetz's protest: ''I know, I know, you were pressed for time.''

Beyond the glass, the one-eyed whale glared at Svetz through murky seawater. Surgeons had removed most of the harpoons, but scars remained along his flanks; and Svetz, awed, wondered how long the beast had been at war with Man. Centuries? How long did sperm whales live?

Ra Chen lowered his voice. ''We'd all be in trouble if the Secretary-General found out that there was once a bigger animal than this. You understand that, don't you, Svetz?''

''Yes, sir.''

''Good.'' Ra Chen's gaze swept across another glass wall, and a fire-breathing Gila monster. Further down, a horse looked back at him along the dangerous spiral horn in its forehead.

''Always we find the unexpected,'' said Ra Chen. ''Sometimes I wonder . . .''

If you'd do your research better, Svetz thought . . .

''Did you know that time travel wasn't even a concept until the first century Ante Atomic? A writer invented it. From then until the fourth century Post Atomic, time travel was pure fantasy. It violates everything the scientists of the time thought were natural laws. Logic. Conservation of matter and energy. Momentum, reaction, any law of motion that makes time a part of the statement. Relativity.

"It strikes me," said Ra Chen, "that every time we push an extension cage past that particular four-century period, we shove it into a kind of fantasy world. That's why you keep finding giant sea serpents and fire-breathing—"

"That's nonsense," said Svetz. He was afraid of his boss, yes; but there were limits.

"You're right," Ra Chen said instantly. Almost with relief. "Take a month's vacation, Svetz, then back to work. The Secretary-General wants a bird."

"A bird?" Svetz smiled. A bird sounded harmless enough. "I suppose he found it in another children's book?"

"That's right. Ever hear of a bird called a *roc*?"

The Horses of Lir
by
Roger Zelazny

Like a number of other writers, Roger Zelazny began publishing in 1962 in the pages of Cele Goldsmith's Amazing. *Many writers in this so-called "class of '62" would eventually achieve prominence, but Zelazny's subsequent career would be one of the most meteoric in the history of SF. By the end of that decade, he had won two Nebula Awards and two Hugo Awards and was widely regarded as one of the most important American SF writers of the sixties. Since then, he has won several more awards, and his series of novels about the enchanted land of Amber has made him one of the best-selling SF and fantasy writers of our time. His books include* This Immortal, The Dream Master, Lord of Light, Isle of the Dead, *and the collection* The Doors of His Face, the Lamps of His Mouth and Other Stories. *His most recent novel is* Sign of Chaos.*

Here he takes us along with him on a suspenseful investigation of a secret that's dark and sinister—and very, very old.

* * *

The moonlight was muted and scattered by the mist above the loch. A chill breeze stirred the white tendrils to a sliding, skating motion upon the water's surface. Staring into the dark depths, Randy smoothed his jacket several times, then stepped forward. He pursed his lips to begin and discovered that his throat was dry.

Sighing, almost with relief, he turned and walked back several paces. The night was especially soundless about him. He seated himself upon a rock, drew his pipe from his pocket and began to fill it.

What am I doing here? he asked himself. How can I . . . ?

As he shielded his flame against the breeze, his gaze fell upon the heavy bronze ring with the Celtic design that he wore upon his forefinger.

It's real enough, he thought, and it had been *his*, and *he* could do it. But this . . .

40

He dropped his hand. He did not want to think about the body lying in a shallow depression ten or twelve paces up the hillside behind him.

His Uncle Stephen had taken care of him for almost two years after the deaths of his parents, back in Philadelphia. He remembered the day he had come over—on that interminable plane flight—when the old man had met him at the airport in Glasgow. He had seemed shorter than Randy remembered, partly because he was a bit stooped now he supposed. His hair was pure white and his skin had the weathered appearance of a man's who had spent his life out-of-doors. Randy never learned his age.

Uncle Stephen had not embraced him. He had simply taken his hand, and his gray eyes had fixed upon his own for a moment as if searching for something. He had nodded then and looked away. It might have been then that Randy first noticed the ring.

"You'll have a home with me, lad," he had said. "Let's get your bags."

There was a brief splashing noise out in the loch. Randy searched its mist-ridden surface but saw nothing.

They know. Somehow they know, he decided. What now?

During the ride to his home, his uncle had quickly learned that Randy's knowledge of Gaelic was limited. He had determined to remedy the situation by speaking it with him almost exclusively. At first, this had annoyed Randy, who saw no use to it in a modern world. But the rudiments were there, words and phrases returned to him, and after several months he began to see a certain beauty in the Old Tongue. Now he cherished this knowledge—another thing he owed the old man.

He toyed with a small stone, cast it out over the waters, listened to it strike. Moments later, a much greater splash echoed it. Randy shuddered.

He had worked at his uncle's boat rental business all that summer. He had cleaned and caulked, painted and mended, spliced . . . He had taken out charters more and more often as the old man withdrew from this end of things.

"As Mary—rest her soul—never gave me children, it will be yours one day, Randy," he had said. "Learn it well, and it will keep you for life. You will need something near here."

"Why?" he had asked.

"One of us has always lived here."

"Why should that be?"

Stephen had smiled.

"You will understand," he said, "in time."

But that time was slow in coming, and there were other things to puzzle him. About once a month, his uncle rose and departed before daybreak. He never mentioned his destination or responded to questions concerning it. He never returned before sundown, and Randy's strongest suspicion did not survive because he never smelled of whisky when he came in.

Naturally, one day Randy followed him. He had never been forbidden to do it, though he strongly suspected it would meet with disapproval. So he was careful. Dressing hastily, he kept the old man in sight through the window as he headed off toward a stand of trees. He put out the Closed sign and moved through the chill pre-dawn in that direction. He caught sight of him once again, briefly, and then Stephen vanished near a rocky area and Randy could find no trace of him after that. Half an hour later, he took the sign down and had breakfast.

Twice again, he tried following him, and he lost him on both occasions. It irritated him that the old man could baffle him so thoroughly, and perhaps it bothered him even more that there was this piece of his life which he chose to keep closed to him— for as he worked with him and grew to know him better he felt an increasing fondness for his father's older brother.

Then, one morning, Stephen roused him early.

"Get dressed," he said. "I want you to come with me."

That morning his uncle hung the Closed sign himself and Randy followed him through the trees, down among the rocks, past a cleverly disguised baffle, and down a long tunnel. Randy heard lapping sounds of water, and even before his uncle put a light to a lantern he knew from the echoes that he was in a fair-sized cave.

His eyes did not adjust immediately when the light spread. When they did, he realized that he was regarding an underground harbor. Nevertheless, it took longer for the possibility to occur to him that the peculiar object to his left might be some sort of boat in a kind of drydock. He moved nearer and examined it while his uncle filled and lit another lantern.

It was flat-bottomed and U-shaped. What he had taken to be some sort of cart beneath it, though, proved a part of the thing itself. It had a wheel on either side. Great metal rings hung loosely on both sides and on the forward end. The vehicle was tilted, resting upon its curved edge. These structural matters, however, aroused but a superficial curiosity, for all other things were overwhelmed within him by a kind of awe at its beauty.

Its gunwales, or sides—depending on exactly what the thing was—were faced with thin bronze plates of amazing design. They looped and swirled in patterns vaguely reminiscent of some of the more abstract figures in the *Book of Kells*, embossed here and there with large studs. The open areas looked to be enameled—green and red in the flickering light.

He turned as his uncle approached.

"Beautiful, isn't it?" he said smiling.

"It—it belongs in a museum!"

"No. It belongs right here."

"What is it?"

Stephen produced a cloth and began to polish the plates.

"A chariot."

"It doesn't look exactly like any chariot I've seen pictures of. For one thing, it's awfully big."

Stephen chuckled.

"Ought to be. 'Tis the property of a god."

Randy looked at him to see whether he was joking. From the lack of expression on his face, he knew that he was not.

"Whose—is it?" he asked.

"Lir, Lord of the Great Ocean. He sleeps now with the other Old Ones—most of the time."

"What is it doing here?"

His uncle laughed again.

"Has to park it someplace now, doesn't he?"

Randy ran his hand over the cold, smooth design on the side.

"I could almost believe you," he said. "But what is your connection with it?"

"I go over it once a month, to clean it, polish it, keep it serviceable."

"Why?"

"He may have need of it one day."

"I mean, why you?"

He looked at his uncle again and saw that he was smiling.

"A member of our family has always done it," he said, "since times before men wrote down history. It is a part of my duty."

Randy looked at the chariot again.

"It would take an elephant to pull something that size."

"An elephant is a land creature."

"Then what . . . ?"

His uncle held up his hand beside the lantern, displaying the ring.

"I am the Keeper of the Horses of Lir, Randy. This is my emblem of office, though they would know me without it after all these years."

Randy looked closely at the ring. Its designs were similar to those on the chariot.

"The Horses of Lir?" he asked.

His uncle nodded.

"Before he went to sleep with the other Old Ones, he put them to pasture here in the loch. It was given to an early ancestor of ours to have charge of them, to see that they do not forget."

Randy's head swam. He leaned against the chariot for support.

"Then all those stories, of—things—in the loch . . . ?"

"Are true," Stephen finished. "There's a whole family, a herd of them out there." He gestured toward the water. "I call them periodically and talk to them and sing to them in the Old Tongue, to remind them."

"Why did you bring me here, Uncle? Why tell me all these secret things?" Randy asked.

"I need help with the chariot. My hands are getting stiff," he replied. "And there's none else but you."

Randy worked that day, polishing the vehicle, oiling enormous and peculiarly contrived harnesses that hung upon the wall. And his uncle's last words bothered him more than a little.

The fog had thickened. There seemed to be shapes moving within it now—great slow shadows sliding by in the distance. He knew they were not a trick of the moonlight, for there had been another night such as this . . .

"Would you get your pullover, lad?" his uncle had said. "I'd like us to take a walk."

"All right."

He put down the book he had been reading and glanced at his watch. It was late. They were often in bed by this hour. Randy had only stayed up because his uncle had kept busy, undertaking a number of one-man jobs about the small cottage.

It was damp outside and somewhat chill. It had been raining

that day. Now the fogs stirred about them, rolling in off the water.

As they made their way down the footpath toward the shore, Randy knew it was no idle stroll that his uncle had in mind. He followed his light to the left past the docking area, toward a secluded rocky point where the land fell away sharply to deep water. He found himself suddenly eager, anxious to learn something more of his uncle's strange commitment to the place. He had grown steadily fonder of the old man in the time they had been together, and he found himself wanting to share more of his life.

They reached the point—darkness and mist and lapping water all about them—and Stephen placed his light upon the ground and seated himself on a stony ledge. He motioned for Randy to sit near him.

"Now, I don't want you to leave my side, no matter what happens," his uncle said.

"Okay."

"And if you must talk, speak the Old Tongue."

"I will."

"I am going to call the Horses now."

Randy stiffened. His uncle placed his hand upon his arm.

"You will be afraid, but remember that you will not be harmed so long as you stay with me and do whatever I tell you. You must be introduced. I am going to call them."

Randy nodded in the pale light.

"Go ahead."

He listened to the strange trilling noises his uncle made, and to the song that followed them. After a time, he heard a splashing, then he saw the advancing shadow . . . Big. Whatever it was, the thing was huge. Large enough to draw the chariot, he suddenly realized. If a person dare harness it . . .

The thing moved nearer. It had a long, thin neck atop its bulky form, he saw, as it suddenly raised its head high above the water, to sway there, regarding them through the shifting mist.

Randy gripped the ledge. He wanted to run but found that he could not move. It was not courage that kept him there. It was a fear so strong it paralyzed him, raising the hair on the back of his neck.

He looked at the Horse, hardly aware that his uncle was speaking softly in Erse now.

The figure continued to move before them, its head occasionally dipping partway toward them. He almost laughed as a wild vision of a snake-charming act passed through his head. The creature's eyes were enormous, with glints of their small light reflected palely within them. Its head moved forward, then back. Forward . . .

The great head descended until it was so close that it was almost touching his uncle, who reached out and stroked it, continuing to speak softly all the while.

He realized abruptly that his uncle was speaking to him. For how long he had been, he did not know.

". . . This one is Scafflech," he was saying, "and the one beside him is Finntag . . ."

Randy had not realized until then that another of the beasts had arrived. Now, with a mighty effort, he drew his eyes from the great reptilian head which had turned toward him. Looking past it, he saw that a second of the creatures had come up and that it, also, was beginning to lean forward. And beyond it there were more splashing sounds, more gliding shadows parting the mists like the prows of Viking ships.

". . . And that one is Garwal. Talk to them, so they'll know the sound of your voice."

Randy felt that he could easily begin laughing hysterically. Instead, he found himself talking, as he would to a large, strange dog.

"That's a good boy . . . Come on now . . . How are you? Good old fellow . . ."

Slowly he raised his hand and touched the leathery muzzle. Stephen had not asked him to. Why he had done it he was not certain, except that it had always seemed a part of the dog-talk he was using and his hand moved almost as if by reflex when he began it.

The first creature's head moved even nearer to his own. He felt its breath upon his face.

"Randy's my name, Scafflech," he heard himself telling it. "Randy . . ."

That night he was introduced to eight of them, of various sizes and dispositions. After his uncle had dismissed them and they had departed, he simply sat there staring out over the water. The fear had gone with them. Now he felt only a kind of numbness.

Stephen stood, stooped, retrieved the light.

"Let's go," he said.

Randy nodded, rose slowly, and stumbled after him. He was certain that he would get no sleep that night, but when he got home and threw himself into bed the world went away almost immediately. He slept later than usual. He had no dreams that he could recall.

They were out there again now, waiting. He had seen them several times since but never alone. His uncle had taught him the songs, the guide-words and phrases, but he had never been called upon to use them this way. Now, on this night so like the first, he was back, alone, and the fear was back, too. He looked down at the ring that he wore. Did they actually recognize it? Did it really hold some bit of the Old Magic? Or was it only a psychological crutch for the wearer?

One of the huge forms—Scafflech, perhaps—drew nearer and then hastily retreated. They had come without being called. They were waiting for his orders, and he clutched his pipe, which had long since gone out, and sat shaking.

Stephen had been ill much of the past month and had finally taken to his bed. At first, Randy had thought it to be influenza. But the old man's condition had steadily worsened. Finally he had determined to get him a doctor.

But Stephen had refused, and Randy had gone along with it until just that morning, when his uncle had taken a turn for the worse.

"No way, lad. This is it," he had finally told him. "A man sometimes has a way of knowing, and *we* always do. It is going to happen today, and it is very important that there be no doctor, that no one know for a time . . ."

"What do you mean?" Randy had said.

"With a doctor there would be a death certificate, maybe an autopsy, a burial. I can't have that. You see, there is a special place set aside for me, for all of the Keepers . . . I want to join my fathers, in the place where the Old Ones sleep . . . It was promised—long ago . . ."

"Where? Where is this place?" he had asked.

"The Isles of the Blessed, out in the open sea . . . You must take me there . . ."

"Uncle," he said, taking his hand, "I studied geography in school. There's no such place. So how can I . . . ?"

"It troubled me once, too," he said, "but I've been there
. . . I took my own father, years ago . . . The Horses know the
way . . ."

"The Horses! How could I—How could they—"

"The chariot . . . You must harness Scafflech and Finntag to
the chariot and place my body within it. Bathe me first, and
dress me in the clothes you'll find in that chest . . ." He nodded
toward an old sea-chest in the corner. "Then mount to the driv-
er's stand, take up the reins, and tell them to take you to the
Isles . . ."

Randy began to weep, a thing he had not done since his parents' deaths—how long ago?

"Uncle, I can't," he said. "I'm afraid of them. They're so
big—"

"You must. I need this thing to know my rest. —And set one
of the boats adrift. Later, tell the people that I took it out . . ."

He wiped his uncle's face with a towel. He listened to his
deepening breathing.

"I'm scared," he said.

"I know," Stephen whispered. "But you'll do it."

"I—I'll try."

"And here . . ." His uncle handed him the ring. "You'll need
this—to show them you're the new Keeper . . ."

Randy took the ring.

"Put it on."

He did.

Stephen had placed his hand upon his head as he had leaned
forward.

"I pass this duty to you," he said, "that you be Keeper of
the Horses of Lir."

Then his hand slipped away and he breathed deeply once
again. He awakened twice after that, but not for long enough to
converse at length. Finally, at sundown, he had died. Randy
bathed him and clothed him as he had desired, weeping the
while and not knowing whether it was for his sadness or his
fear.

He had gone down to the cave to prepare the chariot. By lantern light he had taken down the great harnesses and affixed them
to the rings in the manner his uncle had shown him. Now he
had but to summon the Horses to this pool through the wide

tunnel that twisted in from the loch, and there place the harnesses upon them . . .

He tried not to think about this part of things as he worked, adjusting the long leads, pushing the surprisingly light vehicle into position beside the water. Least of all did he wish to think of aquaplaning across the waves, drawn by those beasts, heading toward some mythical isle, his uncle's body at his back.

He departed the cave and went to the docking area, where he rigged a small boat, unmoored it and towed it out some distance over the loch before releasing it. The mists were already rising by then. In the moonlight, the ring gleamed upon his finger.

He returned to the cottage for his uncle and bore him down to a cove near the water entrance to the cave. Then his nerve had failed, he had seated himself with his pipe and had not stirred since.

The splashing continued. The Horses were waiting. Then he thought of his uncle, who had given him a home, who had left him this strange duty . . .

He rose to his feet and approached the water. He held up his hand with the ring upon it.

"All right," he said. "The time has come. Scafflech! Finntag! To the cave! To the place of the chariot! Now!"

Two forms drifted near, heads raised high upon their great necks.

I should have known it would not be that easy, he thought.

They swayed, looking down at him. He began addressing them as he had that first night. Slowly, their heads lowered. He waved the ring before them. Finally, when they were near enough, he reached out and stroked their necks. Then he repeated the instruction.

They withdrew quickly, turned, and headed off toward the tunnel. He moved away then, making for the land entrance to the place.

Inside, he found them waiting in the pool. He discovered then that he had to unfasten most of the harnessing from the chariot in order to fit it over them, and then secure it once again. It meant clambering up onto their backs. He removed his boots to do it. Their skin was strangely soft and slick beneath his feet, and they were docile now, as if bred to this business. He talked to them as he went about the work, rubbing their necks, humming the refrain to one of the old tunes.

He worked for the better part of an hour before everything was secure and he mounted the chariot and took up the reins.

"Out now," he said. "Carefully. Slowly. Back to the cove."

The wheels turned as the creatures moved away. He felt the reins jerk in his hands. The chariot advanced to the edge of the pool and continued on into the water. It floated. It drifted behind them toward the first bend and around it.

They moved through pitch blackness, but the beasts went carefully. The chariot never touched the rocky walls.

At length, they emerged into moonlight and mist over black water, and he guided them to the cove and halted them there.

"Wait now," he said. "Right here."

He climbed down and waded ashore. The water was cold, but he hardly noticed it. He mounted the slope to the place where his uncle lay and gathered him into his arms. Gently, he bore him down to the water's edge and out again. He took hold of the reins with a surer grip.

"Off now," he said. "You know the way! To the Isles of the Blessed! Take us there!"

They moved, slowly at first, through a long, sweeping turn that bore them out onto the misty breast of the loch. He heard splashings at either hand, and turning his head he saw that the other Horses were accompanying them.

They picked up speed. The beasts did seem to have a definite direction in mind. The mists swept by like a ghostly forest. For a moment, he almost felt as if he rode through some silent, mystical wood in times long out of mind.

The mists towered and thickened. The waters sparkled. He gave the creatures their head. Even if he had known the way, it would have done him little good, for he could not see where they were going. He had assumed that they were heading for the Caledonian Canal, to cut across to the sea. But now he wondered. If the Keepers, down through the ages, had been transported to some strange island, how had it been accomplished in earlier times? The Canal, as he recalled, had only been dug sometime in the nineteenth century.

But as the moonlit mists swirled about him and the great beasts plunged ahead, he could almost believe that there was another way—a way that perhaps only the Horses knew. Was he being borne, somehow, to a place that only impinged occasionally upon normal existence?

How long they rode across the ghostly seascape, he could not tell. Hours, possibly. The moon had long since set, but now the sky paled and a bonfire-like sunrise began somewhere to the right. The mists dispersed and the chariot coursed the waves beneath a clear blue sky with no trace of land anywhere in sight.

The unharnessed Horses played about him as Scafflech and Finntag drew him steadily ahead. His legs and shoulders began to ache and the wind came hard upon him now, but still he gripped the reins, blinking against the drenching spray.

Finally, something appeared ahead. At first he could not be certain, but as they continued on it resolved itself into a clear image. It was an island, green trees upon its hills, white rocks along its wave-swept shores.

As they drew nearer, he saw that the island was but one among many, and they were passing this one by.

Two more islands slipped past before the Horses turned and made their way toward a stone quay at the back of a long inlet at the foot of a high green slope. Giant trees dotted the hillside and there were several near the harbor. As they drew up beside the quay, he could hear birds singing within them.

As he took hold of the stone wall, he saw that there were three men standing beneath the nearest tree, dressed in green and blue and gray. They moved toward him, halting only when they had come alongside. He felt disinclined to look into their faces.

"Pass up our brother Keeper," one of them said in the Old Tongue.

Painfully, he raised his uncle's soaked form and felt them lift it from his arms.

"Now come ashore yourself, for you are weary. Your steeds will be tended."

He told the Horses to wait. He climbed out and followed the three figures along a flagged walk. One of them took him aside and led him into a small stone cottage while the others proceeded on, bearing his uncle's form.

"Your garments are wet," said the man. "Have this one," and he passed him a light green-blue robe of the sort he himself had on, of the sort in which Randy had dressed his uncle for the journey. "Eat now. There is food upon the table," the man continued, "and then there is the bed." He gestured. "Sleep."

Randy stripped and donned the garment he had been given. When he looked about again, he saw that he was alone. He went to the table, suddenly realizing that his appetite was enormous. Afterward, he slept.

It was dark when he awoke, and still. He got up and went to the door of the cottage. The moon had already risen, and the night had more stars in it than he could remember ever having seen before. A fragrant breeze came to him from off the sea.

"Good evening."

One of the men was seated upon a stone bench beneath a nearby tree. He rose.

"Good evening."

"Your Horses are harnessed. The chariot is ready to bear you back now."

"My uncle . . . ?"

"He has come home. Your duty is discharged. I will walk with you to the sea."

They moved back to the path, headed down to the quay. Randy saw the chariot, near to where he had left it, two of the Horses in harness before it. He realized with a start that he was able to tell that they were not Scafflech and Finntag. Other forms moved in the water nearby.

"It is good that two of the others travel the route in harness," the man said, as if reading his mind, "and give the older ones a rest."

Randy nodded. He did not feel it appropriate to offer to shake hands. He climbed down into the chariot and untwisted the reins from the crossbar.

"Thank you," he said, "for—everything. Take good care of him. Goodbye."

"A man who dines and sleeps in the Isles of the Blessed always returns," the other said. "Good night."

Randy shook the reins and the Horses began to move. Soon they were in open water. The new Horses were fresh and spirited. Suddenly Randy found himself singing to them.

They sped east along the path of the moon.

The Mortal
and the Monster
by
Gordon R. Dickson

Here's another look at the traditional lake monster—this one from a very different perspective . . .

Gordon R. Dickson is probably best known for his Dorsai series about mercenary soldiers of the future, but he is also the author of several insightful stories about human-alien interaction, among them "Black Charlie," "Dolphin's Way," and "Jean Dupres." He won a Hugo Award in 1965 for his short novel "Soldier, Ask Not," and a Nebula Award in 1966 for his novelette "Call Him Lord." His novels include Dorsai!, Soldier, Ask Not, The Tactics of Mistake, The Far Call, The Final Encyclopedia, *and* The Way of the Pilgrim *and the collection* The Book of Gordon R. Dickson. *His most recent book is the novel* The Chantry Guild.

* * *

That summer more activity took place upon the shores of the loch and more boats appeared on its waters than at any time in memory. Among them was even one of the sort of boats that went underwater. It moved around in the loch slowly, diving quite deep at times. From the boats, swimmers with various gear about them descended on lines—but not so deep—swam around blindly for a while, and then returned to the surface.

Brought word of all this in her cave, First Mother worried and speculated on disaster. First Uncle, though equally concerned, was less fearful. He pointed out that the Family had survived here for thousands of years; and that it could not all end in a single year—or a single day.

Indeed, the warm months of summer passed one by one with no real disturbance to their way of life.

Suddenly fall came. One night, the first snow filled the air briefly above the loch. The Youngest danced on the surface in the darkness, sticking out her tongue to taste the cold flakes.

Then the snow ceased, the sky cleared for an hour, and the banks could be seen gleaming white under a high and watery moon. But the clouds covered the moon again; and because of the relative warmth of the loch water nearby, in the morning, when the sun rose, the shores were once more green.

With dawn, boats began coming and going on the loch again and the Family went deep, out of sight. In spite of this precaution, trouble struck from one of these craft shortly before noon. First Uncle was warming the eggs on the loch bottom in the hatchhole, a neatly cleaned shallow depression scooped out by Second Mother, near Glen Urquhart, when something heavy and round descended on a long line, landing just outside the hole and raising an almost-invisible puff of silt in the blackness of the deep, icy water. The line tightened and began to drag the heavy thing about.

First Uncle had his huge length coiled about the clutch of eggs, making a dome of his body and enclosing them between the smooth skin of his underside and the cleaned lakebed. Fresh, hot blood pulsed to the undersurface of his smooth skin, keeping the water warm in the enclosed area. He dared not leave the clutch to chill in the cold loch, so he sent a furious signal for Second Mother, who, hearing that her eggs were in danger, came swiftly from her feeding. The Youngest heard also and swam up as fast as she could in mingled alarm and excitement.

She reached the hatchhole just in time to find Second Mother coiling herself around the eggs, her belly skin already beginning to radiate heat from the warm blood that was being shunted to its surface. Released from his duties, First Uncle shot up through the dark, peaty water like a sixty-foot missile, up along the hanging line, with the Youngest close behind him.

They could see nothing for more than a few feet because of the murkiness. But neither First Uncle nor the Youngest relied much on the sense of sight, which was used primarily for protection on the surface of the loch, in any case. Besides, First Uncle was already beginning to lose his vision with age, so he seldom went to the surface nowadays, preferring to do his breathing in the caves, where it was safer. The Youngest had asked him once if he did not miss the sunlight, even the misty and often cloud-dulled sunlight of the open sky over the loch, with its instinctive pull at ancestral memories of the ocean, re-told in the legends. No, he has hold her, he had grown beyond such things. But she found it hard to believe him; for in her, the yearning for the mysterious and fascinating world above the waters was still strong. The Family had no word for it. If they did, they might have called her a romantic.

Now, through the pressure-sensitive cells in the cheek areas of her narrow head, she picked up the movements of a creature no more than six feet in length. Carrying some long, narrow made thing, the intruder was above them, though descending rapidly, parallel to the line.

"Stay back," First Uncle signaled her sharply; and, suddenly fearful, she lagged behind. From the vibrations she felt, their visitor could only be one of the upright animals from the world above that walked about on its hind legs and used "made" things. There was an ancient taboo about touching one of these creatures.

The Youngest hung back, then, continuing to rise through the water at a more normal pace.

Above her, through her cheek cells, she felt and interpreted the turbulence that came from First Uncle's movements. He flashed up, level with the descending animal, and with one swirl of his massive body snapped the taut descending line. The animal was sent tumbling—untouched by First Uncle's bulk (according to the taboo), but stunned and buffeted and thrust aside by the water-blow like a leaf in a sudden gust of wind when autumn sends the dry tears of the trees drifting down upon the shore waters of the loch.

The thing the animal had carried, as well as the lower half of the broken line, began to sink to the bottom. The top of the line trailed aimlessly. Soon the upright animal, hanging limp in the water, was drifting rapidly away from it. First Uncle, satisfied that he had protected the location of the hatchhole for the moment, at least—though later in the day they would move the eggs to a new location, anyway, as a safety precaution—turned and headed back down to release Second Mother once more to her feeding.

Still fearful, but fascinated by the drifting figure, the Youngest rose timidly through the water on an angle that gradually brought her close to it. She extended her small head on its long, graceful neck to feel about it from close range with her pressure-sensitive cheek cells. Here, within inches of the floating form, she could read minute differences, even in its surface textures. It seemed to be encased in an unnatural outer skin—one of those skins the creatures wore which were not actually theirs—made of some material that soaked up the loch water. This soaked-up water was evidently heated by the interior temperature of the creature, much as members of the Family could warm their belly skins with shunted blood, which protected the animal's body inside by cutting down the otherwise too-rapid radiation of its heat into the cold liquid of the loch.

The Youngest noticed something bulky and hard on the creature's head, in front, where the eyes and mouth were. Attached to the back was a larger, doubled something, also hard and almost a third as long as the creature itself. The Youngest had never before seen a diver's wetsuit, swim mask, and air tanks with pressure regulator, but she had heard them described by her elders. First Mother had once watched from a safe distance while a creature so equipped had maneuvered below the surface of the loch, and she had concluded that the things he wore were devices to enable him to swim underwater without breathing as often as his kind seemed to need to, ordinarily.

Only this one was not swimming. He was drifting away with an underwater current of the loch, rising slowly as he traveled toward its south end. If he continued like this, he would come to the surface near the center of the loch. By that time the afternoon would be over. It would be dark.

Clearly, he had been damaged. The blow of the water that had been slammed at him by the body of First Uncle had hurt him in some way. But he was still alive. The Youngest knew this, because she could feel through her cheek cells the slowed beating of his heart and the movement of gases and fluids in his body. Occasionally, a small thread of bubbles came from his head to drift surfaceward.

It was a puzzle to her where he carried such a reservoir of air. She herself could contain enough oxygen for six hours without breathing, but only a portion of that was in gaseous form in her lungs. Most was held in pure form, saturating special tissues throughout her body.

Nonetheless, for the moment the creature seemed to have more than enough air stored about him; and he still lived. However, it could not be good for him to be drifting like this into the open loch with night coming on. Particularly if he was hurt, he would be needing some place safe out in the air, just as members of the Family did when they were old or sick. These upright creatures, the Youngest knew, were slow and feeble swimmers. Not one of them could have fed himself, as she did, by chasing and catching the fish of the loch; and very often when one fell into the water at any distance from the shore, he would struggle only a little while and then die.

This one would die also, in spite of the things fastened to him, if he stayed in the water. The thought raised a sadness in her. There was so much death. In any century, out of perhaps five clutches of a dozen eggs to a clutch, only one embryo might live to hatch. The legends claimed that once, when the Family had lived in the sea, matters had been different. But now, one survivor out of several clutches was the most to be hoped for. A hatchling who survived would be just about the size of this creature, the Youngest thought, though of course not with his funny shape. Nevertheless, watching him was a little like watching a new hatchling, knowing it would die.

It was an unhappy thought. But there was nothing to be done. Even if the diver were on the surface now, the chances were small that his own People could locate him.

Struck by a thought, the Youngest went up to look around. The situation was as she had guessed. No boats were close by. The nearest was the one from which the diver had descended; but it was still anchored close to the location of the hatchhole, nearly half a mile from where she and the creature now were.

Clearly, those still aboard thought to find him near where they had lost him. The Youngest went back down, and found him still drifting, now not more than thirty feet below the surface, but rising only gradually.

Her emotions stirred as she looked at him. He was not a cold life-form like the salmons, eels, and other fishes on which the Family fed. He was warm—as she was—and if the legends were all true, there had been a time and a place on the wide oceans where one of his ancestors and one of her ancestors might have looked at each other, equal and unafraid, in the open air and the sunlight.

So, it seemed wrong to let him just drift and die like this. He had shown the courage to go down into the depths of the loch, this small, frail thing. And such courage required some recognition from one of the Family, like herself. After all, it was loyalty and courage that had kept the Family going all these centuries: their loyalty to each other and the courage to conserve their strength and go on, hoping that someday the ice would come once more, the land would sink, and they would be set free into the seas again. Then surviving hatchlings would once more be numerous, and the Family would begin to grow again into what the legends had once called them, a "True People." Anyone who believed in loyalty and courage, the Youngest told herself, ought to respect those qualities wherever she found them—even in one of the upright creatures.

He should not simply be left to die. It was a daring thought, that she might interfere . . .

She felt her own heart beating more rapidly as she followed him through the water, her cheek cells only inches from his dangling shape. After all, there was the taboo. But perhaps, if she could somehow help him without actually touching him. . . ?

"Him," of course, should not include the "made" things about him. But even if she could move him by these parts alone, where could she take him?

Back to where the others of his kind still searched for him?

No, that was not only a deliberate flouting of the taboo but was very dangerous. Behind the taboo was the command to avoid letting any of his kind know about the Family. To take him back was to deliberately risk that kind of exposure for her People. She would die before doing that. The Family had existed all these centuries only because each member of it was faithful to the legends, to the duties, and to the taboos.

But, after all, she thought, it wasn't that she was actually going to break the taboo. She was only going to do something that went around the edge of it, because the diver had shown courage and because it was not his fault that he had happened to drop his heavy thing right beside the hatchhole. If he had dropped it anyplace else in the loch, he could have gone up and down its cable all summer and the Family members would merely have avoided that area.

What he needed, she decided, was a place out of the water where he could recover. She could take him to one of the banks of the loch. She rose to the surface again and looked around.

What she saw made her hesitate. In the darkening afternoon, the headlights of the cars moving up and down the roadways on each side of the loch were still visible in unusual numbers. From Fort Augustus at the south end of the loch to Castle Ness at the north, she saw more headlights about than ever before at this time of the year, especially congregating by St. Ninian's, where the diver's boat was docked, nights.

No, it was too risky, trying to take him ashore. But she knew of a cave, too small by Family standards for any of the older adults, south of Urquhart Castle. The diver had gone down over the hatchhole, which had been constructed by Second Mother in the mouth of Urquhart Glen, close by St. Ninian's; and he had been drifting south ever since. Now he was below Castle Urquhart and almost level with the cave. It was a good, small cave for an animal his size, with ledge of rock that was dry above the water at this time of year; and during the day even a little light would filter through cracks where tree roots from above had penetrated its rocky roof.

The Youngest could bring him there quite easily. She hesitated again, but then extended her head toward the air tanks on his back, took the tanks in her jaws, and began to carry him in the direction of the cave.

As she had expected, it was empty. This late in the day there was no light inside; but since, underwater, her cheek cells reported accurately on conditions about her and, above water, she had her memory, which was ultimately reliable, she brought him—still unconscious—to the ledge at the back of the cave and reared her head a good eight feet out of the water to lift him up on it. As she set him down softly on the bare rock, one of his legs brushed her neck, and a thrill of icy horror ran through the warm interior of her body.

Now she had done it! She had broken the taboo. Panic seized her.

She turned and plunged back into the water, out through the entrance to the cave and into the open loch. The taboo had never been broken before, as far as she knew—never. Suddenly she was terribly frightened. She headed at top speed for the hatchhole. All she wanted was to find Second Mother, or the Uncle, or anyone, and confess what she had done, so that they could tell her that the situation was not irreparable, not a signal marking an end of everything for them all.

Halfway to the hatchhole, however, she woke to the fact that it had already been abandoned. She turned immediately and began to range the loch bottom southward, her instinct and training counseling her that First Uncle and Second Mother would have gone in that direction, south toward Inverfarigaig, to set up a new hatchhole.

As she swam, however, her panic began to lessen and guilt moved in to take its place. How could she tell them? She almost wept inside herself. Here it was not many months ago that they had talked about how she was beginning to look and think like an adult; and she had behaved as thoughtlessly as if she were still the near-hatchling she had been thirty years ago.

Level with Castle Kitchie, she sensed the new location and homed in on it, finding it already set up off the mouth of the stream which flowed past the castle into the loch. The bed of the loch about the new hatchhole had been neatly swept and the saucer-shaped depression dug, in which Second Mother now lay warming the eggs. First Uncle was close by enough to feel the Youngest arrive, and he swept to speak to her as she halted above Second Mother.

"Where did you go after I broke the line?" he demanded before she herself could signal.

"I wanted to see what would happen to the diver," she signaled back. "Did you need me? I would have come back, but you and Second Mother were both there."

"We had to move right away," Second Mother signaled. She was agitated. "It was frightening!"

"They dropped another line," First Uncle said, "with a thing on it that they pulled back and forth as if to find the first one they dropped. I thought it not wise to break a second one. One break could be a chance happening. Two, and even small animals might wonder."

"But we couldn't keep the hole there with that thing dragging back and forth near the eggs," explained Second Mother. "So we took them and moved without waiting to make the new hole here, first. The Uncle and I carried them, searching as we went. If you'd been here, you could have held half of them while I made the hole by myself, the way I wanted it. But you weren't. We would have sent for First Mother to come from her cave and help us, but neither of us wanted to risk carrying the eggs about so much. So we had to work together here while still holding the eggs."

"Forgive me," said the Youngest. She wished she were dead.

"You're young," said Second Mother. "Next time you'll be wiser. But you do know that one of the earliest legends says the eggs should be moved only with the utmost care until hatching time; and you know we think that may be one reason so few hatch.''

''If none hatch now,'' said First Uncle to the Youngest, less forgiving than Second Mother, even though they were not his eggs, ''you'll remember this and consider that maybe you're to blame.''

''Yes,'' mourned the Youngest.

She had a sudden, frightening vision of this one and all Second Mother's future clutches, failing to hatch and she herself proving unable to lay when her time came. It was almost unheard of that a female of the Family should be barren, but a legend said that such a thing did occasionally happen. In her mind's eye she had a terrible picture of First Mother long dead, First Uncle and Second Mother grown old and feeble, unable to stir out of their caves, and she herself—the last of her line—dying alone, with no one to curl about her to warm or comfort her.

She had intended, when she caught up with the other two members of the Family, to tell them everything about what she had done with the diver. But she could not bring herself to it now. Her confession stuck in her mind. If it turned out that the clutch had been harmed by her inattention while she had actually been breaking the taboo with one of the very animals who had threatened the clutch in the first place . . .

She should have considered more carefully. But, of course, she was still too ignorant and irresponsible. First Uncle and Second Mother were the wise ones. First Mother, also, of course; but she was now too old to see a clutch of eggs through to hatching stage by herself alone, or with just the help of someone presently as callow and untrustworthy as the Youngest.

''Can I— It's dark now,'' she signaled. ''Can I go feed now? Is it all right to go?''

''Of course,'' said Second Mother, who switched her signaling to First Uncle. ''You're too hard sometimes. She's still only half grown.''

The Youngest felt even worse, intercepting that. She slunk off through the underwater, wishing something terrible could happen to her so that when the older ones did find out what she had done they would feel pity for her, instead of hating her. For a while she played with mental images of what this might involve. One of the boats on the surface could get her tangled in their lines in such a way that she could not get free. Then they would tow her to shore, and since she was so tangled in the line she could not get up to the surface, and since she had not breathed for many hours, she would drown on the way. Or perhaps the boat that could go underwater would find her and start chasing her and turn out to be much faster than any of them had ever suspected. It might even catch her and ram her and kill her.

By the time she had run through a number of these dark scenarios, she had begun almost automatically to hunt, for the time was in fact well past her usual second feeding period and she was hungry. As she realized this, her hunt became serious. Gradually she filled herself with salmon; and as she did so, she began to feel better. For all her bulk, she was swifter than any fish in the loch. The wide swim-paddle at the end of each of her four limbs could turn her instantly; and with her long neck and relatively small head outstretched, the streamlining of even her twenty-eight-foot body parted the waters she displaced with an absolute minimum of resistance. Last, and most important of all, was the great engine of her enormously powerful, lashing tail: that was the real drive behind her ability to flash above the loch bottom at speeds of up to fifty knots.

She was, in fact, beautifully designed to lead the life she led, designed by evolution over the generations from that land-dwelling, omnivorous early mammal that was her ancestor. Actually, she was herself a member of the mammalian sub-class prototheria, a large and distant cousin of monotremes like the platypus and the echidna. Her cretaceous forebears had drifted over and become practicing carnivores in the process of readapting to life in the sea.

She did not know this herself, of course. The legends of the Family were incredibly ancient, passed down by the letter-perfect memories of the individual generations; but they actually were not true memories of what had been, but merely deductions about the past gradually evolved as her People had acquired communication and intelligence. In many ways, the Youngest was very like a human savage: a member of a Stone Age tribe where elaborate ritual and custom directed every action of her life except for a small area of individual freedom. And in that area of individual freedom she was as prone to ignorance and misjudgments about the world beyond the waters of her loch as any Stone Age human primitive was in dealing with the technological world beyond his familiar few square miles of jungle.

Because of this—and because she was young and healthy—by the time she had filled herself with salmon, the exercise of hunting her dinner had burned off a good deal of her feelings of shame and guilt. She saw, or thought she saw, more clearly that her real fault was in not staying close to the hatchhole after the first incident. The diver's leg touching her neck had been entirely accidental; and besides, the diver had been unconscious and unaware of her presence at that time. So no harm could have been done. Essentially, the taboo was still unbroken. But she must learn to stay on guard as the adults did, to anticipate additional trouble, once some had put in an appearance, and to hold herself ready at all times.

She resolved to do so. She made a solemn promise to herself not to forget the hatchhole again—ever.

Her stomach was full. Emboldened by the freedom of the night-empty waters above, for the loch was always clear of boats after sundown, she swam to the surface, emerging only a couple of hundred yards from shore. Lying there, she watched the unusual number of lights from cars still driving on the roads that skirted the loch.

But suddenly her attention was distracted from them. The clouds overhead had evidently cleared, some time since. Now it was a clear, frosty night and more than half the sky was glowing and melting with the northern lights. She floated, watching them. So beautiful, she thought, so beautiful. Her mind evoked pictures of all the Family who must have lain and watched the lights like this since time began, drifting in the arctic seas or resting on some skerry or ocean rock where only birds walked. The desire to see all the wide skies and seas of all the world swept over her like a physical hunger.

It was no use, however. The mountains had risen and they held the Family here, now. Blocked off from its primary dream, her hunger for adventure turned to a more possible goal. The temptation came to go and investigate the loch-going "made" things from which her diver had descended.

She found herself up near Dores, but she turned and went back down opposite St. Ninian's. The dock to which this particular boat was customarily moored was actually a mile below the village and had no illumination. But the boat had a cabin on its deck, amidships, and through the square windows lights now glowed. Their glow was different from that of the lights shown by the cars. The Youngest noted this difference without being able to account for it, not understanding that the headlights she had been watching were electric, but the illumination she now saw shining out of the cabin windows of the large, flat-hulled boat before her came from gas lanterns. She heard sounds coming from inside the cabin.

Curious, the Youngest approached the boat from the darkness of the lake, her head now lifted a good six feet out of the water so that she could look over the side railing. Two large, awkward-looking shapes rested on the broad deck in front of the cabin—one just in front, the other right up in the bow with its far end overhanging the water. Four more shapes, like the one in the bow but smaller, were spaced along the sides of the foredeck, two to a side. The Youngest slid through the little waves until she was barely a couple of dozen feet from the side of the boat. At that moment, two men came out of the cabin, strode onto the deck, and stopped by the shape just in front of the cabin.

The Youngest, though she knew she could not be seen against the dark expanse of the loch, instinctively sank down until only her head was above water. The two men stood, almost overhead, and spoke to each other.

Their voices had a strangely slow, sonorous ring to the ears of the Youngest, who was used to hearing sound waves traveling through the water at four times the speed they moved in air. She did understand, of course, that they were engaged in meaningful communication, much as she and the others of the Family were when they signaled to each other. This much her People had learned about the upright animals: they communicated by making sounds. A few of these sounds—the *"Ness"* sound, which, like the other sound, *"loch,"* seemed to refer to the water in which the Family lived—were by now familiar. But she recognized no such noises among those made by the two above her; in fact, it would have been surprising if she had, for while the language was the one she was used to hearing, the accent of one of the two was Caribbean English, different enough from that of those living in the vicinity of the loch to make what she heard completely unintelligible.

". . . poor bastard," the other voice said.

"Man, you forget that 'poor bastard' talk, I tell you! He knew what he doing when he go down that line. He know what a temperature like that mean. A reading like that big enough for a blue whale. He just want the glory—he all alone swimming down with a speargun to drug that great beast. It the newspaper headlines, man; that's what he after!''

"Gives me the creeps, anyway. Think we'll ever fish up the sensor head?''

"You kidding. Lucky we find *him*. No, we use the spare, like I say, starting early tomorrow. And I mean it, early!''

"I don't like it. I tell you, he's got to have relatives who'll want to know why we didn't stop after we lost him. It's his boat. It's his equipment. They'll ask who gave us permission to go on spending money they got coming, with him dead.''

"You pay me some heed. We've got to try to find him, that's only right. We use the equipment we got—what else we got to use? Never mind his rich relatives. They just like him. He don't never give no damn for you or me or what it cost him, this expedition. He was born with money and all he want to do is write the book about how he an adventurer. We know what we hunt be down there, now. We capture it, then everybody happy. And you and me, we get what's in the contract, the five thousand extra apiece for taking it. Otherwise we don't get nothing—you back to that machine shop, me to the whaling, with the pockets empty. We out in the cold then, you recall that!''

"All right.''

"You damn right, it all right. Starting tomorrow sun-up.''

"I said *all right*!'' The voice paused for a second before going on. "But I'm telling you one thing. If we run into it, you better get it fast with a drug spear; because I'm not waiting. If I see it, I'm getting on the harpoon gun.''

The other voice laughed.

"That's why he never let you near the gun when we out before. But I don't care. Contract, it say alive or dead we get what he promise us. Come on now, up the inn and have us food and drink.''

"I want a drink! Christ, this water's empty after dark, with that law about no fishing after sundown. Anything could be out there!''

"Anything is. Come on, mon.''

The Youngest heard the sound of their footsteps backing off

the boat and moving away down the dock until they became inaudible within the night of the land.

Left alone, she lifted her head gradually out of the water once more and cautiously examined everything before her: big boat and small ones nearby, dock and shore. There was no sound or other indication of anything living. Slowly, she once more approached the craft the two had just left and craned her neck over its side.

The large shape in front of the cabin was box-like like the boat, but smaller and without any apertures in it. Its top sloped from the side facing the bow of the craft to the opposite side. On that sloping face she saw circles of some material that, although as hard as the rest of the object, still had a subtly different texture when she pressed her cheek cells directly against them. Farther down from these, which were in fact the glass faces of meters, was a raised plate with grooves in it. The Youngest would not have understood what the grooves meant, even if she had had enough light to see them plainly; and even if their sense could have been translated to her, the words "caloric sensor" would have meant nothing to her.

A few seconds later, she was, however, puzzled to discover on the dock beside this object another shape which her memory insisted was an exact duplicate of the heavy round thing that had been dropped to the loch bed beside the old hatchhole. She felt all over it carefully with her cheek cells, but discovered nothing beyond the dimensions of its almost plumb-bob shape and the fact that a line was attached to it in the same way a line had been attached to the other. In this case, the line was one end of a heavy coil that had a farther end connected to the box-like shape with the sloping top.

Baffled by this discovery, the Youngest moved forward to examine the strange object in the bow of the boat with its end overhanging the water. This one had a shape that was hard to understand. It was more complex, made up of a number of smaller shapes both round and boxy. Essentially, however, it looked like a mound with something long and narrow set on top of it, such as a piece of waterlogged tree from which the limbs had long since dropped off. The four smaller things like it, spaced two on each side of the foredeck, were not quite like the big one, but they were enough alike so that she ignored them in favor of examining the large one. Feeling around the end of the object that extended over the bow of the boat and hovered above the water, the Youngest discovered the log shape rotated at a touch and even tilted up and down with the mound beneath it as a balance point. On further investigation, she found that the log shape was hollow at the water end and was projecting beyond the hooks the animals often let down into the water with little dead fish or other things attached, to try to catch the larger fish of the loch. This end, however, was attached not to a curved length of metal, but to a straight metal rod lying loosely in the hollow log space. To the rod part, behind the barbed head, was joined the end of another heavy coil of line wound about a round thing on the deck. This line was much thicker than the one attached to the box with the sloping top. Experimentally, she tested it with her teeth. It gave—but did not cut when she closed her jaws on it—then sprang back, apparently unharmed, when she let it go.

All very interesting, but puzzling—as well it might be. A harpoon gun and spearguns with heads designed to inject a powerful tranquilizing drug on impact were completely outside the reasonable dimensions of the world as the Youngest knew it. The heat-sensing equipment that had been used to locate First Uncle's huge body as it lay on the loch bed warming the eggs was closer to being something she could understand. She and the rest of the Family used heat sensing themselves to locate and identify one another, though their natural abilities were nowhere near as sensitive as those of the instrument she had examined on the foredeck. At any rate, for now, she merely dismissed from her mind the question of what these things were. Perhaps, she thought, the upright animals simply liked to have odd shapes of "made" things around them. That notion reminded her of her diver; and she felt a sudden, deep curiosity about him, a desire to see if he had yet recovered and found his way out of the cave to shore.

She backed off from the dock and turned toward the south end of the loch, not specifically heading for the cave where she had left him but traveling in that general direction and turning over in her head the idea that perhaps she might take one more look at the cave. But she would not be drawn into the same sort of irresponsibility she had fallen prey to earlier in the day, when she had taken him to the cave! Not twice would she concern herself with one of the animals when she was needed by others

of the Family. She decided, instead, to go check on Second
Mother and the new hatchhole.

When she got to the hole, however, she found that Second
Mother had no present need of her. The older female, tired from
the exacting events of the day and heavy from feeding later than
her usual time—for she had been too nervous, at first, to leave
the eggs in First Uncle's care and so had not finished her feeding
period until well after dark—was half asleep. She only untucked
her head from the coil she had made of her body around and
above the eggs long enough to make sure the Youngest had not
brought warning of some new threat. Reassured, she coiled up
tightly again about the clutch and closed her eyes.

The Youngest gazed at her with a touch of envy. It must be a
nice feeling, she thought, to shut out everything but yourself and
your eggs. There was plainly nothing that Youngest was wanted
for, here—and she had never felt less like sleeping herself. The
night was full of mysteries and excitements. She headed once
more north, up the lake.

She had not deliberately picked a direction, but suddenly she
realized that unconsciously she was once more heading toward
the cave where she had left the diver. She felt a strange sense of
freedom. Second Mother was sleeping with her eggs. First Uncle by this time would have his heavy bulk curled up in his
favorite cave and his head on its long neck resting on a ledge at
the water's edge, so that he had the best of both the worlds of
air and loch at the same time. The Youngest had the loch to
herself, with neither Family nor animals to worry about. It was
all hers, from Fort Augustus clear to Castle Ness.

The thought gave her a sense of power. Abruptly, she decided
that there was no reason at all why she should not go see what
had happened to the diver. She turned directly toward the cave,
putting on speed.

At the last moment, however, she decided to enter the cave
quietly. If he was really recovered and alert, she might want to
leave again without being noticed. Like a cloud shadow moving
silently across the surface of the waves, she slid through the
underwater entrance of the cave, invisible in the blackness, her
cheek cells reassuring her that there was no moving body in the
water inside.

Once within, she paused again to check for heat radiation that
would betray a living body in the water even if it was being held

perfectly still. But she felt no heat. Satisfied, she lifted her head silently from the water inside the cave and approached the rock ledge where she had left him.

Her hearing told that he was still here, though her eyes were as useless in this total darkness as his must be. Gradually, that same, sensitive hearing filled in the image of his presence for her.

He still lay on the ledge, apparently on his side. She could hear the almost rhythmic scraping of a sort of metal clip he wore on the right side of his belt. It was scratching against the rock as he made steady, small movements. He must have come to enough to take off his head-things and back-things, however, for she heard no scraping from these. His breathing was rapid and hoarse, almost a panting. Slowly, sound by sound, she built up a picture of him, there in the dark. He was curled up in a tight ball, shivering.

The understanding that he was lying, trembling from the cold, struck the Youngest in her most vulnerable area. Like all the Family, she had vivid memories of what it had been like to be a hatchling. As eggs, the clutch was kept in open water with as high an oxygen content as possible until the moment for hatching came close. Then they were swiftly transported to one of the caves so that they would emerge from their shell into the land and air environment that their warm-blooded, air-breathing ancestry required. And a hatchling could not drown on a cave ledge. But, although he or she was protected there from the water, a hatchling was still vulnerable to the cold; and the caves were no warmer than the water—which was snow-fed from the mountains most of the year. Furthermore, the hatchling would not develop the layers of blubber-like fat that insulated an adult of the Family for several years. The life of someone like the Youngest began with the sharp sensations of cold as a newborn, and ended the same way, when aged body processes were no longer able to generate enough interior heat to keep the great hulk going. The first instinct of the hatchling was to huddle close to the warm belly skin of the adult on guard. And the first instinct of the adult was to warm the small, new life.

She stood in the shallow water of the cave, irresolute. The taboo, and everything that she had ever known, argued fiercely in her against any contact with the upright animal. But this one had already made a breach in her cosmos, had already been promoted from an "it" to a "he" in her thoughts; and her instincts cried out as strongly as her teachings, against letting him chill there on the cold stone ledge when she had within her the heat to warm him.

It was a short, hard, internal struggle; but her instincts won. After all, she rationalized, it was she who had brought him here to tremble in the cold. The fact that by doing so she had saved his life was beside the point.

Completely hidden in the psychological machinery that moved her toward him now was the lack in her life that was the result of being the last, solitary child of her kind. From the moment of hatching on, she had never had a playmate, never known anyone with whom she could share the adventures of growing up. An unconscious part of her was desperately hungry for a friend, a toy, anything that could be completely and exclusively hers, apart from the adult world that encompassed everything around her.

Slowly, silently, she slipped out of the water and up onto the ledge and flowed around his shaking form. She did not quite dare to touch him; but she built walls about him and a roof over him out of her body, the inward-facing skin of which was already beginning to pulse with hot blood pumped from deep within her.

Either dulled by his semi-consciousness or else too wrapped up in his own misery to notice, the creature showed no awareness that she was there. Not until the warmth began to be felt did he instinctively relax the tight ball of his body and, opening out, touch her—not merely with his wetsuit-encased body, but with his unprotected hands and forehead.

The Youngest shuddered all through her length at that first contact. But before she could withdraw, his own reflexes operated. His chilling body felt warmth and did not stop to ask its source. Automatically, he huddled close against the surfaces he touched.

The Youngest bowed her head. It was too late. It was done.

This was no momentary, unconscious contact. She could feel his shivering directly now through her own skin surface. Nothing remained but to accept what had happened. She folded herself close about him, covering as much of his small, cold, trembling body as possible with her own warm surface, just as she would have if he had been a new hatchling who suffered from the chill. He gave a quavering sigh of relief and pressed close against her.

Gradually he warmed and his trembling stopped. Long before that, he had fallen into a deep, torpor-like slumber. She could hear the near-snores of his heavy breathing.

Grown bolder by contact with him and abandoning herself to an affection for him, she explored his slumbering shape with her sensitive cheek cells. He had no true swim paddles, of course—she already knew this about the upright animals. But she had never guessed how delicate and intricate were the several-times split appendages that he possessed on his upper limbs where swim paddles might have been. His body was very narrow, its skeleton hardly clothed in flesh. Now that she knew that his kind were as vulnerable to cold as new hatchlings, she did not wonder that it should be so with them: they had hardly anything over their bones to protect them from the temperature of the water and air. No wonder they covered themselves with non-living skins.

His head was not long at all, but quite round. His mouth was small and his jaws flat, so that he would be able to take only very small bites of things. There was a sort of protuberance above the mouth and a pair of eyes, side by side. Around the mouth and below the eyes his skin was full of tiny, sharp points; and on the top of his head was a strange, springy mat of very fine filaments. The Youngest rested the cells of her right cheek for a moment on the filaments finding a strange inner warmth and pleasure in the touch of them. It was a completely inexplicable pleasure, for the legends had forgotten what old, primitive parts of her brain remembered: a time when her ancestors on land had worn fur and known the feel of it in their close body contacts.

Wrapped up in the subconscious evocation of ancient companionship, she lay in the darkness spinning impossible fantasies in which she would be able to keep him. He could live in this cave, she thought, and she would catch salmon—since that was what his kind, with their hooks and filaments, seemed most to search for—to bring to him for food. If he wanted "made" things about him, she could probably visit docks and suchlike about the loch and find some to bring here to him. When he got to know her better, since he had the things that let him hold his breath underwater, they could venture out into the loch together. Of course, once that time was reached, she would have to tell Second Mother and First Uncle about him. No doubt it would disturb them greatly, the fact that the taboo had been broken; but once they had met him underwater, and seen how sensible and friendly he was—how wise, even, for a small animal like himself . . .

Even as she lay dreaming these dreams, however, a sane part of her mind was still on duty. Realistically, she knew that what she was thinking was nonsense. Centuries of legend, duty, and taboo were not to be upset in a few days by any combination of accidents. Nor, even if no problem arose from the Family side, could she really expect him to live in a cave, forsaking his own species. His kind needed light as well as air. They needed the freedom to come and go on shore. Even if she could manage to keep him with her in the cave for a while, eventually the time would come when he would yearn for the land under his feet and the open sky overhead, at one and the same time. No, her imaginings could never be; and, because she knew this, when her internal time sense warned her that the night was nearly over, she silently uncoiled from around him and slipped back into the water, leaving the cave before the first light, which filtered in past the tree roots in the cave roof, could let him see who it was that had kept him alive through the hours of darkness.

Left uncovered on the ledge but warm again, he slept heavily on, unaware.

Out in the waters of the loch, in the pre-dawn gloom, the Youngest felt fatigue for the first time. She could easily go twenty-four hours without sleep; but this twenty-four hours just past had been emotionally charged ones. She had an irresistible urge to find one of the caves she favored herself and to lose herself in slumber. She shook it off. Before anything else she must check with Second Mother.

Going swiftly to the new hatchhole, she found Second Mother fully awake, alert, and eager to talk to her. Evidently Second Mother had awakened early and spent some time thinking.

"You're young," she signaled the Youngest, "far too young to share the duty of guarding a clutch of eggs, even with someone as wise as your First Uncle. Happily, there's no problem physically. You're mature enough so that milk would come, if a hatchling should try to nurse from you. But, sensibly, you're still far too young to take on this sort of responsibility. Nonetheless, if something should happen to me, there would only be you and the Uncle to see this clutch to the hatching point. Therefore, we have to think of the possibility that you might have to take over for me.''

''No. No, I couldn't,'' said the Youngest.

''You may have to. It's still only a remote possibility; but I should have taken it into consideration before. Since there're only the four of us, if anything happened to one of us, the remaining would have to see the eggs through to hatching. You and I could do it, I'm not worried about that situation. But with a clutch there must be a mother. Your uncle can do everything but that, and First Mother is really too old. Somehow, we must make you ready before your time to take on that duty.''

''If you say so . . .'' said the Youngest, unhappily.

''Our situation says so. Now, all you need to know, really, is told in the legends. But knowing them and understanding them are two different things . . .''

Then Second Mother launched into a retelling of the long chain of stories associated with the subject of eggs and hatchlings. The Youngest, of course, had heard them all before. More than that, she had them stored, signal by signal, in her memory as perfectly as had Second Mother herself. But she understood that Second Mother wanted her not only to recall each of these packages of stored wisdom, but to think about what was stated in them. Also—so much wiser had she already become in twenty-four hours—she realized that the events of yesterday, had suddenly shocked Second Mother, giving her a feeling of helplessness should the upright animals ever really chance to stumble upon the hatchhole. For she could never abandon her eggs, and if she stayed with them the best she could hope for would be to give herself up to the land-dwellers in hope that this would satisfy them and they would look no further.

It was hard to try and ponder the legends, sleepy as the Youngest was, but she tried her best; and when at last Second Mother turned her loose, she swam groggily off to the nearest cave and curled up. It was now broad-enough daylight for her early feeding period, but she was too tired to think of food. In seconds, she was sleeping almost as deeply as the diver had been when she left him.

She came awake suddenly and was in motion almost before her eyes were open. First Uncle's signal of alarm was ringing all through the loch. She plunged from her cave into the outer waters. Vibrations told her that he and Second Mother were headed north, down the deep center of the loch as fast as they could travel, carrying the clutch of eggs. She drove on to join them, sending ahead her own signal that she was coming.

"Quick! Oh, quick!" signaled Second Mother.

Unencumbered, she began to converge on them at double their speed. Even in this moment her training paid off. She shot through the water, barely fifty feet above the bed of the loch, like a dolphin in the salt sea; and her perfect shape and smooth skin caused no turbulence at all to drag at her passage and slow her down.

She caught up with them halfway between Inverfarigaig and Dores and took her half of the eggs from Second Mother, leaving the older female free to find a new hatchhole. Unburdened, Second Mother leaped ahead and began to range the loch bed in search of a safe place.

"What happened?" signaled Youngest.

"Again!" First Uncle answered. "They dropped another 'made' thing, just like the first, almost in the hatchhole this time!" he told her.

Second Mother had been warming the eggs. Luckily he had been close. He had swept in; but not daring to break the line a second time for fear of giving clear evidence of the Family, he had simply scooped a hole in the loch bed, pushed the thing in, buried it and pressed down hard on the loch bed material with which he had covered it. He had buried it deeply enough so that the animals above were pulling up on their line with caution, for fear that they themselves might break it. Eventually, they would get it loose. Until then, the Family had a little time in which to find another location for the eggs.

A massive shape loomed suddenly out of the peaty darkness, facing them. It was First Mother, roused from her cave by the emergency.

"I can still carry eggs. Give them here and you go back," she ordered First Uncle. "Find out what's being done with that 'made' thing you buried and what's going on with those creatures. Two hatchholes stumbled on in two days is too much for chance."

First Uncle swirled about and headed back.

The Youngest slowed down. First Mother was still tremendously powerful, of course, more so than any of them; but she no longer had the energy reserves to move at the speed at which First Uncle and the Youngest had been traveling. Youngest felt a surge of admiration for First Mother, battling the chill of the open loch water and the infirmities of her age to give help now, when the Family needed it.

"Here! This way!" Second Mother called.

They turned sharply toward the east bank of the loch and homed in on Second Mother's signal. She had found a good place for a new hatchhole. True, it was not near the mouth of a stream; but the loch bed was clean and this was one of the few spots where the rocky slope underwater from the shore angled backward when it reached a depth below four hundred feet, so that the loch at this point was actually in under the rock and had a roof overhead. Here, there was no way that a "made" thing could be dropped down on a line to come anywhere close to the hatchhole.

When First Mother and the Youngest got there, Second Mother was already at work making and cleaning the hole. The hole had barely been finished and Second Mother settled down with the clutch under her, when First Uncle arrived.

"They have their 'made' thing back," he reported. "They pulled on its line with little, repeated jerkings until they loosened it from its bed, and then they lifted it back up."

He told how he had followed it up through the water until he was just under the "made" thing and rode on the loch surface. Holding himself there, hidden by the thing itself, he had listened, trying to make sense out of what the animals were doing, from what he could hear.

They had made a great deal of noise after they hoisted the thing back on board. They had moved it around a good deal and done things with it, before finally leaving it alone and starting back toward the dock near St. Ninian's. First Uncle had followed them until he was sure that was where they were headed; then he had come to find the new hatchhole and the rest of the Family.

After he was done signaling, they all waited for First Mother to respond, since she was the oldest and wisest. She lay thinking for some moments.

"They didn't drop the 'made' thing down into the water again, you say?" she asked at last.

"No," signaled First Uncle.

"And none of them went down into the water, themselves?"
"No."

"It's very strange," said First Mother. "All we know is that they've twice almost found the hatchhole. All I can guess is that this isn't a chance thing, but that they're acting with some purpose. They may not be searching for our eggs, but they seem to be searching for *something*."

The Youngest felt a sudden chilling inside her. But First Mother was already signaling directly to First Uncle.

"From now on, you should watch them, whenever the thing in which they move about the loch surface isn't touching shore. If you need help, the Youngest can help you. If they show any signs of coming close to here, we must move the eggs immediately. I'll come out twice a day to relieve Second Mother for her feeding, so that you can be free to do that watching. No"— she signaled sharply before they could object—"I *will* do this. I can go for some days warming the eggs for two short periods a day, before I'll be out of strength; and this effort of mine is needed. The eggs *should* be safe here, but if it proves that the creatures have some means of finding them, wherever the hatchhole is placed in the open loch, we'll have to move the clutch into the caves."

Second Mother cried out in protest.

"I know," First Mother said, "the legends counsel against ever taking the eggs into the caves until time for hatching. But we may have no choice."

"My eggs will die!" wept Second Mother.

"They're your eggs, and the decision to take them inside has to be yours," said First Mother. "But they won't live if the animals find them. In the caves there may be a chance of life for them. Besides, our duty as a Family is to survive. It's the Family we have to think of, not a single clutch of eggs or a single individual. If worse comes to worst and it turns out we're not safe from the animals even in the caves, we'll try the journey of the Lost Father from Loch Morar before we'll let ourselves all be killed off."

"What Lost Father?" the Youngest demanded. "No one ever told me a legend about a Lost Father from Loch Morar. What's Loch Morar?"

"It's not a legend usually told to those too young to have full wisdom," said First Mother. "But these are new and dangerous times. Loch Morar is a loch a long way from here, and some of our People were also left there when the ice went and the land rose. They were of our People, but a different Family.''

"But what about a Lost Father?'' the Youngest persisted, because First Mother had stopped talking as if she would say no more about it. "How could a Father be lost?''

"He was lost to Loch Morar,'' First Mother explained, "because he grew old and died here in Loch Ness.''

"But how did he get here?''

"He couldn't, that's the point,'' said First Uncle grumpily. "There are legends *and* legends. That's why some are not told to young ones until they've matured enough to understand. The journey the Lost Father's supposed to have made is impossible. Tell it to some youngster and he or she's just as likely to try and duplicate it.''

"But you said we might try it!'' The Youngest appealed to First Mother.

"Only if there were no other alternative,'' First Mother answered. "I'd try flying out over the mountains if that was the only alternative left, because it's our duty to keep trying to survive as a Family as long as we're alive. So, as a last resort, we'd try the journey of the Lost Father, even though as the Uncle says, it's impossible.''

"Why? Tell me what it was. You've already begun to tell me. Shouldn't I know all of it?''

"I suppose . . .'' said First Mother, wearily. "Very well. Loch Morar isn't surrounded by mountains as we are here. It's even fairly close to the sea, so that if a good way could be found for such as us to travel over dry land, members of the People living there might be able to go home to the sea we all recall by the legends. Well, this legend says that there once was a Father in Loch Morar who dreamed all his life of leading his Family home to the sea. But we've grown too heavy nowadays to travel any distance overland, normally. One winter day, when a new snow had just fallen, the legend says this Father discovered a way of traveling on land that worked.''

In sparse sentences, First Mother rehearsed the legend to a fascinated Youngest. It told that the snow provided a slippery surface over which the great bodies of the People could slide under the impetus of the same powerful tail muscles that drove them through the water, their swim paddles acting as rudders—

or brakes—on downslopes. Actually, what the legend described was a way of swimming on land. Loch Ness never froze and First Mother therefore had no knowledge of ice-skating, so she could not explain that what the legend spoke of was the same principle that makes a steel ice blade glide over ice—the weight upon it causing the ice to melt under the sharp edge of the blade so that, effectively, it slides on a cushion of water. With the People, their ability to shunt a controlled amount of warmth to the skin in contact with the ice and snow did the same thing.

In the legend, the Father who discovered this tried to take his Family from Loch Morar back to the sea, but they were all afraid to try going, except for him. So he went alone and found his way to the ocean more easily than he had thought possible. He spent some years in the sea, but found it lonely and came back to land to return to Loch Morar. However, though it was winter, he could not find enough snow along the route he had taken to the sea in order to get back to Loch Morar. He hunted northward for a snow-covered route inland, north past the isle of Sleat, past Glenelg; and finally, under Benn Attow, he found a snow route that led him ultimately to Glen Moriston and into Loch Ness.

He went as far back south through Loch Ness as he could go, even trying some distance down what is now the southern part of the Caledonian Canal before he became convinced that the route back to Loch Morar by that way would be too long and hazardous to be practical. He decided to return to the sea and wait for snow to make him a way over his original route to Morar.

But, meanwhile, he had become needed in Loch Ness and grown fond of the Family there. He wished to take them with him to the sea. The others, however, were afraid to try the long overland journey; and while they hesitated and put off going, he grew too old to lead them; and so they never did go. Nevertheless, the legend told of his route and, memories being what they were among the People, no member of the Family in Loch Ness, after First Mother had finished telling the legend to the Youngest, could not have retraced the Lost Father's steps exactly.

"I don't think we should wait," the Youngest said eagerly, when First Mother was through. "I think we should go now—I mean, as soon as we get a snow on the banks of the loch so that we can travel. Once we're away from the loch, there'll be snow all the time, because it's only the warmth of the loch that keeps the snow off around here. Then we could all go home to the sea, where we belong, away from the animals and their 'made' things. Most of the eggs laid there would hatch—''

''I told you so,'' First Uncle interrupted, speaking to First Mother. ''Didn't I tell you so?''

''And what about my eggs now?'' said Second Mother.

''We'll try something like that only if the animals start to destroy us,'' First Mother said to the Youngest with finality. ''Not before. If it comes to that, Second Mother's present clutch of eggs will be lost, anyway. Otherwise, we'd never leave them, you should know that. Now, I'll go back to the cave and rest until late feeding period for Second Mother.''

She went off. First Uncle also went off, to make sure that the animals had really gone to the dock and were still there. The Youngest, after asking Second Mother if there was any way she could be useful and being told there was none, went off to her delayed first feeding period.

She was indeed hungry, with the ravenous hunger of youth. But once she had taken the edge off her appetite, an uneasy feeling began to grow inside her, and not even stuffing herself with rich-fleshed salmon made it go away.

What was bothering her, she finally admitted to herself, was the sudden, cold thought that had intruded on her when First Mother had said that the creatures seemed to be searching for something. The Youngest was very much afraid she knew what they were searching for. It was their fellow, the diver she had taken to the cave. If she had not done anything, they would have found his body before this; but because she had saved him, they were still looking; and because he was in a cave, they could not find him. So they would keep on searching, and sooner or later they would come close to the new hatchhole; and then Second Mother would take the clutch into one of the caves, and the eggs would die, and it would be her own fault, the Youngest's fault alone.

She was crying inside. She did not dare cry out loud because the others would hear and want to know what was troubling her. She was ashamed to tell them what she had done. Somehow, she must put things right herself, without telling them—at least until some later time, when it would be all over and unimportant.

The diver must go back to his own people—if he had not already.

She turned and swam toward the cave, making sure to approach it from deep in the loch. Through the entrance of the cave, she stood up in the shallow interior pool and lifted her head out of the water; and he was still there.

Enough light was filtering in through the ceiling cracks of the cave to make a sort of dim twilight inside. She saw him plainly—and he saw her.

She had forgotten that he would have no idea of what she looked like. He had been sitting up on the rock ledge; but when her head and its long neck rose out of the water, he stared and then scrambled back—as far back from her as he could get, to the rock wall of the cave behind the ledge. He stood pressed against it, still staring at her, his mouth open in a soundless circle.

She paused, irresolute. She had never intended to frighten him. She had forgotten that he might consider her at all frightening. All her foolish imaginings of keeping him here in the cave and of swimming with him in the loch crumbled before the bitter reality of his terror at the sight of her. Of course, he had had no idea of who had been coiled about him in the dark. He had only known that something large had been bringing the warmth of life back into him. But surely he would make the connection, now that he saw her?

She waited.

He did not seem to be making it. He simply stayed where he was, as if paralyzed by her presence. She felt an exasperation with him rising inside her. According to the legends, his kind had at least a share of intelligence, possibly even some aspect of wisdom, although that was doubtful. But now, crouched against the back of the cave, he looked like nothing more than another wild animal—like one of the otters, strayed from nearby streams, she had occasionally encountered in these caves. And as with such an otter, for all its small size ready to scratch or bite, she felt a caution about approaching him.

Nevertheless, something had to be done. At any moment now, the others like him would be out on the loch in their "made" thing, once more hunting for him and threatening to rediscover the hatchhole.

Cautiously, slowly, so as not to send him into a fighting reflex, she approached the ledge and crept up on it sideways, making an arc of her body and moving in until she half surrounded him, an arm's length from him. She was ready to pull back at the first sign of a hostile move, but no action was triggered in him. He merely stayed where he was, pressing against the rock wall as if he would like to step through it, his eyes fixed on her and his jaws still in the half-open position. Settled about him, however, she shunted blood into her skin area and began to radiate heat.

It took a little while for him to feel the warmth coming from her and some little while more to understand what she was trying to tell him. But then, gradually, his tense body relaxed. He slipped down the rock against which he was pressed and ended up sitting, gazing at her with a different shape to his eyes and mouth.

He made some noises with his mouth. These conveyed no sense to the Youngest, of course, but she thought that at least they did not sound like unfriendly noises.

"So now you know who I am," she signaled, although she knew perfectly well he could not understand her. "Now, you've got to swim out of here and go back on the land. Go back to your People."

She had corrected herself instinctively on the last term. She had been about to say "go back to the other animals"; but something inside her dictated the change—which was foolish, because he would not know the difference, anyway.

He straightened against the wall and stood up. Suddenly, he reached out an upper limb toward her.

She flinched from his touch instinctively, then braced herself to stay put. If she wanted him not to be afraid of her, she would have to show him the same fearlessness. Even the otters, if left alone, would calm down somewhat, though they would take the first opportunity to slip past and escape from the cave where they had been found.

She held still, accordingly. The divided ends of his limb touched her and rubbed lightly over her skin. It was not an unpleasant feeling, but she did not like it. It had been different when he was helpless and had touched her unconsciously.

She now swung her head down close to watch him and had the satisfaction of seeing him start when her own eyes and jaws came within a foot or so of his. He pulled his limbs back quickly, and made more noises. They were still not angry noises, though, and this fact, together with his quick withdrawal, gave her an impression that he was trying to be conciliatory, even friendly.

Well, at least she had his attention. She turned, backed off the ledge into the water, then reached up with her nose and pushed toward him the "made" things he originally had had attached to his back and head. Then, turning, she ducked under the water, swam out of the cave into the loch, and waited just under the surface for him to follow.

He did not.

She waited for more than enough time for him to reattach his things and make up his mind to follow, then she swam back inside. To her disgust, he was now sitting down again and his "made" things were still unattached to him.

She came sharply up to the edge of the rock and tumbled the two things literally on top of him.

"Put them on!" she signaled. "Put them on, you stupid animal!"

He stared at her and made noises with his mouth. He stood up and moved his upper limbs about in the air. But he made no move to pick up the "made" things at his feet. Angrily, she shoved them against his lower limb ends once more.

He stopped making noises and merely looked at her. Slowly, although she could not define all of the changes that signaled it to her, an alteration of manner seemed to take place in him. The position of his upright body changed subtly. The noises he was making changed; they became slower and more separate, one from another. He bent down and picked up the larger of the things, the one that he had had attached to his back; but he did not put it on.

Instead, he held it up in the air before him as if drawing her attention to it. He turned it over in the air and shook it slightly, then held it in that position some more. He rapped it with the curled-over sections of one of his limb-ends, so that it rang with a hollow sound from both its doubled parts. Then he put it down on the ledge again and pushed it from him with one of his lower limb ends.

The Youngest stared at him, puzzled, but nonetheless hopeful for the first time. At last he seemed to be trying to communicate something to her, even though what he was doing right now seemed to make no sense. Could it be that this was some sort of game the upright animals played with their "made" things; and he either wanted to play it, or wanted her to play it with him, before he would put the things on and get in the water? When she was much younger, she had played with things herself—interesting pieces of rock or waterlogged material she found on the loch bed, or flotsam she had encountered on the surface at night, when it was safe to spend time in the open.

No, on second thought that explanation hardly seemed likely. If it was a game he wanted to play with her, it was more reasonable for him to push the things at her instead of just pushing the bigger one away and ignoring it. She watched him, baffled. Now he had picked up the larger thing again and was repeating his actions, exactly.

The creature went though the same motions several more times, eventually picking up and putting the smaller ''made'' thing about his head and muzzle, but still shaking and pushing away the larger thing. Eventually he made a louder noise which, for the first time, sounded really angry; threw the larger thing to one end of the ledge; and went off to sit down at the far end of the ledge, his back to her.

Still puzzled, the Youngest stretched her neck up over the ledge to feel the rejected ''made'' thing again with her cheek cells. It was still an enigmatic, cold, hard, double-shaped object that made no sense to her. What he's doing can't be playing, she thought. Not that he was playing at the last, there. And besides, he doesn't act as if he liked it and liked to play with it, he's acting as if he hated it—

Illumination came to her, abruptly.

''Of course!'' she signaled at him.

But of course the signal did not even register on him. He still sat with his back to her.

What he had been trying to tell her, she suddenly realized, was that for some reason the ''made'' thing was no good for him any longer. Whether he had used it to play with, to comfort himself, or, as she had originally guessed, it had something to do with making it possible for him to stay underwater, for some reason it was now no good for that purpose.

The thought that it might indeed be something to help him stay underwater suddenly fitted in her mind with the fact that he no longer considered it any good. She sat back on her tail, mentally berating herself for being so foolish. Of course, that was what he had been trying to tell her. It would not help him stay underwater anymore; and to get out of the cave he had to go underwater—not very far, of course, but still a small distance.

On the other hand, how was he to know it was only a small

distance? He had been unconscious when she had brought him here.

Now that she had worked out what she thought he had been trying to tell her, she was up against a new puzzle. By what means was she to get across to him that she had understood?

She thought about this for a time, then picked up the thing in her teeth and threw it herself against the rock wall at the back of the ledge.

He turned around, evidently alerted by the sounds it made. She stretched out her neck, picked up the thing, brought it back to the water edge of the ledge, and then threw it at the wall again.

Then she looked at him.

He made sounds with his mouth and turned all the way around. Was it possible he had understood? she wondered. But he made no further moves, just sat there. She picked up and threw the "made" thing a couple of more times; then she paused once again to see what he might do.

He stood, hesitating, then inched forward to where the thing had fallen, picked it up and threw it himself. But he threw it, as she had thrown it—at the rock wall behind the ledge.

The Youngest felt triumph. They were finally signaling each other—after a fashion.

But now where did they go from here? She wanted to ask him if there was anything they could do about the "made" thing being useless, but she could not think how to act that question out.

He, however, evidently had something in mind. He went to the edge of the rock shelf, knelt down and placed one of his multi-divided limb ends flat on the water surface, but with its inward-grasping surface upward. Then he moved it across the surface of the water so that the outer surface, or back, of it was in the water but the inner surface was still dry.

She stared at him. Once more he was doing something incomprehensible. He repeated the gesture several more times, but still it conveyed no meaning to her. He gave up, finally, and sat for a few minutes looking at her; then he got up, went back to the rock wall, turned around, walked once more to the edge of the ledge, and sat down.

Then he held up one of his upper limb ends with all but two of the divisions curled up. The two that were not curled up he pointed downward, and lowered them until their ends rested on the rock ledge. Then, pivoting first on the end of one of the divisions, then on the other, he moved the limb end back toward the wall as far as he could stretch, then turned it around and moved it forward again to the water's edge, where he folded up the two extended divisions, and held the limb end still.

He did this again. And again.

The Youngest concentrated. There was some meaning here; but with all the attention she could bring to bear on it, she still failed to see what it was. This was even harder than extracting wisdom from the legends. As she watched, he got up once more, walked back to the rock wall, came forward again and sat down. He did this twice.

Then he did the limb-end, two-division-movement thing twice.

Then he walked again, three times.

Then he did the limb-end thing three more times—

Understanding suddenly burst upon the Youngest. He was trying to make some comparison between his walking to the back of the ledge and forward again, and moving his limb ends in that odd fashion, first backward and then forward. The two divisions, with their little joints, moved much like his two lower limbs when he walked on them. It was extremely interesting to take part of your body and make it act like your whole body, doing something. Youngest wished that her swim paddles had divisions on the ends, like his, so she could try it.

She was becoming fascinated with the diver all over again. She had almost forgotten the threat to the eggs that others like him posed as long as he stayed hidden in this cave. Her conscience caught her up sharply. She should check right now and see if things were all right with the Family. She turned to leave, and then checked herself. She wanted to reassure him that she was coming back.

For a second only she was baffled for a means to do this; then she remembered that she had already left the cave once, thinking he would follow her, and then come back when she had given up on his doing so. If he saw her go and come several times, he should expect that she would go on returning, even though the interval might vary.

She turned and dived out through the hole into the loch, paused for a minute or two, then went back in. She did this two more times before leaving the cave finally. He had given her no real sign that he understood what she was trying to convey, but he had already showed signs of that intelligence the legends credited his species with. Hopefully, he would figure it out. If he did not—well, since she was going back anyway, the only harm would be that he might worry a bit about being abandoned there.

She surfaced briefly, in the center of the loch, to see if many of the "made" things were abroad on it today. But none were in sight and there was little or no sign of activity on the banks. The sky was heavy with dark, low-lying clouds; and the hint of snow, heavy snow, was in the sharp air. She thought again of the journey of the Lost Father of Loch Morar, and of the sea it could take them to—their safe home, the sea. They should go. They should go without waiting. If only she could convince them to go . . .

She dropped by the hatchhole, found First Mother warming the eggs while Second Mother was off feeding, and heard from First Mother that the craft had not left its place on shore all day. Discussing this problem almost as equals with First Mother—of whom she had always been very much in awe—emboldened the Youngest to the point where she shyly suggested she might try warming the clutch herself, occasionally, so as to relieve First Mother from these twice-daily stints, which must end by draining her strength and killing her.

"It would be up to Second Mother, in any case," First Mother answered, "but you're still really too small to be sure of giving adequate warmth to a full clutch. In an emergency, of course, you shouldn't hesitate to do you best with the eggs, but I don't think we're quite that desperate, yet."

Having signaled this, however, First Mother apparently softened.

"Besides," she said, "the time to be young and free of responsibilities is short enough. Enjoy it while you can. With the Family reduced to the four of us and this clutch, you'll have a hard enough adulthood, even if Second Mother manages to produce as many as two hatchlings out of the five or six clutches she can still have before her laying days are over. The odds of hatching females over males are four to one; but still, it could be that she might produce only a couple of males—and then everything would be up to you. So, use your time in your own way while it's still yours to use. But keep alert. If you're called, come immediately!"

The Youngest promised that she would. She left First Mother and went to find First Uncle, who was keeping watch in the neighborhood of the dock to which the craft was moored. When she found him, he was hanging in the loch about thirty feet deep and about a hundred feet offshore from the craft, using his sensitive hearing to keep track of what was happening in the craft and on the dock.

"I'm glad you're here," he signaled to the Youngest when she arrived. "It's time for my second feeding; and I think there're none of the animals on the 'made' thing, right now. But it wouldn't hurt to keep a watch, anyway. Do you want to stay here and listen while I go and feed?"

Actually, Youngest was not too anxious to do so. Her plan had been to check with the Uncle, then do some feeding herself and get back to her diver while daylight was still coming into his cave. But she could hardly explain that to First Uncle.

"Of course," she said. "I'll stay here until you get back."

"Good," said the Uncle; and went off.

Left with nothing to do but listen and think, the Youngest hung in the water. Her imagination, which really required very little to start it working, had recaptured the notion of making friends with the diver. It was not so important, really, that he had gotten a look at her. Over the centuries a number of incidents had occurred in which members of the Family were seen briefly by one or more of the animals, and no bad results had come from those sightings. But it was important that the land-dwellers not realize there was a true Family. If she could just convince the diver that she was the last and only one of her People, it might be quite safe to see him from time to time—of course, only when he was alone and when they were in a safe place of her choosing, since though he might be trustworthy, his fellows who had twice threatened the hatchhole clearly were not.

The new excitement about getting to know him had come from starting to be able to "talk" with him. If she and he kept at it, they could probably work out ways to tell all sorts of things to each other eventually.

That thought reminded her that she had not yet figured out why it was important to him that she understand that moving his divided limb ends in a certain way could stand for his walking. He must have had some reason for showing her that. Maybe it was connected with his earlier moving of his limb ends over the surface of the water?

Before she had a chance to ponder the possible connection, a sound from above, reaching down through the water, alerted her to the fact that some of the creatures were once more coming out onto the dock. She drifted in closer, and heard the sounds move to the end of the dock and onto the craft.

Apparently, they were bringing something heavy aboard, because along with the noise of their lower limb ends on the structure came the thumping and rumbling of something which ended at last—to judge from the sounds—somewhere up on the forward deck where she had examined the box with the sloping top and the other "made" thing in the bow.

Following this, she heard some more sounds moving from the foredeck area into the cabin.

A little recklessly, the Youngest drifted in until she was almost under the craft and only about fifteen feet below the surface, and so verified that it was, indeed, in that part of the boat where the box with the sloping top stood that most of the activity was going on. Then the noise in that area slowed down and stopped, and she heard the sound of the animals walking back off the craft, down the dock and ashore. Things became once more silent.

First Uncle had not yet returned. The Youngest wrestled with her conscience. She had not been specifically told not to risk coming up to the surface near the dock; but she knew that was simply because it had not occurred to any of the older members of the Family that she would be daring enough to do such a thing. Of course, she had never told any of them how she had examined the foredeck of the craft once before. But now, having already done so, she had a hard time convincing herself it was too risky to do again. After all, hadn't she heard the animals leave the area? No matter how quiet one of them might try to be, her hearing was good enough to pick up little sounds of his presence, if he was still aboard.

In the end, she gave in to temptation—which is not to say she moved without taking every precaution. She drifted in, underwater, so slowly and quietly that a little crowd of curious minnows formed around her. Approaching the foredeck from the loch side of the craft, she stayed well underwater until she was right up against the hull. Touching it, she hung in the water, listening. When she still heard nothing, she lifted her head quickly, just enough for a glimpse over the side; then she ducked back under again and shot away and down to a safe distance.

Eighty feet deep and a hundred feet offshore, she paused to consider what she had seen.

Her memory, like that of everyone in the Family, was essentially photographic when she concentrated on remembering, as she had during her brief look over the side of the craft. But being able to recall exactly what she had looked at was not the same thing as realizing its import. In this case, what she had been looking for was what had just been brought aboard. By comparing what she had just seen with what she had observed on her night visit earlier, she had hoped to pick out any addition to the "made" things she had noted then.

At first glance, no difference had seemed visible. She noticed the box with the sloping top and the thing in the bow with the barbed rod inside. A number of other, smaller, things were about the deck, too, some of which she had examined briefly the time before and some that she had barely noticed. Familiar were several of the doubled things like the one the diver had thrown from him in order to open up communications between them at first. Largely unfamiliar were a number of smaller boxes, some round things, other things that were combinations of round and angular shapes, and a sort of tall open frame, upright and holding several rods with barbed ends like the ones which the thing in the bow contained.

She puzzled over the assortment of things—and then without warning an answer came. But provokingly, as often happened with her, it was not the answer to the question she now had, but to an earlier one.

It had suddenly struck her that the diver's actions in rejecting the "made" thing he had worn on his back, and all his original signals to her, might mean that for some reason it was not the one he wanted, or needed, in order to leave the cave. Why there should be that kind of difference between it and these things left her baffled. The one with him now in the cave had been the right one; but maybe it was not the right one, today. Perhaps—she had a sudden inspiration—"made" things could die like animals or fish, or even like People, and the one he now had was dead. In any case, maybe what he needed was another of that particular kind of thing.

Perhaps this insight had come from the fact that several of these same "made" things were on the deck; and also, there was obviously only one diver, since First Uncle had not reported any of the other animals going down into the water. She was immediately tempted to go and get another one of the things, so that she could take it back to the diver. If he put it on, that meant she was right. Even if he did not, she might learn something by the way he handled it.

If it had been daring to take one look at the deck, it was inconceivably so to return now and actually try to take something from it. Her sense of duty struggled with her inclinations but slowly was overwhelmed. After all she knew now—knew positively—that none of the animals were aboard the boat and none could have come aboard in the last few minutes because she was still close enough to hear them. But if she went, she would have to hurry if she was going to do it before the Uncle got back and forbade any such action.

She swam back to the craft in a rush, came to the surface beside it, rose in the water craned her neck far enough inboard to snatch up one of the things in her teeth and escape with it.

A few seconds later, she had it two hundred feet down on the bed of the loch and was burying it in silt. Three minutes later she was back on station watching the craft, calmly enough but with her heart beating fast. Happily, there was still no sign of First Uncle's return.

Her heartbeat slowed. She went back to puzzling over what it was on the foredeck that could be the thing she had heard the creatures bring aboard. Of course, she now had three memory images of the area to compare . . .

Recognition came.

There *was* a discrepancy between the last two mental images and the first one, a discrepancy about one of the "made" things to which he had devoted close attention, that first time.

The difference was the line attached to the box with the sloping top. It was not the same line at all. It was a drum of other line at least twice as thick as the one which had connected the heavy thing and the box previously—almost as thick as the thick line connecting the barbed rod to the thing in the bow that contained it. Clearly, the animals of the craft had tried to make sure that they would run no danger of losing their dropweight if it became buried again. Possibly they had foolishly hoped that it was so strong that not even First Uncle could break it as he had the first.

That meant they were not going to give up. Here was clear evidence they were going to go on searching for their diver. She *must* get him back to them as soon as possible.

She began to swim restlessly, to and fro in the underwater, anxious to see the Uncle return so that she could tell him what had been done.

He came not long afterward, although it seemed to her that she had waited and worried for a considerable time before he appeared. When she told him about the new line, he was concerned enough by the information so that he barely reprimanded her for taking the risk of going in close to the craft.

"I must tell First Mother, right away—" He checked himself and looked up through the twenty or so feet of water that covered them. "No, there're only a few more hours of daylight left. I need to think, anyway. I'll stay on guard here until dark, then I'll go see First Mother in her cave. Youngest, for right now don't say anything to Second Mother, or even to First Mother if you happen to talk to her. I'll tell both of them myself after I've had time to think about it."

"Then I can go now?" asked the Youngest, almost standing on her tail in the underwater in her eagerness to be off.

"Yes, yes," signaled the Uncle.

The Youngest turned and dove toward the spot where she had buried the "made" thing she had taken and about which she had been careful to say nothing to First Uncle. She had no time to explain about the diver now, and any mention of the thing would bring demands for a full explanation from her elders. Five minutes later, the thing in her teeth, she was splitting the water in the direction of the cave where she had left the diver.

She had never meant to leave him alone this long. An irrational fear grew in her that something had happened to him in the time she had been gone. Perhaps he had started chilling again and had lost too much warmth, like one of the old ones, and was now dead. If he was dead, would the other animals be satisfied just to have his body back? But she did not want to think of him dead: He was not a bad little animal, in spite of his acting in such an ugly fashion when he had seen her for the first time. She should have realized that in the daylight, seeing her as he had without warning for the first time—

The thought of daylight reminded her that First Uncle had talked about there being only a few hours of it left. Surely there must be more than that. The day could not have gone so quickly.

She took a quick slant up to the surface to check. No, she was right. There must be at least four hours yet before the sun would sink below the mountains. However, in his own way the Uncle had been right, also, because the clouds were very heavy now. It would be too dark to see much, even long before actual nightfall. Snow was certain by dark, possibly even before. As she floated for a moment with her head and neck out of water, a few of the first wandering flakes came down the wind and touched her right cheek cells with tiny, cold fingers.

She dived again. It would indeed be a heavy snowfall; the Family could start out tonight on their way to the sea, if only they wanted to. It might even be possible to carry the eggs, distributed among the four of them, just two or three carried pressed between a swim paddle and warm body skin. First Mother might tire easily; but after the first night, when they had gotten well away from the loch, and with new snow falling to cover their footsteps, they could go by short stages. There would be no danger that the others would run out of heat or strength. Even the Youngest, small as she was, had fat reserves for a couple of months without eating and with ordinary activity. The Lost Father had made it to Loch Ness from the sea in a week or so.

If only they would go now. If only she were old enough and wise enough to convince them to go. For just a moment she gave herself over to a dream of their great sea home, of the People grown strong again, patrolling in their great squadrons past the white-gleaming berg ice or under the tropic stars. Most of the eggs of every clutch would hatch, then. The hatchlings would have the beaches of all the empty islands of the world to hatch on. Later, in the sea, they would grow up strong and safe, with their mighty elders around to guard them from anything that moved in the salt waters. In their last years, the old ones would bask under the hot sun in warm, hidden places and never need to chill again. The sea. That was where they belonged. Where they must go home to, someday. And that day should be soon . . .

The Youngest was almost to the cave now. She brought her thoughts, with a wrench, back to the diver. Alive or dead, he too must go back—to his own kind. Fervently, she hoped that she was right with another "made" thing being what he needed before he would swim out of the cave. If not, if he just threw this one away as he had the other one, then she had no choice. She would simply have to pick him up in her teeth and carry him out of the cave without it. Of course, she must be careful to hold him so that he could not reach her to scratch or bite; and she must get his head back above water as soon as they got out of the cave into the open loch, so that he would not drown.

By the time she had gotten this far in her thinking, she was at the cave. Ducking inside, she exploded up through the surface of the water within. The diver was seated with his back against the cave wall, looking haggard and savage. He was getting quite dark-colored around the jaws, now. The little points he had there seemed to be growing. She dumped the new "made" thing at his feet.

For a moment he merely stared down at it, stupidly. Then he fumbled the object up into his arms and did something to it with those active little divided sections of his two upper limb ends. A hissing sound came from the thing that made her start back, warily. So, the "made" things were alive, after all!

The diver was busy attaching to himself the various things he had worn when she had first found him—with the exception that the new thing she had brought him, rather than its old counter-part, was going on his back. Abruptly, though, he stopped, his head-thing still not on and still in the process of putting on the paddle-like things that attached to his lower limb ends. He got up and came forward to the edge of the water, looking at her.

He had changed again. From the moment he had gotten the new thing to make the hissing noise, he had gone into yet a different way of standing and acting. Now he came within limb reach of her and stared at her so self-assuredly that she almost felt she was the animal trapped in a cave and he was free. Then he crouched down by the water and once more began to make motions with his upper limbs and limb ends.

First, he made the on-top-of-the-water sliding motion with the back of one limb end that she now began to understand must mean the craft he had gone overboard from. Once she made the connection it was obvious: the craft, like his hand, was in the water only with its underside. Its top side was dry and in the air. As she watched, he circled his "craft" limb end around in the water and brought it back to touch the ledge. Then, with his other limb end, he "walked" two of its divisions up to the "craft" and continued to "walk" them onto it.

She stared. He was apparently signaling something about his getting on the craft. But why?

However, now he was doing something else. He lifted his walking-self limb end off the "craft" and put it standing on its two stiff divisions, back on the ledge. Then he moved the "craft" out over the water, away from the ledge, and held it there. Next, to her surprise, he "walked" his other limb end right off the ledge into the water. Still "walking" so that he churned the still surface of the cave water to a slight roughness, he moved that limb end slowly to the unmoving "craft." When the "walking" limb end reached the "craft," it once more stepped up onto it.

The diver now pulled his upper limbs back, sat crouched on the ledge, and looked at the Youngest for a long moment. Then he made the same signals again. He did it a third time, and she began to understand. He was showing himself swimming to his craft. Of course, he had no idea how far he actually was from it, here in the cave—an unreasonable distance for as weak a swimmer as one of his kind was.

But now he was signaling yet something else. His "walking" limb end stood at the water's edge. His other limb end was not merely on the water, but in it, below the surface. As she watched, a single one of that other limb end's divisions rose through the surface and stood, slightly crooked, so that its upper joint was almost at right angles to the part sticking through the surface. Seeing her gaze on this part of him, the diver began to move that solitary joint through the water in the direction its crooked top was pointing. He brought it in this fashion all the way to the rock ledge and halted it opposite the "walking" limb end standing there.

He held both limb ends still in position and looked at her, as if waiting for a sign of understanding.

She gazed back, once more at a loss. The joint sticking up out of the water was like nothing in her memory but the limb of a waterlogged tree, its top more or less looking at the "walking" limb end that stood for the diver. But if the "walking" limb end was *he*—? Suddenly she understood. The division protruding from the water signalized *her*!

To show she understood, she backed off from the ledge,

crouched down in the shallow water of the cave until nothing but her upper neck and head protruded from the water, and then—trying to look as much like his crooked division as possible—approached him on the ledge.

He made noises. There was no way of being sure, of course, but she felt she was beginning to read the tone of some of the sounds he made; and these latest sounds, she was convinced, sounded pleased and satisfied.

He tried something else.

He made the ''walking'' shape on the ledge, then added something. In addition to the two limb-end divisions standing on the rock, he unfolded another—a short, thick division, one at the edge of that particular limb end, and moved it in circular fashion, horizontally. Then he stood up on the ledge himself and swung one of his upper limbs at full length, in similar circular fashion. He did this several times.

In no way could she imitate that kind of gesture, though she comprehended immediately that the movement of the extra, short division above the ''walking'' form was supposed to indicate him standing and swinging his upper limb like now. She merely stayed as she was and waited to see what he would do next.

He got down by the water, made the ''craft'' shape, ''swam'' his ''walking'' shape to it, climbed the ''walking'' shape up on the ''craft'' then had the ''walking'' shape turn and make the upper-limb swinging motion.

The Youngest watched, puzzled, but caught up in this strange game of communication she and the diver had found to play together. Evidently he wanted to go back to his craft, get on it, and then wave his upper limb like that, for some reason. It made no sense so far—but he was already doing something more.

He now had the ''walking'' shape standing on the ledge, making the upper-limb swinging motion, and he was showing the crooked division that was she approaching through the water.

That was easy: he wanted her to come to the ledge when he swung his upper limb.

Sure enough, after a couple of demonstrations of the last shape signals, he stood on the ledge and swung his arm. Agreeably, she went out in the water, crouched down, and approached the ledge. He made pleased noises. This was all rather ridiculous, she thought, but enjoyable nonetheless. She was standing half her length out from the edge, where she had stopped, and was trying to think of a body signal she could give that would make him swim to her, when she noticed that he was going on to further signals.

He had his "walking" shape standing on the "craft" shape, in the water out from the ledge, and signaling "Come." But then he took his "walking" shape away from the "craft" shape, put it under the water a little distance off, and came up with it as the "her" shape. He showed the "her" shape approaching the "craft" shape with her neck and head out of the water.

She was to come to his craft? In response to his "Come" signal?

No!

She was so furious with him for suggesting such a thing that she had no trouble at all thinking of a way to convey her reaction. Turning around, she plunged underwater, down through the cave entrance and out into the loch. Her first impulse was to flash off and leave him there to do whatever he wanted—stay forever, go back to his kind, or engage in any other nonsensical activity his small head could dream up. Did he think she had no wisdom at all? To suggest that she come right up to his craft with her head and neck out of water when he signaled—as if there had never been a taboo against her People having anything to do with his! He must not understand her in the slightest degree.

Common sense caught up with her, halted her, and turned her about not far from the cave mouth. Going off like this would do her no good—more, it would do the Family no good. On the other hand, she could not bring herself to go back into the cave, now. She hung in the water, undecided, unable to conquer the conscience that would not let her swim off, but also unable to make herself re-enter.

Vibrations from the water in the cave solved her problem. He had evidently put on the "made" thing she had brought him and was coming out. She stayed where she was, reading the vibrations.

He came to the mouth of the cave and swam slowly, straight up, to the surface. Level with him, but far enough away to be out of sight in the murky water, the Youngest rose, too. He lifted his head at last into the open air and looked around him.

He's looking for me, thought the Youngest, with a sense of satisfaction that he would see no sign of her and would assume she had left him for good. Now, go ashore and go back to your own kind, she commanded in her thoughts.

But he did not go ashore, though shore was only a matter of feet from him. Instead, he pulled his head underwater once more and began to swim back down.

She almost exploded with exasperation. He was headed toward the cave mouth! He was going back inside!

"You stupid animal!" she signaled to him. *"Go ashore!"*

But of course he did not even perceive the signal, let alone understand it. Losing all patience, the Youngest swooped down upon him, hauled him to the surface once more, and let him go.

For a second he merely floated there, motionless, and she felt a sudden fear that she had brought him up through the water too swiftly. She knew of some small fish that spent all their time down in the deepest parts of the loch, and if you brought one of them too quickly up the nine hundred feet or so to the surface, it twitched and died, even though it had been carried gently. Sometimes part of the insides of these fish bulged out through their mouths and gill slits after they were brought up quickly.

After a second, the diver moved and looked at her.

Concerned for him, she had stayed on the surface with him, her head just barely out of the water. Now he saw her. He kicked with the "made" paddles on his lower limbs to raise himself partly out of the water and, a little awkwardly, with his upper limb ends made the signal of him swimming to his craft.

She did not respond. He did it several more times, but she stayed stubbornly non-communicative. It was bad enough that she had let him see her again after his unthinkable suggestion.

He gave up making signals. Ignoring the shore close at hand, he turned from her and began to swim slowly south and out into the center of the loch.

He was going in the wrong direction if he was thinking of swimming all the way to his craft. And after his signaling it was pretty clear that this was what he had in mind. Let him find out his mistake for himself, the Youngest thought, coldly.

But she found that she could not go through with that. Angrily, she shot after him, caught the thing on his back with her teeth, and, lifting him by it enough so that his head was just above the surface, began to swim with him in the right direction.

She went slowly—according to her own ideas of speed—but even so a noticeable bow wave built up before him. She lifted

him a little higher out of the water to be on the safe side; but
she did not go any faster: perhaps he could not endure too much
speed. As it was, the clumsy shape of his small body hung about
with ''made'' things was creating surprising turbulence for its
size. It was a good thing the present hatchhole (and, therefore,
First Mother's current resting cave and the area in which First
Uncle and Second Mother would do their feeding) was as distant
as they were; otherwise First Uncle, at least, would certainly
have been alarmed by the vibrations and have come to investigate.

It was also a good thing that the day was as dark as it was,
with its late hour and the snow that was now beginning to fall
with some seriousness; otherwise she would not have wanted to
travel this distance on the surface in daylight. But the snow was
now so general that both shores were lost to sight in its white,
whirling multitudes of flakes, and certainly no animal on shore
would be able to see her and the diver out here.

There was privacy and freedom, being hidden by the snow
like this—like the freedom she felt on dark nights when the whole
loch was free of the animals and all hers. If only it could be this
way all the time. To live free and happy was so good. Under
conditions like these, she could not even fear or dislike the animals, other than her diver, who were a threat to the Family.

At the same time, she remained firm in her belief that the
Family should go, now. None of the others had ever before told
her that any of the legends were untrustworthy, and she did not
believe that the one about the Lost Father was so. It was not that
the legend was untrustworthy, but that they had grown conser-
vative with age and feared to leave the loch; while she, who was
still young, still dared to try great things for possibly great re-
wards.

She had never admitted it to the older ones, but one midwinter
day when she had been very young and quite small—barely old
enough to be allowed to swim around in the loch by herself—
she had ventured up one of the streams flowing into the loch. It
was a stream far too shallow for an adult of the Family; and
some distance up it, she found several otters playing on an ice
slide they had made. She had joined them, sliding along with
them for half a day without ever being seen by any upright animal. She remembered this all very well, particularly her scram-
bling around on the snow to get to the head of the slide; and

that she had used her tail muscles to skid herself along on her warm belly surface, just as the Lost Father had described.

If she could get the others to slip ashore long enough to try the snowy loch banks before day-warmth combined with loch-warmth to clear them of the white stuff . . . But even as she thought this, she knew they would never agree to try. They would not even consider the journey home to the sea until, as First Mother said, it became clear that that was the only alternative to extinction at the hands of the upright animals.

It was a fact, and she must face it. But maybe she could think of some way to make plain to them that the animals had, indeed, become that dangerous. For the first time, it occurred to her that her association with the diver could turn out to be something that would help them all. Perhaps, through him, she could gain evidence about his kind that would convince the rest of the Family that they should leave the loch.

It was an exciting thought. It would do no disservice to him to use him in that fashion, because clearly he was different from others of his kind: he had realized that not only was she warm as he was, but as intelligent or more so than he. He would have no interest in being a danger to her People, and might even cooperate—if she could make him understand what she wanted—in convincing the Family of the dangers his own race posed to them. Testimony from one of the animals directly would be an argument to convince even First Uncle.

For no particular reason, she suddenly remembered how he had instinctively huddled against her when he had discovered her warming him. The memory roused a feeling of tenderness in her. She found herself wishing there were some way she could signal that feeling to him. But they were almost to his craft, now. It and the dock were beginning to be visible—dark shapes lost in the dancing white—with the dimmer dark shapes of trees and other things ashore behind them.

Now that they were close enough to see a shore, the falling snow did not seem so thick, nor so all-enclosing as it had out in the middle of the loch. But there was still a privacy to the world it created, a feeling of security. Even sounds seemed to be hushed.

Through the water, Youngest could feel vibrations from the craft. At least one, possibly two, of the other animals were aboard it. As soon as she was close enough to be sure her diver could see the craft, she let go of the thing on his back and sank abruptly to about twenty feet below the surface, where she hung and waited, checking the vibrations of his movements to make sure he made it safely to his destination.

At first, when she let him go, he trod water where he was and turned around and around as if searching for her. He pushed himself up in the water and made the "Come" signal several times; but she refused to respond. Finally, he turned and swam to the edge of the craft.

He climbed on board very slowly, making so little noise that the two in the cabin evidently did not hear him. Surprisingly, he did not seem in any hurry to join them or to let them know he was back.

The Youngest rose to just under the surface and lifted her head above to see what he was doing. He was still standing on the foredeck, where he had climbed aboard, not moving. Now, as she watched, he walked heavily forward to the bow and stood beside the "made" thing there, gazing out in her direction.

He lifted his arm as if to make the "Come" signal, then dropped it to his side.

The Youngest knew that in absolutely no way could he make out the small portion of her head above the waves, with the snow coming down the way it was and day drawing swiftly to its dark close. She stared at him. She noticed something weary and sad about the way he stood. I should leave now, she thought. But she did not move. With the other two animals unaware in the cabin, and the snow continuing to fall, there seemed no reason to hurry off. She would miss him, she told herself, feeling a sudden pang of loss. Looking at him, it came to her suddenly that from the way he was acting he might well miss her, too.

Watching, she remembered how he had half lifted his limb as if to signal and then dropped it again. Maybe his limb is tired, she thought.

A sudden impulse took her. I'll go in close, underwater, and lift my head high for just a moment, she thought, so he can see me. He'll know then that I haven't left him for good. He already understands I wouldn't come on board that thing of his under any circumstance. Maybe if he sees me again for a second, now, he'll understand that if he gets back in the water and swims to me, we can go on learning signals from each other. Then, maybe, someday, we'll know enough signals together so that he can convince the older ones to leave.

Even as she thought this, she was drifting in, underwater, until she was only twenty feet from the craft. She rose suddenly and lifted her head and neck clear of the water.

For a long second she saw he was staring right at her but not responding. Then she realized that he might not be seeing her, after all, just staring blindly out at the loch and the snow. She moved a little sideways to attract his attention, and saw his head move. Then he *was* seeing her? Then why didn't he do something?

She wondered if something was wrong with him. After all, he had been gone for nearly two days from his own People and must have missed at least a couple of his feeding periods in that time. Concern impelled her to a closer look at him. She began to drift in toward the boat.

He jerked upright suddenly and swung an upper limb at her.

But he was swinging it all wrong. It was not the "Come" signal he was making, at all. It was more like the "Come" signal in reverse—as if he was pushing her back and away from him. Puzzled, and even a little hurt, because the way he was acting reminded her of how he had acted when he first saw her in the cave and did not know she had been with him earlier, the Youngest moved in even closer.

He flung both his upper limbs furiously at her in that new, "rejecting" motion and shouted at her—a loud, angry noise. Behind him, came an explosion of different noise from inside the cabin, and the other two animals burst out onto the deck. Her diver turned, making noises, waving both his limbs at them the way he had just waved them at her. The Youngest, who had been about to duck down below the safety of the loch surface, stopped. Maybe this was some new signal he wanted her to learn, one that had some reference to his two companions?

But the others were making noises back at him. The taller one ran to one of the "made" things that were like, but smaller than, the one in the bow of the boat. The diver shouted again, but the tall one ignored him, only seizing one end of the thing he had run to and pulling that end around toward him. The Youngest watched, fascinated, as the other end of the "made" thing swung to point at her.

Then the diver made a very large angry noise, turned, and

seized the end of the largest "made" thing before him in the bow of the boat.

Frightened suddenly, for it had finally sunk in that for some reason he had been signaling her to get away, she turned and dived. Then, as she did so, she realized that she had turned, not away from, but into line with, the outer end of the thing in the bow of the craft.

She caught a flicker of movement, almost too fast to see, from the thing's hollow outer end. Immediately, the loudest sound she had ever heard exploded around her, and a tremendous blow struck her behind her left shoulder as she entered the underwater.

She signaled for help instinctively, in shock and fear, plunging for the deep bottom of the loch. From far off, a moment later, came the answer of First Uncle. Blindly, she turned to flee to him.

As she did, she thought to look and see what had happened to her. Swinging her head around, she saw a long, but shallow, gash across her shoulder and down her side. Relief surged in her. It was not even painful yet, though it might be later; but it was nothing to cripple her, or even to slow her down.

How could her diver have done such a thing to her? The thought was checked almost as soon as it was born—by the basic honesty of her training. *He* had not done this. *She* had done it, by diving into the path of the barbed rod cast from the thing in the bow. If she had not done that, it would have missed her entirely.

But why should he make the thing throw the barbed rod at all? She had thought he had come to like her, as she liked him.

Abruptly, comprehension came; and it felt as if her heart leaped in her. For all at once it was perfectly clear what he had been trying to do. She should have had more faith in him. She halted her flight toward the Uncle and turned back toward the boat.

Just below it, she found what she wanted. The barbed rod, still leaving a taste of her blood in the water, was hanging point down from its line, in about two hundred feet of water. It was being drawn back up, slowly but steadily.

She surged in close to it, and her jaws clamped on the line she had tried to bite before and found resistant. But now she was serious in her intent to sever it. Her jaws scissored and her teeth ripped at it, though she was careful to rise with the line and put no strain upon it that would warn the animals above about what she was doing. The tough strands began to part under her assault.

Just above her, the sound of animal noises now came clearly through the water: her diver and the others making sounds at each other.

". . . I tell you we're through!" It was her diver speaking. "It's over. I don't care what you saw. It's my boat. I paid for it; and I'm quitting."

"It not *your* boat, man. It a boat belong to the company, the company that belong all three of us. We got contracts."

"I'll pay off your damned contracts."

"There's more to this than money, now. We know that great beast in there, now. We get our contract money, and maybe a lot more, going on the TV telling how we catch it and bring it in. No, man, you don't stop us now."

"I say, it's my boat. I'll get a lawyer and court order—"

"You do that. You get a lawyer and a judge and a pretty court order, and we'll give you the boat. You do that. Until then, it belong to the company and it keep after that beast."

She heard the sound of footsteps—her diver's footsteps, she could tell, after all this time of seeing him walk his lower limbs—leaving the boat deck, stepping onto the dock, going away.

The line was almost parted. She and the barbed rod were only about forty feet below her.

"What'd you have to do that for?" That was the voice of the third creature. "He'll do that! He'll get a lawyer and take the boat and we won't even get our minimum pay. Whyn't you let him pay us off, the way he said?"

"Hush, you fooking fool. How long you think it take him get a lawyer, a judge, and a writ? Four days, maybe five—"

The line parted. She caught the barbed rod in her jaws as it started to sink. The ragged end of the line lifted and vanished above her.

"—and meanwhile, you and me, we go hunting with this boat. We know the beast there, now. We know what to look for. We find it in four, five days, easy."

"But even if we get it, he'll just take it away from us again with his lawyer—"

"I tell you, no. We'll get ourselves a lawyer, also. This company formed to take the beast; and he got to admit he tried to call off the hunt. And we both seen what he do. He've fired that harpoon gun to scare it off, so I can't get it with the drug lance and capture it. We testify to that, we got him—Ah!"

"What is it?"

"What is it? You got no eyes, man? The harpoon gone. It in the beast after all, being carried around. We don't need no four, five days, I tell you now. That be a good, long piece of steel, and we got the locators to find metal like that. We hunt that beast and bring it in tomorrow. Tomorrow, man, I promise you! It not going to go too fast, too far, with that harpoon."

But he could not see below the snow and the black surface of the water. The Youngest was already moving very fast indeed through the deep loch to meet the approaching First Uncle. In her jaws she carried the harpoon, and on her back she bore the wound it had made. The elders could have no doubt, now, about the intentions of the upright animals (other than her diver) and their ability to destroy the Family.

They must call First Mother, and this time there would be no hesitation. She would see the harpoon and the wound and decide for them all. Tonight they would leave by the route of the Lost Father, while the snow was still thick on the banks of the loch. They might have to leave the eggs behind, after all; but if so, Second Mother could have more clutches, and maybe later they would even find a way ashore again to Loch Morar and meet others of their own People at last.

But, in any case, they would go now to live free in the sea; and in the sea most of Second Mother's future eggs would hatch and the Family would grow numerous and strong again.

She could see them in her mind's eye, now. They would leave the loch by the mouth of Glen Moriston—First Mother, Second Mother, First Uncle, herself—and take to the snow-covered banks when the water became too shallow . . .

They would travel steadily into the mountains, and the new snow falling behind them would hide the marks of their going from the eyes of the animals. They would pass by deserted ways through the silent rocks to the ocean. They would come at last to its endless waters, to the shining bergs of the north and the endless warmth of the Equator sun. The ocean, their home, was welcoming them back, at last. There would be no more doubt, no more fear or waiting. They were going home to the sea . . . they were going home to the sea . . .

Man Overboard

by
John Collier

The late John Collier was a novelist and poet, but is perhaps best remembered as a writer of short, acerbic, slyly witty stories like "The Touch of Nutmeg Makes It," "Green Thoughts," and "Thus I Refute Beelzy"—stories which brought him international critical acclaim. The bulk of them have been collected in Fancies and Goodnights, *which won the International Fantasy Award, and* The John Collier Reader. *His other books include the novel* His Monkey Wife *and the postholocaust novel* Tom's A-Cold. *Collier died in 1980.*

Here he gives us the gripping drama of a man who devotes his life to searching for a dream—and is unlucky enough to find it.

* * *

Glenway Morgan Abbott had the sort of face that is associated with New England by those who like New England. It was so bony, so toothy even, so modest, so extremely serious, and so nearly flinchingly unflinching, that one hardly noticed that he was actually a very good-looking man.

He also had the yacht *Zenobia*, which was handsome enough to take one's breath away at the very first glance; it showed its seriousness only on closer inspection. Once in a very great while, I used to go on a long cruise with Glenway. I was his best, and his only intimate, friend.

Those who have seen the *Zenobia*, or its picture in books on sailing, may be impolite enough to wonder how I came to be so specially friendly with the owner of a three-masted schooner which is certainly among the dozen, perhaps among the half-dozen, most famous of the great yachts of the world.

Such people should realize that, though I may lack wealth and grace and charm, I do so in a special and superior way. Moreover, in spite of the glorious *Zenobia* and the impressive associations of his name, Glenway's way of life was far from being sophisticated or luxurious. His income, though still very large, was only just large enough to pay for his yacht's upkeep and her numerous crew. When he wanted to get a piece of research done, he had to dip into his capital.

The fact is, Glenway had at one time been married, and to a filmstar, and in highly romantic circumstances. As if this wasn't enough, he had at once been divorced. The star in question was Thora Vyborg, whose beauty and personality are among the legends, or the myths, of our time. All this happened before I met him, but I had gathered, though not from Glenway, that the divorce had been distinguished, by a settlement such as can result only from the cruelest heartbreak, the bitterest injury, and the most efficient lawyers on the one side and honest eyes and rather prominent front teeth on the other.

Therefore, if the word "yacht" suggests music, ladies, awnings, white-jacketed stewards, caviar, and champagne, the suggestion is altogether misleading. The only music was the wind in the rigging; there were no ladies; the solitary steward wore no jacket; and the crew wore no shirts, either. They were all natives of different parts of the Pacific with different complexions and different tongues. The language used on board was a sort of sub-Basic English, adequate for work, expressive in song, but not very suitable for conversation. Glenway might have had an American or a British captain or mate; however, he did not.

Anyway, every man on board knew his job. It was a pity that the cook's job was all too often only the opening of cans of frankfurters or baked beans. This was not so much due to New English frugality as to the gastronomical absentmindedness which is so often found linked with honesty, teeth, etc., and especially with devotion to a cause.

Glenway was devoted to a cause, and so was the *Zenobia*. All these great yachts are, of course, capable of ocean cruising; this one was used for it, and for nothing else at all. She was used and hard-used, and, though as clean as a pin, she was by no means as shiny. On the horizon, she looked like a cloud; at her mooring, like a swan to the poetically-minded, or, to the materialistic, like a boating palace. But, as soon as you stepped aboard, she had more the appearance of something sent out by an oceanographical institute. All manner of oddly-shaped nets and trawls and scoops were hung, or spread, or stowed around her deck. On either side of the foremast, there were two objects on pedestals, shoulder-high, and made of that ugly, gray, rust-resisting alloy which was used everywhere on this boat in place of brass or chromium. These objects were not ventilators. They had rotating tops; these tops were hooded or cowled, or whatever you'd call it; and closely shuttered against the salty spray. If you turned one of the tops towards you, and slid open the shutter, and looked inside, you would find yourself being looked back at, quietly, by the darkly gleaming eye of a movie camera.

Up in the bows, there was a bulky object lashed down under quickly removable canvas. This was a searchlight. Long chests, seat-high, almost as high as the low gunwale into which they were built, contained rockets and flares. Glenway was hoping to photograph something which he believed might be nocturnal in its habits. He thought that, otherwise, being a very large, noticeable creature, and being a reptile, and therefore breathing air, it would have been seen more often by daylight.

Glenway, in a word, was looking for the sea serpent. As he detested the sensational newspaper stories and the tiresome jokes associated with the term, he preferred to think of it as a "large marine saurian." For short, we called it, not inaptly, "It."

People all over the Pacific knew of Glenway's quest. They were, though tactful about it, rather too obviously so. Something about Glenway caused them to refrain from guffaws; or, if they took the matter seriously, they seriously sought to reclaim him from his folly. Either way, they made it all too clear that they thought him a crank and perhaps a zany because he believed in the existence of such a creature. For this reason, he avoided ports as far as possible, and, when taking in supplies or docked for overhaul, he avoided the society of his kind. Now, it so happens that, though I am of a skeptical nature in most matters, I am strongly inclined to suspend disbelief when it comes to a large marine saurian. Without at least the possibility of such a creature, it seems to me that the world would be a poor and a narrow place. Glenway perceived this at our very first meeting, and it was the reason for the beginning of our friendship. I was forced to tell him I thought the chances were a million-to-one against his ever seeing his quarry, and I thought he was crazy to waste his time and his lovely money on hunting for it. This didn't worry him in the least.

"I shall find it sooner or later," said he, when first we debated the question, "because I know where to look."

His theory was a simple one, and made sense up to a point.

If you know how an animal is constructed, you can deduce a great deal as to how it lives, and especially as to what it lives on. When you know what it eats, and where that particular abounds, you have already a very good clue as to where to look for it.

Glenway had taken all the best authenticated reports, and he had had an outline drawn up from each of them. Almost all these reports, from whatever corner of the world they may come, describe more or less the same sort of creature, so he had no trouble in getting a composite picture made by an expert hand. This, of course, showed a reptile of the plesiosaur type, but very much larger than any of the fossil plesiosaurs, being only a few inches under eighty feet in length. But here there was a snag.

Glenway had every reason to know what each extra foot on the length of a yacht adds to its maintenance bills, and he knew that an eighty-foot plesiosaur is not a practical proposition. It was not hard to calculate what its weight would be, or the size of its bite, or how large a fish could pass down its narrow gullet. ''It would spend more energy just picking up fish of that size one by one,'' said Glenway, ''than it would gain by eating them. Also, schools of herrings, mackerel, haddock, and so forth are mostly found in coastal waters, and fishermen have been after them by day and by night ever since fishermen existed. An air-breathing creature has to show itself on the surface fairly often; if it followed fish of that sort it would be as familiar to us as the basking shark. And, finally, it would be extinct, because with those jaws it couldn't defend itself against killer whales, or threshers, if it hadn't been finished off by carcharodon, and the other big sharks of the Miocene.''

''Glenway, if all this is correct, you've slain your own goddam Jabberwock.''

''I was afraid I had,'' said he. ''It depressed the Hell out of me. But one day it struck me that people who see something very surprising, and see it suddenly, briefly, in bad visibility and so forth, will naturally tend to exaggerate the most surprising aspect of whatever it is they see. Thus, an astonishing long, snaky neck will look longer and snakier than it actually is, a small head smaller, and so forth. So, I had a couple of young chaps from Uncle Fred's Institute of Industrial Psychology do a series of tests. They found a deviation running up to about twenty-five percent. Then I told them what I wanted it for, and asked them to modify this outline accordingly. We got this.'' He handed me a second sheet. ''We can take it this is what was actually seen.''

''Why, this damned thing is only six feet long!'' said I, rather discontentedly. ''It seems to me you're correcting eyewitness reports on pure speculation.''

''No, I'm not,'' said he. ''I double-checked it. I hired a reptile man and an icthyologist, and I asked them to work out what the nearest thing to sixty-foot plesiosaur would be like if it were to be a practical proposition in terms of food, energy, defense, and all that. They came up with two or three alternatives. The one that interested me was this.'' He pulled out a third outline. ''If you put this on top of the psychologists' corrected version,'' said he, ''you'll see they correspond in everything essential.''

''All the same, if I'm going to believe in a large marine saurian, I'd rather have an eighty-footer.''

''This one weighs more than an eighty-footer,'' said Glenway, ''and he's probably ten times as powerful. Those jaws have a bite of over three feet. This fellow could swallow a big barracuda at a gulp. He might have to make two snaps at a porpoise. He'll follow schools of tuna, albacore, any sort of fish ranging from fifty to a hundred-and-fifty pounds. Not cod, of course.''

''And why not cod?''

''Fishermen. He'd have been seen.''

''Oh!''

''So, evidently, he doesn't follow cod.''

''And, evidently, you can sweat a positive out of a couple of demolished negatives. Even so, it may make some sort of sense.''

Glenway accepted this, which at least was better than he got from other people. He eagerly showed me innumerable charts he had drawn up, and had emended by his own observation. These showed the seasonal movements of deep-sea fish in the East Pacific, and, where these movements weren't known, he had what data there was on the smaller fish that the larger ones preyed on. He went on down through the food chains, and down to plankton drifts and current temperatures and so forth, and, with all these, modified by all sorts of other factors, he had marked out a great oval, with dates put in here and there, which tilted through those immense solitudes of ocean which stretch from the coast of Chile up to the Aleutians.

This was his beat, and two or three times I sailed it with him.

There were almost no islands, almost no shipping lanes. I used to take a regular spell in the crow's nest; two hours in the morning and two more in the late afternoon. You can't sit day after day looking for something without an admission, deep in your mind, of the possibility of seeing it. Anyway, I was extremely fond of Glenway, and it would have given me great pleasure to have been the one who sighted his saurian for him somewhere far out on the flat green or the rolling blue. The very wish lent a sinewy twist to every water-logged palm trunk that drifted across our bows, and every distant dolphin leap offered the arc of a black, wet, and leathery neck.

At the first sight of such things, my hand, more wishful even than my thoughts, would move towards the red button on the rail of the crow's nest. This, like another in the bow, and a third by the wheel, was connected with a loud buzzer in Glenway's cabin. However, the buzzer remained silent; the immense horizon, day after day, was empty.

Glenway was an excellent navigator. One morning, when I was aloft, he called up to ask if I could see anything ahead. I told him there was nothing, but I had no sooner raised my glasses again than I discerned a thickening, a long hump gathering itself in the infinitely faint pencil line that marked the juncture of sky and sea. "There's something. It's land! Land ahead!"

"That's Paumoy."

He had not bothered to mention that he was going to touch at Paumoy, the main island of an isolated group northeast of the Marquesas. I had heard of the place; there were eight or ten Americans there, and someone had said that, since the war, they almost never got their mail. Glenway's beat took him within fifty miles of the island, and he now told me he had agreed to touch there as he passed. Sensitive as he was to crude jokes about the sea serpent, he was still a New Englander, and he felt that people should have their mail.

The island, as we drew nearer, revealed itself as several miles of whaleback, covered with that hot froth of green which suggests coconut palms and boredom. I put down the light binoculars I was using and took up the telescope, which had a much greater range. I could see the harbor, the white bungalows spaced out around it, and I could even see the people quite clearly. Before long I saw a man catch sight of the yacht. He stared under his hand, and waved, and pointed; another man came out of a bungalow with a pair of glasses. I saw the two of them go off at a run to where a jeep was standing. The jeep crawled off around the harbor, stopped at another bungalow; someone got out, someone got in. The jeep moved on again, disappeared into a grove, came out on the other side, and went toiling up a little thread-like track until it went out of sight over the ridge.

By this time, other people on the shore level had turned out to look at us. They had plenty of time to do so, for the breeze fell off almost to nothing as we stood in towards the island. It was already late afternoon when the *Zenobia*, with every sail set, floated as softly as an enormous thistledown to her anchorage in the harbor of Paumoy.

"What a dreary-looking dump!" I said. "What do they do here? Copra?"

"That, and shell. One fellow dries a sort of sea slug and sells it to Chinese dealers all over the world. There was a Gauguin from San Francisco, but he didn't stay very long."

"You'd think they'd cut each other's throats out of sheer boredom."

"Well, they play poker every night of their lives, and I guess they've developed a technique of not getting on each other's nerves."

"They must need it." There seemed to be nothing on the island but coconut palms, which I don't like, and the blistering bungalows, all of which might have been prefabricated by the same mail-order house. What I had taken from a greater distance to be banks of vari-colored flowers beside the bungalows were now recognizable as heaps of tin cans, some rusty, some with their labels still on. But I had no more time to look about me; we were on the quay, and being greeted by men in shorts and old-fashioned sun helmets, and the greeting was hearty.

"Now, listen to me," said Victor Brewer, "we've got two new guys here who've been in Java. We've had them working like dogs ever since we sighted you, fixing a *rijsttafel*. So you've got to stay to dinner. Or those guys are going to be hurt. Hell, you're not going to insult a couple of fellows who are slaving over a hot stove, fixing you a dinner!"

Glenway wanted nothing but to pick up the outgoing mailbag and be gone. On the other hand, he hated the idea of hurting anyone. He looked at me as if in the faint hope that I might step in and do it for him. It was at such moments, very rare with

Glenway, that I felt Fitzgerald was right about the rich being
different. This thought, and the thought of the *rijsttafel*, pre-
vented me from obliging him. Instead, I pointed out there'd
probably be no wind till nightfall, so we'd be losing hardly any
time. Glenway at once surrendered, and we settled down to
drinks and chat and to watch the sun go down.

Listening to the chat, I remembered Glenway's remark about
the technique of not getting on each other's nerves. It seemed
to me that this technique was being exercised, and especially for
Glenway's benefit. At the end of almost every remark our host
made, I felt myself dropping into the air pocket of a pulled
punch; I experienced that disconcerting absence of impact which
is the concomitant of velvet paws. It was clear they knew what
Glenway was after, and they even referred to it, but with such
collective tact that, if one of them seemed likely to dwell on it
for more than a few seconds, he would be steamrollered out of
the conversation, generally by Mr. Brewer. It was he who asked,
very casually, when we had been sitting some time at dinner, if
Glenway was sailing the same course as usual; if he was going
to pass, give or take a hundred miles, the northern extremity of
Japan.

Glenway having replied that he always followed the same
course: "You know," said Vic Brewer, letting the words fall as
casually as one lets fall the poker chips when the hands are high
and the stakes are higher, "you know, you could do the Hell of
a good turn to a guy. If you felt like it, that is."

"What sort of turn?" asked Glenway. "And which guy?"

"You don't know him," said the man on Brewer's left. "He's
a fellow called Geisecker. He's Charlie's brother-in-law's brother-
in-law, if you can work that one out."

"He dropped in here to say hello," said the next man. "He
came on the copra boat and he didn't know the mailboat doesn't
call anymore. So he's stuck."

"The point is, this poor guy is going to be in big trouble if
he doesn't get to Tokyo in the next few weeks."

"When you get up in those latitudes you're certainly going to
sight some boat or other bound for Japan."

"Any little tramp, or oiler, or fishing boat, or anything. He'll
be tickled to death."

They spoke one after another all the way round the table, and
remembering that Glenway had said they played poker every

night of their lives, I was irresistibly reminded of the process of doubling up.

"We hate to see him go," said Brewer, collecting the whole matter into his hands with the genial authority of the dealer. "He's wonderful company, Bob Geisecker. But it's almost life or death for him, poor fellow! Look, he'll pay for his passage— anything you like—if *that's* the obstacle."

"It ain't that," said Glenway. "But, I haven't seen him yet."

"He's over on the other side of the island," said Brewer. "He went off with Johnny Ray in the jeep less than half an hour before we sighted you."

"That's funny," said I, thinking of what I'd seen through the telescope.

"Damned funny," said Brewer, "if going off to give Johnny a hand makes him miss his chance of a passage." And, turning to Glenway, he added, "If you'd only seen old Bob, I know you'd have been glad to help him."

"I'll take him," said Glenway, "if he's back in time. But the wind's been failing us, and we're behind schedule, and . . ."

"Fair enough," said Brewer. "If he's back in time, you'll take him. If he isn't, that's his hard luck. More rice? More chicken? More shrimp? Boy, fill up that glass for Mr. Abbott."

The dinner went on and on, and not another word was said about Mr. Geisecker. At last, the heavy frondage above the table drew a deep breath and began to live and move. The wind was up, and Glenway said we could wait no longer. We all walked together down to the quay. Glenway and I were just stepping into the dinghy when someone pointed, and looking back, as people were rightly warned not to do in the old stories, we saw, like a moonrise, the glow of headlights in the sky. The jeep was coming up the far side of the ridge. "That's Bob," said Brewer. "But don't wait. We'll get him packed up in no time, and bring him out in the launch before you can up-anchor."

Sure enough, just as we were ready to move out, the launch came alongside with Mr. Bob Geisecker and his bags. The latter had pieces of pajamas hanging out at their sides like the tongues of panting dogs. Geisecker himself seemed a little breathless. His face, as he came up the steps into the light hanging above, had something strange about it. At first, I thought it was just the flustered and confused expression of a man who had to pack and get off in such a hurry; then, I thought it was the fact that, after weeks and months under an equatorial sun, this considerable face still peeled and glowed as if fresh from a weekend at Atlantic City. Finally, still unsatisfied, I thought of that massive, opulently curved, wide-mouthed instrument which is included in every brass band, and which, when it is not playing full blast, looks as if it ought to be, or at least is about to be. Mr. Geisecker greatly resembled this instrument, but he was very silent, and it was this that was strange.

There was a quick introduction, a brief welcome from Glenway, who was busy, an uncertain mumble of thanks from our guest, and a very hasty farewell from Brewer. Glenway had to give all his attention to taking the yacht out, and Geisecker stood neglected on deck, staring after the launch, his mouth open, looking something worse than lost. I took him down to his cabin, told him we breakfasted at seven, and asked him if there was anything he wanted before turning in. He seemed only vaguely aware that I was talking to him.

"Those guys," said he, speaking like a man in a state of shock, "I kept them in stitches. In stitches—all the time!"

"Good night," I said. "I'll see you in the morning."

Next morning Geisecker joined us at breakfast. He acknowledged our greeting soberly, sat down, and looked at his plate. Glenway apologized for having been so much occupied overnight and began to discuss where and when we might hope to encounter a boat headed for Tokyo or Yokohama. Geisecker lifted a face on which dawning enlightenment made me think of the rapid change from the blue-gray hush of the tropic night to the full glare and blare of tropic day; light, warmth, life, and laughter all came flooding in faster than one would think believable or even desirable.

"I knew it all the time!" said he exultantly. "Only I just didn't happen to think of it. I knew it was a gag. When those guys hustled me aboard this lugger I got the idea they were—you know—giving me the brush-off. They just about had me fooled. Now, I get it. Anything for a laugh! They swore to me last night you were heading for Lima, Peru."

"They told me very definitely," said Glenway, staring, "that it was of the greatest importance that you should get to Tokyo."

Geisecker slapped his plump and crimson thigh with startling effect. "Those guys," said he, "they'd ship a fellow to the moon on one of those goddam spaceships if they could get a laugh out of it. And that's what they've done to me! Tokyo's where I came from. Lima, Peru is where I was going to move on to. *That's* why they kept me all day over on the other side of the island. So I couldn't hear which way you were going.''

''We're short of time,'' said Glenway, ''but I'll put about and take you back to Paumoy if you want me to.''

''Not on your life,'' said Geisecker. ''It's a good gag and I'll be goddamned if I spoil it. All I'm doing is just going around the world saying hello to people, and, to tell you the truth, there's a little kimono lady back in Tokyo I won't mind saying hello to once again.'' With that, he obliged us with a few bars from *Madame Butterfly.*

''Glenway,'' said I, ''it's just on eight. I think I'll be getting up aloft.''

''Aloft?'' cried Geisecker. ''That sounds like the real saltwater stuff. I've never been on one of these windjammers before. You've got to give me the dope on marline spikes, splicing the main brace, and all the rest of the crap. I tell you, boys, I'm going to learn to be a sailor. Now, what's all this about going up aloft?''

''I'm just going up to the crow's nest for a couple of hours.''

''What for? Looking for something?'' Even as he asked the question, he turned, first to me and then on Glenway, a face which now resembled a Thespian as well as a porcine ham, it so overacted the simple feat of putting two and two together. Fixing his eyes on Glenway, he slowly raised and extended an index finger of great substance. The lower joint of this finger was adorned with curving hairs, very strong and serviceable, and of a ruddy gold which glinted in the morning sun. The finger stopped about a foot short of Glenway's ribs, but its quality was so potent that it seemed to make itself felt there. In fact, I even felt it in my own.

''Abbott!'' cried Geisecker triumphantly. ''Now, that shows you how miffed I was last night when I thought those guys had given me the brush—it didn't ring any sort of bell. Glenway Morgan Abbott! Christ, I've heard about you, pal. These birds told me all sorts of yarns. *You're* the guy who got married to Thora Vyborg! *You're* the guy who goes around looking for the sea serpent!''

At this point he became aware of Glenway's regard, which was, for one naked moment at least, quite deadly. Geisecker drew back a little. "But, maybe," said he, "maybe they were pulling my leg. I ought to have seen it right away. A fellow with your education wouldn't fall for that cheesy old bit of hokum."

By this time Glenway had recovered himself, which is to say that he was once more subject to his customary inhibitions and compulsions. These forbade him to be discourteous to a guest, and forced him to bear witness like a zealot in favor of his large marine saurian. "Perhaps," said he, after a painful swallow or two, "you haven't considered the evidence."

He went on to summarize the affidavits of numbers of worthy citizens, all describing what was obviously the same sort of creature, seen at widely dispersed times and places. He stressed especially the sworn evidence of naval officers and sea captains, and crowned the list with a reference to the reptile clearly seen by the bearded and impeccable gentlemen in charge of Queen Victoria's own yacht, the *Osborne*.

Geisecker, who had been listening with a widening smile, here heartily slapped Glenway on the back. "You know what it was *they* saw, brother? They saw the old girl herself, flopped overboard for a dip. What do you say, boys?" said he, addressing the question to me and to the man who was clearing the table. "That's about the size of it, believe you me! *Splash me, Albert!*"

He accompanied this last sentence with a flapping mimicry of regal and natatory gambols, which, considering he was neither on a throne nor in the water, seemed to me to show talent. Glenway, like the august personage represented, was not amused. There was such a contest between displeasure and hospitality visible on his face that it looked for a moment like a wrestling match seen on television, except, of course, that the pain was genuine.

This, and the thought that I had rather let him down over the dinner on Paumoy, moved me to an unwonted self-sacrifice. "Glenway," said I, "you take my spell in the crow's nest, and I'll take the wheel this morning."

Glenway, being one of nature's martyrs, refused this handsome offer, and elected to stay down in the arena. As I went aloft, I realized how those patricians must have felt, who, though inclined to Early Christian sympathies, were nevertheless pressured into taking a box in the Colosseum on a gala night in Nero's Rome.

Every now and then I heard a roar below me, and it was not merely that of a lion; it was that of Geisecker's laughter. Before long I saw Glenway come forward, and pretend to busy himself with the little nets that were used for taking up plankton and algae. In a very few minutes, Geisecker came after him, smiling, and spoke with jovial camaraderie to the two sailors who were spreading the nets. These men looked uneasily at Glenway before they laughed; it was sufficiently obvious that the jests were concerned with the sea serpent. Glenway then dropped his work and went aft, and below. Geisecker went bellowing along the deck and, getting no response, he went down after Glenway. There was a period of calm—deceptive calm, which is calmer than the other sort. Then, Glenway burst up out of the forward hatch and looked around him as if for refuge. But there is no refuge on a yacht, not even on a yacht like the *Zenobia*. I realized that he must have slipped through the pantry, into the galley, and thence into the men's quarters, leaving Geisecker ditched in the saloon. Geisecker was, of all men, the least likely to remain ditched more than three minutes. At the expiration of that time, I leaned far out and looked back, and saw his mighty, sweating torso emerge from the companionway.

There are certain big, fat men who, when they joke with you, seem almost to enfold you in a physical embrace. This caused me to wish we were farther from the equator, but it did not prevent me going to try to run a little interference for Glenway.

I soon found that it was next door to impossible to draw Geisecker away from Glenway. There are certain people who, if they become dimly aware they are offensive to another, will fasten on that unfortunate with all the persistence of a cat which seeks out the one cat hater in a crowded room. They can't believe it; they think you really love them; they are tickled and fascinated and awesomely thrilled by the fantastic improbability of your dislike. They'll pluck at your attention and finger your very flesh for the unbelievable spectacle of your recoil, and they'll press yet closer for the marvel of your shudder, for all the world as if recoil and shudder were rapturous spasms induced by some novel form of lovemaking, to be evoked in wonder and in triumph again and again and again.

"Good old Glen!" said Geisecker, one afternoon when Glenway had jumped up with what I can only call a muttered exclamation, and sought refuge in his cabin. "I love that guy. I love

the way he takes a bit of ribbing. You know—straight, deadpan—
and yet you can tell that underneath he just loves it.''

"Not on that subject," I said. "He detests it. And so do I.
It's making him miserable. It's driving him just about crazy."

"Ah, don't give me that baloney!" said he with a good-
humored flap of his hand. Geisecker was not in the least interested in what I said about my own reaction. Sensitive to nothing
else on earth, he had, unconsciously, of course, better than a
dog's nose for the exact nature of the feeling he inspired. This
keen sense told him that I am of a type not offended by his sort
of humor, and that my mounting anger was entirely on behalf
of Glenway. To him, therefore, it was vicarious, secondhand,
and as flavorless as a duenna's kiss. It gave him no sort of thrill,
and he had no itch to increase it. I felt quite rejected.

I went down to see if I could be more effective with Glenway.
I said, "If you had the least sense of humor, you'd enjoy this
monster. After all, he's the sort of thing you're looking for. He
belongs to a species thought to be extinct."

"I wish to god he was," said Glenway.

"He may not come from the Cretaceous, but he's at least a
survival from the Jokebook Age. He's a human coelacanth. He's
a specimen of Comic Picture Postcard Man. He's a living Bab-
bitt. You ought to turn your cameras on him. Otherwise, people
won't believe he exists."

It was like trying to skip and run over soft sand. Each new
sentence got off to a worse start and sank deeper into Glenway's
depression. At last I was altogether bogged down, and we sat
there just looking at each other. Then, like the last trump, there
arose an urgent, heart-stopping stridulation in the buzzer box on
the wall over the bed. Glenway was out of his depression, out
of his chair, into the doorway, and up the companionway so
quickly that one felt certain intervening movements must have
been left out. I followed as fast as I could; after all, it was either
the sea serpent or Geisecker, and in either case I thought I'd
better be there.

It was Geisecker. He was standing by the wheel, hooting with
laughter, pointing out over the ocean, shouting, "That she blows!
Flukes on the starboard bow!"

Then the laughter doubled him up completely. I noticed that
it can be true about people getting purple in the face. I noticed

also that, even doubled up, Geisecker seemed bigger—there seemed to be more of him than at other times.

Sadder still, there seemed to be less of Glenway. He seemed to be shrunken and concentrated into a narrower and grayer column of tissue than was natural. I had time to think, He'll be driven completely out of his mind if this continues, and then he turned and went down the companionway out of sight.

I went over to Geisecker, wondering on the way what sort of words could possibly pierce his thick hide. "Jesus Christ!" said he. "I knew it was true. When those boys on Paumoy told me, I knew it was true, but I just felt I had to check up on it."

"What the Hell are you talking about?" I asked, cursing myself as I spoke for asking anything.

"About old Glen and Thora Vyborg," replied Geisecker, still gasping with mirth. "Don't you know about Glen and Thora Vyborg?"

I knew they had been married. I vaguely remembered something about a dramatic love-at-first-sight encounter in Honolulu. I had some sort of a picture in my mind of the more than famous filmstar—of her unfathomable personality, her unknowable beauty, and the fact that she talked to no one and traveled with no one and dined with no one except her Svengali, her current director, and her publicity man. I had a fairly clear idea of what these types were like, and I could imagine that Glenway—younger then, tall, angular, already dedicated, with the ocean behind him, winged with sail and haloed with sun and money—must have seemed to offer her a part in a rather better production.

I remembered, too, that the marriage had been extremely short-lived. Someone had said something about them sailing away with the sunset and returning with the dawn. No statement had been made by either party. There had been rumors, as there always are, but these were weak, uncertain; they had been drowned in a flood of better authenticated adulteries long before I ever knew Glenway. Now, it seemed that some of them had been washed ashore, horribly disfigured, swollen and salty, on the ultimate beaches of Paumoy. "You know what the boys there told me?" said Geisecker, watching me closely. "Seems they got married in no time flat and started out on this very same boat, on a big, front-page honeymoon. Believe it or not, the very first night out—round about eleven o'clock, if you get what

I mean, pal—some fellow on deck sees something or other, maybe porpoises or kelp or any damn thing you like, and he gets the idea it's the old brontosaurus in person. So he presses the buzzer, and Glen comes rushing on deck in ten seconds flat. Don't ask me any questions, pal; all I know is that first thing next morning the lugger was turned right around, and it's full steam ahead back to Honolulu, and Reno, and points in opposite directions.''

I realized at once that this was true, and had a certain beauty. However, that was for my private contemplation and had nothing to do with Geisecker. He was regarding me with a sort of arrested gloat, his eye triumphant and his nose tilted up ready to join in the expected peal of laughter. ''Geisecker,'' I said, and for the first time I heard, and he heard, a note of direct and personal hatred in my voice, ''Geisecker, I'm not going to discuss the whys and wherefores, but from now on you're going to stay right away from Glenway. You can come on deck; you can have a chair on the port side there, between the masts. But if you step one inch . . .''

''Hold it!'' said Geisecker. ''Who's talking? The owner? Skipper? First mate? Or what the Hell else do you think you are? I'd like to hear what old Glen's got to say.''

I am no good at all at a row. When my first damp squib of wrath has exploded, I am always overwhelmed by an immense weariness and blankness. At that moment I had neither the will nor the power to go on. But Geisecker obligingly came to my assistance. I could never decide whether he was a sadist, avid for the discomfort of his victim, or a masochist, indecently eager for the wound of being disliked. Whichever it was, he watched me with his little eyes, and he actually passed his tongue over his lips. ''Anyway,'' said he, ''I'm going down to ask him if there's any truth in that goddamn yarn or not.''

The lip-licking was so crude and so banal that it transposed everything into a different key. There was a sailor of great good nature and phenomenal size, a man called Wiggam, a native of Hawaii, who was mending a net a little way along the deck. I called him and told him, in phrases which normally appear only in balloons in comic strips, to take his net and work on it outside Abbott's door, and, in the event of Geisecker approaching that door, to cut his belly open.

I gave these deplorable instructions in a rather cold, staccato tone, assumed in order to overcome a tendency to squeakiness, and I was reminded, even as I heard myself speak, of a small boy's imitation of a tommy gun. Had Geisecker laughed, or had the sailor looked surprised or reluctant, I should have been in a very ludicrous situation. However, it seems that sailors are simple folk; this one showed alacrity, his teeth, and a spring knife that seemed all the more purposeful for being of very moderate dimensions. He glanced at Geisecker, or rather at the belly in question, as if making certain precise and workmanlike calculations, and then he went and gathered up the long net and carried it below. Geisecker watched all this with growing seriousness.

"Look," said he, "maybe I got things wrong somehow, but . . ."

"Listen, Fatso," said I, "if you get anything else wrong you're going to be put on a little Jap crab-fisher boat, see? And the name of that boat's going to be screwed up when we write it down in the log. 'Cause it'll be a Japanese name that means 'the boat that never returned.' Or never existed. Work that one out next time you feel like kidding."

I went down and found Glenway lying on his bed, not reading. I said, "I've fixed him. I can't believe it, but I have."

"How?" said Glenway, not believing it, either.

When I had told him, he said, "He won't stay fixed, not by that sort of thing."

I said, "You think so because I've related it with a twinkle. When I spoke to Geisecker, my voice was cold and dead, like steel, and I let my eyelids droop a little. Like this."

"He certainly won't stay fixed," said Glenway.

"In that case, his belly will be cut open," said I. "Because to Hill Wiggam, who is sitting right out there in the passage, this is his moment of fulfillment. Or, it will be, if Geisecker tries to get past him. It's a case of a man suddenly finding his vocation."

"I don't want Wiggam getting into trouble," said Glenway.

"Nor," said I, "does Geisecker." With that, I went up and did my afternoon spell in the crow's nest, and later I had a drink with Geisecker, to whom I said as little as possible, not knowing what to say nor how to say it. I then dined with Glenway, in his cabin, and then had a smoke with Geisecker on the port deck, and, at about ten o'clock, I went to spend the last hour of the evening with Glenway, who was still extremely tense.

"What's the night like?" he asked.

I said, "It's the most wonderful night of the whole cruise. The moon's just on full, and someone's let it down on an invisible wire, and you can see the curve of the stars going up behind it. The wind's light, but there's a Hell of a big swell rolling in from somewhere. She's still got everything on but her balloon jib, and she's riding it like a steeplechaser. Why don't you go up and take the wheel for a bit?"

"Where's Geisecker?" asked Glenway.

"Amidships, on the port side, fenced in invisibly by threats," I said with some pride.

"I'll stay down here," said Glenway.

"Glenway," said I, "you're making altogether too much of this. The fact is, you've led a sheltered life; people like Geisecker have always treated you with far too much respect. It sets you apart, which I find rather offensive. It reminds me of what Fitzgerald said about the rich. He said you are different. Think of that! It's almost worse than being the same."

"You forget what Hemingway said," replied Glenway, who perhaps found little attraction in either alternative.

"The Hemingway rebuttal," said I, "proves only what it was intended to prove. That is, that Hemingway is a fine, upstanding, independent citizen, and probably with a magnificent growth of hair on his chest. All the same, Fitzgerald had a point. Just because your iniquitous old grandfather happened to build a few railways . . ."

"First of all," interrupted Glenway, "it was not my grandfather, but my great-grandfather. What's more . . ."

And, at that moment, just as I was exulting in having induced him to unclench his hands, and look out of his eyes, and stick his neck out, the buzzer sounded again. I had forgotten to have it disconnected.

What was quite pathetic was that Glenway couldn't control an instinctive movement towards leaping off the bed. He arched up like a tetanus victim, and then collapsed as flat as an empty sack. The buzzer went on. I had a panicky feeling that he might arch up again at any moment. I lost my head and picked up a stool that stood in front of the dressing table and pounded that rattlesnake box into silence.

The silence, once achieved, seemed deep and complete. This was an illusion; we soon noticed that there were all sorts of noises here and there in the large emptiness left by the death of the outrageous buzzer. We could hear the patter of running feet on deck, and voices, and especially Geisecker's voice, spouting large jets of urgent sound.

I opened the door and the words came rushing in. "Glen! Glen! Come up, for God's sake! Can't you hear me? Come on! Come up, quick!"

"My God!" I said. "Maybe they are cutting his belly open."

With that, I ran up. Geisecker was at the head of the companionway. He turned his head briefly to send another shout down the stairs; then he turned it back again to stare out over the sea. I barged into him. He blindly clutched at my arm and dragged me to the side of the boat, and pointed.

I saw something already disappearing into the great smooth side of one of the enormous waves. It was black, wet, shining, and very large. These words can be applied to a whale or a whale shark, and maybe to two or three other things. I can summon up with absolute precision the way Geisecker's face was turning as I came up the companionway; I can remember exactly how his shout went on a little after he had turned his head back to look over the sea again. But I haven't the same perfect mental photograph of what I saw disappearing into the wave. To the very best of my recollection, I saw the hinder half of an enormous back and, following on a curve, already half-lost in the black and moon-glitter, a monstrous tail.

The men who had run up were standing three or four paces away. I looked at them, and they nodded. As they did so, I heard Glenway's voice speaking to the men. "You saw it?" He had come up, after all, and had seen my look and their response as he came toward us. One of them said, "Yes, but he shout," pointing to Geisecker. "He shout, shout, shout, and it go under."

Glenway stepped toward Geisecker, thus turning his back on the men. They couldn't see his face, but I could see it, and so could Geisecker. I don't think Glenway even raised his hand. Geisecker stepped backwards, which brought him, at what I would have thought a very slight and harmless angle, against the low gunwale. His big, fat, heavy torso went on and over; his feet went up, and he was gone. He was overboard.

I don't remember putting my hand on the life belt, but I can remember flinging it, skimming it almost parallel with the side of the boat, and feeling sure it hit the water within a very few feet of Geisecker. Then the boat, whose six knots or so had been like nothing at all a moment earlier, seemed to be racing ahead faster than any boat had ever gone before.

Glenway shouted; the helmsmen put the helm over and spilled the wind out of her sails. There was always a boat ready to be lowered at record speed. Two men were at the oars, Glenway took the tiller, and I stood in the bows looking for Geisecker, who could be no more than two or three hundred yards away.

The night was clear beyond all description. The enormous, smooth swells gleamed and flashed under the moon. The yacht, when we had drawn away from it, stood up like a snowy Alp on the water, and when at the top of each swell, the men lifted their oars for a moment, it was a moment of unbelievable silence, as if some tremendous creature was holding its breath.

Then I saw Geisecker. We were lifted high on one of the great, glassy hills of sea, and he was beginning to slide down the slope of another. He had the life belt. I couldn't see his real features at that distance, but the white moonlight gave him such great, hollow, black eyes, and made such a crater of his open mouth, that I got the picture of a clown in comic distress. Then he went down, and we went down, and two or three ridges ten feet high humped themselves between us.

I said, "He's ahead of us; a couple of hundred feet. You'll see him from the top of the next one."

But we didn't. I began to wonder do a man and a life belt rise and fall faster or slower on a rolling sea than a fourteen-foot boat. Before I could work out the answer, we had gone up and down again and had arrived at a spot which certainly was extremely close to where I had seen him.

"You misjudged the distance," said Glenway, after perhaps half a puzzled minute.

"I must have. Anyway, he's got the life buoy. He'll be all right. Let's row around in a circle."

One of the men put out a bailing can as a marker. The giant swells were so smooth that, ballasted with a couple of inches of water, the can floated up and down without shipping another drop. We went round it on a hundred-foot radius and then at a hundred-and-fifty feet. Geisecker was not to be seen. And we could see, at one time or another, every square foot of water where he could possibly be.

"He's sunk!" said Glenway. "A cramp . . . A shark . . ."

"No shark would have taken the life belt down. It'd be floating right here. We'd see it."

The words were scarcely out of my mouth when we saw it. It breached up, right out of the water—it must have come up from god knows how many fathoms—and it fell back with a splash just a boat's-length ahead of us. Next moment, it was beside our bow and I reached out and lifted it aboard. I turned, holding it in my hands, and showed it to Glenway. It was easier than speaking, and not so silly. We both knew perfectly well that no known creature, except possibly a sperm whale, could have taken Geisecker and the life belt down to that sort of depth. And we knew that what I had seen, and what the men had seen, was not a sperm whale.

We rowed around in circles for a little longer, and then we pulled back to the yacht. When we were aboard again, I said to Glenway, "You didn't so much as touch him. You didn't even mean to touch him. You didn't even raise your hand."

"And some of the men were watching," said Glenway with the utmost calm. "They can testify to that."

If not the railway tycoon, his great-grandfather, it might certainly have been his grandfather, the banker, speaking. He saw my surprise, and smiled. "From the most scrupulous legal point of view," said he, "it was a pure accident. And we'll make a report accordingly. Of course, I killed the man."

"Now, wait a minute," said I.

"Excuse me," said he. We were near the wheel. He took it from the man who was steering, and said something to him, and the man ran forward calling to the rest of the crew who were still on deck. Next minute, the helm went up, the booms swung over, the sails bellied out on the other side, and the great boat jibbed and sweeping round on to a new course.

"Where are we heading now?" said I to Glenway.

"Due east," said he. "To San Francisco."

"To make the report? Can't you . . . ?"

"To put the boat up for sale."

I said, "Glenway, you're upset. You've got to see this business in proportion."

He said, "He was alive and enjoying himself, and now he's

dead. I didn't like him—I detested him. But that's got nothing to do with it.''

I said, ''Don't be completely psychological illiterate. It's got everything in the world to do with it. You hated his guts, a little too intensely, perhaps, but very understandably. You wished he was dead. In fact, you more or less said so. Now you've got guilt feelings. You're going to take the blame for it. Glenway, you're an obsessive type; you're a Puritan, a New Englander, and Early Christian. Be reasonable. Be moderate.''

''Suppose you were driving a car,'' said Glenway, ''and you knocked a man down and killed him?''

''I'd be very sorry, but I think I'd go on driving.''

''If you were a speed demon, and it was because of that? Or a drunk? Or if there was reason to believe you were mentally unfit to handle a car?''

''Well . . .'' I said.

But Glenway wasn't listening. He beckoned the man who had been steering, and turned the wheel over to him. He gave him the course and told him who was to relieve him in each watch. Then he turned away and walked forward. He walked like a passenger. He walked like a man walking on a street. He was walking away from his mania, and in the very hour of its justification.

I followed him, eager to bring him back to himself, but he walked away from me, too.

I said to him considerably later, ''I've found out something very interesting, talking to the men. Shall I tell you?''

''Please do,'' said he.

I said, ''I thought they rather liked Geisecker because he made them laugh. But they didn't. Not a bit. Are you listening?''

''Of course,'' said he as politely as a banker who has already decided not to make a loan.

I said, ''They hated him almost as much as you did, and for the same reason—for making fun of It. They believed in It, all the time. They've all got different names for It, according to where they come from. Almost every man's got an uncle who's seen It, or a wife's grandfather, or someone. And it's quite clear It's the same sort of beast.''

Glenway said, ''I've decided I'm going to buy a farm or a ranch as far from the ocean as I can get. I'll breed cattle or hybridize corn or something.''

I said, "You've been over seven years on this boat with these men, or most of them. Did you know they believed in It?"

"No," said he. "Or I might go in for soil biology. There's still a tremendous amount to be discovered in that field."

This made me feel very sick. I felt Glenway was indeed different—different from me, different from himself. The beautiful *Zenobia* was to be sold, the crew disbanded, and the large marine saurian left to dwindle into a figure on an old map, distant and disregarded in its watery solitude. As for myself, all my friendship with Glenway had been aboard the boat—I was part of it; I was one of these things. I had been nothing but the accomplice of his obsession, and now he was, in a way I didn't like, cured. I felt that I, too, was up for sale, and we talked amiably and politely and quite meaninglessly all the way back to San Francisco, and there we said good-bye to each other and promised to write.

We didn't write in over three years. One can't write to the ghost of a banker, nor expect a letter from one. But, this summer, when I was in New York, I got home one night and found a letter awaiting me. The postmark was Gregory, South Dakota, which is about as far from either ocean as you can get.

He was there; he wondered if I knew those parts; he wondered if I was likely to be free; there were some interesting things to talk about. The lines were extremely few, but there was all the more space to read between them. I took up the telephone.

It was nearly midnight, but, of course, it was two hours earlier in South Dakota. All the same, Glenway was a very long time coming to the phone. "I hope I didn't get you out of bed," I told him.

"Heavens, no!" said he. "I was on the roof. We get wonderful nights here; as clear as Arizona."

I remembered that clear night in the Pacific, and the flash and glitter of the enormous, glassy waves, and the silence, and the boat rising and falling so high and so low, and the yacht like a hill of snow in the distance, and the little bailing can visible at over a hundred feet. I said, "I'd like to come out right away."

"I rather hoped you would," said Glenway, and began to tell me about planes and trains.

I asked him if there was anything he wanted from New York.

"There most certainly is," said he. "There's a man called Emil Schroeder; you'll find his address in the book; he's out in

Brooklyn; he's the best lens grinder that ever got out of Germany, and he's got a package for me that I don't want sent through the mail because it's fragile.''

"What is it?" I asked. "A microscope? Did you go in for soil biology after all?"

"Well, I did for a time," said Glenway. "But this is something different. It's lenses for a binocular telescope a fellow's designed for me. You see, a single eyepiece is no good for following anything that moves at all fast. But this binocular thing will be perfect. I can use it on the roof, or I can set in a mounting I've had built into the plane.''

"Glenway, do you mind telling me what the hell you're talking about?"

"Haven't you read the government report on unidentified flying objects? Hello! Are you there?"

"Yes, I'm here, Glenway. And you're there. You're there, sure enough!''

"Listen, if you haven't read that report, do please get hold of it first thing tomorrow, and read it on the way out here. I don't want to hear you talking like that unfortunate fellow fell overboard that night. Will you do that? Will you read it?"

"All right, Glenway, I will. I most certainly will."

The Dakwa
by
Manly Wade Wellman

The late Manly Wade Wellman was one of the finest modern practitioners of the "dark fantasy" or "supernatural horror" tale. He was probably best known for his stories about John the Minstrel or "Silver John," scary and vividly evocative tales set against the background of a ghost-and-demon haunted rural Appalachia that, in Wellman's hands, is as bizarre and beautiful as many another writer's entirely imaginary fantasy world. The "Silver John" stories have been collected in Who Fears the Devil, *generally perceived as Wellman's best book. In recent years, there were "Silver John" novels as well:* The Old Gods Waken, After Dark, The Lost and the Lurking, The Hanging Stones, *and, most recently,* Voice of the Mountain. *Wellman's non-"Silver John" stories were assembled in the mammoth collection* Worse Things Waiting, *which won a World Fantasy Award as the Best Anthology/Collection of 1975. Wellman himself has won the prestigious World Fantasy Award for Life Achievement. He died in 1986 at the age of 82. His most recent book is the posthumously published collection* Mountain Valley Stories.

Here he gives us the kind of story he did best: one lone, unflinching man pitted against evil, forced to rely only on his own brains and muscle and courage, face to face and grip to grip with the forces of darkness . . .

*　　　*　　　*

Night had fallen two hours ago in these mountains, but Lee Cobbett remembered the trail up from Markum's Fork over Dogged Mountain and beyond. Too, he had the full moon and a blazing skyful of stars to help him. Finally he reached the place where Long Soak Hollow had been, where now lay a broad stretch of water among the heights, water struck to quivering radiance by the moonlight.

Shaggy trees made the last of the trail dark and uneasy under his boot soles. He half-groped his way to the grassy brink and looked across to something he recognized. On an island that

once had been the top of a broad rise in the hollow stood a
square cabin in a tuft of trees. Light from the open door beat
upon a raftlike dock and a boat tied up there.

Dropping his pack and bedroll, Cobbett cupped his big hands
into a trumpet at his mouth.

"Hello!" he shouted. "Hello, the house, hello, Mr. Luns
Lamar, I'm here! Come over and get me!"

A shadow slid into the doorway. A man tramped down to
where that dock was visible. He held a lantern high.

"Who's that a-bellowing?" came back a call across the water.

"Lee Cobbett—come get me!"

"No, sir," echoed to his ears. "Can't do it tonight."

"But—"

"Not tonight!" The words were sharp, they meant that thing.
"No way. You wait there for me till sunup."

The figure plodded back to the doorway and sat down on the
threshold with the lantern beside it.

Cobbett cursed to himself, there on the night shore. He was
a blocky man in denim jacket and slacks, with a square, seamed
face and a mane of dark hair. Scowling, he estimated the distance across. Fifty yards? Not much more than that. If Luns
Lamar wouldn't come, Lee Cobbett would go.

He put the pack and roll together next to a laurel bush and sat
on them to drag off his boots and socks. He stripped away slacks,
jacket, blue shirt, underwear, and stood up naked. Walking to
the edge of the lake, he tested it with his toe. Chill, like most
mountain water. He set his whole foot in, found bottom, and
waded forward to his knees. Two more steps, and he was waist
deep. He shivered as he moved out along the clay bottom until
he could wade no longer. He struck out for the light of the cabin
door.

The coldness of the water bit him, and he swam more strongly
to fight against it. Music seemed to be playing somewhere,
a song he had never heard, like a muted woodwind. A hum in his
head—no, it came from somewhere away from the cabin and the
island, somewhere on the moonbright water. It grew stronger,
more audible.

On he swam with powerful strokes. His body glided swiftly,
but a current sprang up around him, more of a current than he
had thought possible. And the melody heightened in his ears,
still nothing he could remember, but tuneful, haunting.

Then a sudden shuddering impact, a blow like a club against his side and shoulder.

He almost whirled under. He kicked at whatever it was, shouting aloud as he did so. Next moment he was at the poles that supported the dock, grabbing at them with both hands. Luns Lamar stooped above him and caught his thick wrists.

"You damned fool," grumbled Lamar, heaving away.

Cobbett scrambled up on the split slabs, kneeling.

"Whatever in hell made you swim over here?" Lamar scolded him.

"What else was there for me to do?" Cobbett found breath to say. "You said you wouldn't come and fetch me, even when you'd written that letter wanting me to bring you those books. I don't know why I should have moped over there until tomorrow, not when I can swim."

"I wouldn't go out on this lake tonight, even in the boat." Lamar helped Cobbett to his feet. "Hey, you're scraped. Bleeding."

It was true. Cobbett's sinewy shoulder looked red and raw.

"There's a log or snag right out from the dock," he said, heading for the cabin's open door.

"No," said Lamar. "That wasn't any log or snag."

They went inside together. The front half of the cabin was a single room, raftered overhead. Cobbett knew its rawhide-seated chairs, the plank table, the oil stove, tall shelves of books, a fireplace with a strew of winking coals and a glowing kerosene lamp on the mantel board. Against the wall, an ancient army cot with brown blankets. In a rear corner, a tool chest, and upon that a scuffed banjo case. Lamar brought him a big, frayed towel. Cobbett winced as he rubbed himself down.

"That's a real rough raking you got," said Lamar, peering.

He, too, was known to Cobbett, old and small but sure of movement, with spectacles closely set on his shrewd face. He wore a dark blue pullover, khaki pants, and scuffed house slippers.

"We'd better do something about that," he said and went to a shelf by the stove. He took down a big, square bottle and worried out the cork, then came back. "Just hold still."

He filled his palm with dark, oily liquid from the bottle and spread it over the torn skin of Cobbett's ribs and shoulder.

"What's in that stuff?" Cobbett asked.

"There's some sap of three different trees in it," replied Lamar. "And boiled tea of three different flowers, and some crushed seeds, and the juice of what some folks call a weed, but the Indians used to prize it."

He brought an old blue bathrobe with GOLDEN GLOVES in faded yellow letters across the back. "Put this on till we can go over tomorrow and get your clothes," he said.

"Thanks." Cobbett drew the robe around him and sat down in a chair. "Now," he said, "if that wasn't a log or snag, what was it?"

Lamar wiped his spectacles. "You won't believe it."

"Not without hearing it."

"I asked you to fetch me some books," Lamar reminded.

"Mooney's study for the Bureau of Anthology, *Myths of the Cherokee*," said Cobbett. "And Skinner's *Myths and Legends of Our Own Land*. And *The Kingdom of Madison*. All right, they're over yonder in my pack. If you hadn't flooded Long Soak Hollow, I could have brought them right into this cabin without even wetting my feet. If you'd come with the boat, they'd be here now. Why don't you get to telling me what this is all about?"

Lamar studied him. "Lee, did you ever hear about the Dakwa?"

"Dakwa," Cobbett said after him. "Sounds like Dracula."

"It's not Dracula, but it happens to be terrible in its own way. It's what rubbed up against you while you were out there swimming." Lamar scowled. "Look here, let's have a drink. I reckon maybe we both need one."

He sought the shelf again and opened a fruit jar of clear, white liquid and poured generous portions into two glasses. "This is good blockade whiskey," he said, handing a glass to Cobbett. The liquid tingled sharply on Cobbett's tongue and warmed him all the way down.

Lamar sipped in turn. "It's hard to explain, even though we've known each other nearly all our lives."

"You've known me nearly all my life," said Cobbett, "but I haven't known you nearly all yours. I've heard that you studied law, then you taught in a country school, then you edited a little weekly paper. After that, I don't know why, you quit everything and built this cabin. You don't ever come out of it except to listen to mountain songs and mountain tales, and sometimes you write about them for folklore journals.'' Cobbett studied his friend. ''Why not start by telling me what you've done, drowning Long Soak Hollow like this?''

''It wasn't my doing,'' growled Lamar. ''Some resort company did it, to make a lake amongst the summer cottages they're building for visitors. You remember how this place of mine was set—high above the little creek down in the hollow, safe from any flood. I wouldn't sell out, but that company bought up all the land round about and put in a dam, and here it is, filled in. I'm like Robinson Crusoe on my island, but I'm not studying to go ashore till tomorrow.''

Cobbett drank again. ''Because of what?''

''Because of one of those same old tales that makes a noise like the truth.'' Lamar showed his gold-wired teeth. ''The Dakwa,'' he said again. ''It's in those books I asked you to fetch along with you.''

''And I said they're across that water that scares you,'' said Cobbett. ''What,'' he asked patiently, ''is the Dakwa?''

''It's what tried to grab you just now,'' Lamar flung out. ''It used to be penned up in the little creek they called Long Soak, penned up there for centuries. And now, by God, it's out again in this lake they've dammed up, a-looking for what it may devour.'' His face clamped desperately. ''Devour it whole,'' he said.

''You say it's out again,'' said Cobbett. ''What do you mean by again? How long has this been going on?''

''Centuries, I told you,'' said Lamar. ''The tale was here with the Cherokee Indians when the first settlers came, before the Revolutionary War. And the Dakwa's hungry. Two men and a boy—Del Hungant and Steve Biggins and a teenager from somewhere in the lowlands named McIlhenny—they just sort of went out of sight along this new lake. Folks came up from town and dragged for them, and nothing whatever dragged up.''

''Not even the Dakwa,'' suggested Cobbett.

''Especially not the Dakwa. It's too smart to be hooked.''

''And you believe in it,'' said Cobbett.

''Sure enough I believe in it. I've seen it again and again, just an ugly hunch of it in the water out there. I've heard it humming.''

''So that's what I heard,'' said Cobbett.

''Yes, that's what. And once, the last time I've ever been out in the boat at night, it shoved against the boat and damn near turned it over with me. You'd better believe in it yourself, the way it rasped your skin like that."

Cobbett went over to the bookshelf and studied the titles. He took down Thompson's *Mysteries and Secrets of Magic* and leafed through the index pages.

"You won't read about it in there," Lamar told him sourly. "That's only about old-world witches and devils, with amulets and charms against them, and all the names of God to defeat them. The Dakwa doesn't believe in God. It's an Indian thing— Cherokee. Something else has to go to work against it. That's why I wanted those books, hoping to find something in them. They're the only published notices of the Dakwa."

Cobbett slid Thompson's volume back into place and went to the door and opened it.

"You fixing to do something foolish?" grumbled Lamar.

"No, nothing foolish if I can help it," Cobbett assured him. "I just thought I'd go and look at the stars before bedtime."

He stepped across the threshold log into grass. Dew splashed his bare feet. He paced to the dock and gazed up at the moon, a great pallid blotch of radiance. Gazing, he heard something again.

Music, that was all it could be. Perhaps it had words, but words so soft that they were like a faint memory.

Out upon the dock he stepped. Ripples broke against its supporting poles. Something made a dark rush in the water, close up almost to the boat. Whatever it was glinted shinily beneath the surface. Cobbett stared down at it, trying to make out its shape. It vanished. He turned and paced back to the cabin door, that faint sense of the music still around him.

"All right, what did you find out there?" Lamar demanded.

"Nothing to speak of," said Cobbett. "Now then, I had a long uphill trudge getting here. How about showing me where I'll sleep?"

"Over yonder, as usual." Lamar nodded toward the cot.

"And we'll get up early tomorrow morning and go get my gear and those books of yours."

"Not until the sun's up," insisted Lamar.

"Okay," grinned Cobbett. "Not until the sun's up."

* * *

When Cobbett woke, Lamar was at the oil stove, cooking breakfast. Cobbett got into the robe, washed his face and hands and teeth and unclasped the banjo case. He took out Lamar's old banjo, tuned it briefly and softly began to pick a tune, the tune he had heard the night before.

"You cut that right out!" Lamar yelled at him. "You want to call that thing out of the water, right up to the door?"

Cobbett put the banjo away and came to the table. Breakfast was hearty and good—flapjacks drenched in molasses, eggs and home-cured bacon, and black coffee so strong you'd expect a hatchet to float in it. Cobbett had two helpings of everything. Afterward, he washed the dishes while Lamar wiped.

"And now the sun's up," Cobbett said, peering at it through the window. "It's above those trees on the mountain. What do you say we get me back into my clothes?"

Wearing the GOLDEN GLOVES bathrobe, he walked out to the dock with Lamar. He had his first good look at the boat. It was well made of calked planks, canoe style, pointed fore and aft, with two seats and two paddles. It was painted a deep brown.

"I built that thing," said Lamar. "Built it when they started in to fill up the hollow. Can you paddle? Bow or stern?"

"Let me take stern."

Getting in, they pushed off. Lamar, dipping his paddle, gazed at something far out toward the middle of the lake. Cobbett gazed too. Whatever it was it hung there on the water, something dark and domed. It might have been a sort of head. As Cobbett looked, the thing slipped underwater. The light of the rising sun twinkled on a bit of foam.

Lamar's mouth opened as if to speak, but closed again on silence. A score of determined strokes took them across to a shallow place. Cobbett hopped ashore, picked up his clothes and pack and blanket roll, and came back to stow everything in the waist of the boat. Around they swung and headed back toward the island. Out there across the gentle stir of the water's surface, the dark, domed object was visible again.

"Whatever it is, it's watching us," ventured Cobbett. "It doesn't seem to want to come close."

"That's because there's a couple of us," grunted Lamar, paddling. "I don't expect it would tackle two people at a time, by daylight."

That seemed to put a stop to the conversation. They nosed in against the dock. Tying up, Lamar helped Cobbett carry his things into the cabin. Cobbett rummaged in the pack.

"All right, here are those books of yours," he said. "Now, I'll get dressed."

While he did so, Lamar leafed through Mooney's book about Cherokee myths.

"Sure enough, here we are," he said. "Dakwa—it's a water spirit, and it used to drag Cherokee hunters down and eat them. It's said to have been in several streams."

"Including Long Soak," supplied Cobbett.

"Mooney doesn't mention Long Soak but, yes, here too." Lamar turned pages. "It's still here, and well you know that's a fact." He took up two smaller volumes. "Now, look in this number two book of Skinner's *Myths and Legends of Our Own Land*. Hmmm," he crooned.

"More Dakwa?" asked Cobbett, picking up the other book he had brought.

"Skinner titles it, 'The Siren of the French Broad.' This time it's not as grotesque as in Mooney. It's supposed to be a beautiful naked woman rising up to sing to you. So, if you're a red-blooded American he-man, you stoop close to see and hear better and it quits being beautiful, it suddenly has a skull and two bony arms to drag you down." He snapped the book shut. "I judge the white settlers prettied the tale up to sound like the Lorelei. But not much in any of these books to tell how to fight it. What are you reading there in *The Kingdom of Madison*?"

"I'm looking at page thirteen, which I hope isn't unlucky," replied Cobbett. "Here's what it says about a deep place on the French Broad River: 'There, the Cherokees said, lurked the *dakwa*, the gigantic fish-monster that caught men at the riverside and dragged them down, swallowed them whole.' And it has that other account, too: 'The story would seem to inspire another fable, this time of a lovely water-nymph, who smiled to lure the unwary wanderer, reached up her arms to him, and dragged him down to be seen no more.'"

"Not much help, either. That's about what Mooney and Skinner say, and it's no fable, no legend." Lamar studied his guest. "How do you feel today, after that gouging it gave you in the water last night?"

"I feel fine." Cobbett buttoned up his shirt. "Completely healed. It didn't hurt me too much for you to cure me."

"Maybe if it had been able to get you into its mouth, swallow you up—"

"Didn't you say that was an old Indian preparation you sloshed on me?"

"It's something I got from a Cherokee medicine man," said Lamar. "A valued old friend of mine. He has a degree in philosophy from the University of North Carolina, but he worships his people's old gods, is afraid of their evil spirits, carries out their old formulas and rituals, and I admire him for it."

"So do I," said Cobbett. "But you mentioned certain plants in that mixture."

"Well, for the most part there were smashed-up seeds of viper's bugloss and some juice of campion, what the country folks call rattlesnake plant."

Both of those growths had snake names to them, reflected Cobbett. "I think you might have mentioned to me why you wanted these books," he said.

"Why mention it?" groaned Lamar, adjusting his spectacles. "You wouldn't have believed me then. Anyway, I don't see how this extra information will help. It doesn't do more than prove things, more or less. Well, I've got errands to do."

He walked out to the dock. Cobbett followed him.

"I'm paddling across and going down the trail to meet old Snave Dalbom," Lamar announced. "This is his day to drive down to the county seat to wag back a week's supplies. He lets me go with him to do my shopping."

He got into the boat and began to cast off.

"Let me paddle you over," offered Cobbett, but Lamar shook his head violently.

"I'll paddle myself over and tie up the boat yonder," he declared. "I'm not a-going to have you out on this lake, maybe getting yourself yanked overboard and down there where they can't drag for you, like those three others who never came up."

"How do you know I won't go swimming?" Cobbett teased him.

"Because I don't reckon your mother raised any such fool. Listen, just sit around here and take it easy. Snave and I will probably get a bite in town, so fix your own noon dinner and look for me back sometime before sundown. There's some pretty good canned stuff in the house—help yourself. And maybe you can read the whole tariff on the Dakwa, figure out something to help us. But I'm leaving you here so you'll stay here.''

He shoved out from the dock and paddled for the shore opposite.

Cobbett strolled back to the cabin, and around it. Clumps of cedar brush stood at the corner, and locusts hung above the old tin roof. The island itself was perhaps an acre in extent, with cleared ground behind the cabin. A well had been dug there. Lamar's well-kept garden showed two rows of bright green cornstalks, the tops of potatoes and tomatoes and onions. Cobbett inspected the corn. At noon he might pick a couple of ears and boil them to eat with butter and salt and pepper. On the far side of the garden was the shore of the island, dropping abruptly to the water. Kneeling, Cobbett peered. He could see that the bottom was far down there, a depth of many feet. Below the clear surface he saw a shadowy patch, a drowned tree that once had grown there, that had been overwhelmed by the lake.

That crooning music, or the sense of it, seemed to hang over the gentle ripples.

He returned to the cabin and sat down with Mooney's book. The index gave him several page references to the Dakwa and he looked them up, one by one. The Dakwa had been reported where the creek called Toco, and before that called the Dakwai, flowed into the Little Tennessee River. Again, it was supposed to lurk in a low-churned stretch of the French Broad River, six miles upstream from Hot Springs. There were legends. A hunter, said one, had been swallowed whole by a Dakwa and had fought his way out to safety, but his hair had been scalded from his head. Mooney's notes referred to Jonah in the Bible, to the swallowing of an Ojibwa hero named Mawabosho. That reminded Cobbett of Longfellow's poem, where the King of Fishes had swallowed Hiawatha.

But Hiawatha had escaped, and Jonah and Mawabosho had escaped. The devouring monster of the deep, whatever it might be, was not inescapable.

Again he studied the index. He could not find any references to the plants Lamar had mentioned, but there was a section called "Plant Lore." He read it carefully:

> . . . the cedar is held sacred above all other trees . . . the small green twigs are thrown upon the fire in certain cere-

monies . . . as it is believed that the anisgina or malevolent ghosts cannot endure the smell . . .

Below that, a printed name jumped to his eye:

. . . the white seeds of the viper's bugloss *(Echium vulgara)* were formerly used in many important ceremonies . . .

And, a paragraph or so beyond:

The campion *(silene stellata)* . . . the juice is held to be a sovereign remedy for snake bites . . .

He shut up the book with a snap and began to take off his clothes.

He searched a pair of bathing trunks out of his pack and put them on. Next, he explored Lamar's tool chest. Among the things at the bottom he found a great cross-hilted hunting knife and drew it from its riveted sheath. The blade was fully a foot long, whetted sharp on both edges. Then he went out to the woodpile and chose a stafflike length of hickory, about five feet in length. There was plenty of fishing line in the cabin, and he lashed the knife to the end of the pole like a spearhead. From the shelf he took the bottle of ointment that had healed him so well and rubbed palmsful on himself from head to foot. Remembering the Indian warrior who had been swallowed and came out bald, he lathered the mixture into his dark, shaggy hair. He smeared more on the blade and the pole. When he was done, the bottle was two-thirds empty.

Finally he walked out with his makeshift spear. He paused at the corner of the cabin, gazing at what grew there.

Those cedar bushes. *The anisgina or malevolent ghosts cannot endure the smell,* Mooney had written, and Mooney, the scholarly friend of the Cherokees, must have known. Cobbett found a match and gathered a sheaf of dry twigs to make a fire. Then he plucked bunches of the dark green cedar leaves and heaped them on top of the blaze. Up rose a dull, vapory smoke. He stood in it, eyes and nose tingling from the fumes, until the fire burned down and the smoke thinned away.

Spear in hand, he paced around the cabin and past the garden and to the place where the margin shelved steeply down into the lake.

He gazed at the sunken tree, then across the lake. No motion there. He looked again at the tree. He could see enough of it to remember it, from times before Long Soak was dammed up. It was a squat oak, thick-stemmed, with sprawling roots driven in among rocks, twenty feet below him.

Yet again he looked out over the water. Still no sign upon it. He began to hum the tune he had heard before, the tune Lamar had forbidden him to pick on the banjo.

Humming, he heard the song outside himself, faint as a song in a dream. It made his skin creep.

From the deep shadowy bottom something came floating upward, straight toward where he knelt.

A woman, thought Cobbett at once, certainly a woman, certainly what the myth in Skinner's book said, not terrible at all. He saw her streaming banner of dark hair, saw her round, lithe arms, her oval, wide-eyed face, and her plump breasts, her skin as smooth and as richly brown as some tropical fruit. Her eyes sought him, her red lips moved as though they sang. Closer she came. Her head with its soaking hair broke clear of the water. Her hand reached to him, both her hands. Those beautiful arms spread wide for him.

He felt light-headed. He almost leaned within the reach of the arms when she drew back and away, still on the surface. His homemade spear had drooped between them. Her short, straight nose twitched as though she would sneeze.

A moment, and then back she came, to the very brink. And changed suddenly. Her eyes spread into shadowed caverns, her mouth opened to show stockades of long, stale teeth. Her arms, round and lithe no longer, drove a taloned clutch at him.

He thrust with the spear, and again she slid swiftly back and away. Off balance, Cobbett fell floundering into the water.

He plunged deep with the force of his fall. In the shimmering blur above him he saw a vast, winnowing shape, far larger than the woman had seemed. It was dark and somehow ribbed, something like a parachute fluttering in a gale. He rose under it, trying to stab and failing again. He could not dart a swift thrust under that impeding water. He clamped the hickory shaft so that it lay tight along his forearm and made a pushing prod with it. The point struck something, seemed to pierce. The broad shape slid away with a flutter that churned the lake all around. Cobbett rose to the surface, gratefully gulping a mighty lungful of breath.

The Dakwa, whatever it was, whatever it truly looked like, had dived out of sight as he came up. Cobbett swam for the shore, one-handed, as another surging wave struck him. He dived deeply, as deeply as he could swim without letting go of his spear.

There it was, stretched overhead again. The dimness of the water, the hampering slowness put upon his movements, seemed like a struggling nightmare. He turned over as he swam. The dark blotch extended itself and came settling down upon him, like a seine dropped to secure a prey. Clamping his spear to his right arm from elbow to wrist, he stabbed, not swiftly but powerfully. Again he felt something at the point. He slid clear and swam upward until his head broke the surface and he could breathe.

He thought no longer of winning to shore. He was here in the lake, he had to fight the Dakwa, do something to it somehow. Underwater was best, where he could see his adversary beneath the surface. Huckleberry Finn had counted on a whole minute to swim without breath under a steamboat. He, Lee Cobbett, ought to do better than that.

But before he went under, ripples and waves. His charging enemy broke into sight, making a veering turn. He saw the slanting spread of it, suddenly rising high, like the murky sail of a scudding catboat. At waterline skimmed the jut of a woman's semblance, a sort of grotesque figurehead, hair in a whirl, teeth bare and big.

Cobbett dived, as straight down as he could manage. The cavern-eyed head was almost at him as he dipped under. Groping talons touched his leg and he felt the stab of them, but he twitched clear. As he swam strivingly down, headfirst, he saw the shape of the water-whelmed oak there, standing where the lake had swallowed it. Its trunk looked bigger than arms could clasp, its roots clutched crookedly at rocks. He slid toward it and went behind as that sprawling shape descended to engulf him. It did not want him there below, poking and stabbing. Cobbett's left hand found and seized a stubby branch of the oak. He rose a trifle. As the Dakwa came gliding toward him and just beneath him, he drove down hard with the spear.

The force of the blow would have pushed him upward if he

had not held the branch. That solid anchor helped him bring
weight and power into his stab as it went home.

All around him the water suddenly rippled and pulsed, as
though with an explosion. Darkness flooded out around him, like
sepia expelled by a great cuttlefish, but he clung to the branch
and forced the spear grindingly into what it had found, and
through and beyond into something as hard and tough as wood.
As oak wood. He had spiked the Dakwa to the root of the tree.

The spear lodged there as though clamped in a vise. He let
go of it and swam upward. It seemed miles to the surface, to
air. He knew he was very tired. He came up at the grassy shag
that fringed the island's shore.

With both hands he caught the edge. It began to crumble, but
he heaved himself out with almost the last of his strength.
Sprawling on the grass, he squirmed dully around and looked
down to see what he had done.

No seeing it. Just bubbles and ripples, in water gone poison-
ously dark, as with some dull infusion. Cobbett panted and
moaned for air. At last he got to his hands and knees, and finally
stood shakily upright.

His thigh was gashed and the skin on his arm and chest looked
rasped, although he could not remember how that last contact
had come. He almost fell in as he stooped and tried to see into
the lake. If he could not see, he could sense. The Dakwa was
down there and it was not coming up. Strength began to return
to his muscles. He scowled to himself as he summoned his nerve.
Drawing a deep breath into himself, he dived in again. Down
he swam, determinedly down.

There it was, writhed around the roots of the oak like a blown
tarpaulin. It stirred and trembled. He could make out that forward part, the part shaped with head and arms and breasts to
lure its prey. There was where his spear had struck. The knife
that had been lashed on for a point was driven in, clear to the
cross hilt, at the very region of the spine, if the Dakwa had a
spine. It was solidly nailed down there, the Dakwa, like some
gigantic, loathsome specimen on a collector's pin. It could not
get away and come after him. He hoped not.

Slowly, laboriously, he swam up again, and dragged himself
out as before. Getting to his feet, he half-staggered to the cabin
and inside. Blood from his wounded leg dripped to the floor.
He found the fruit jar full of blockade whiskey, screwed off the

lid, put it to his mouth and drank and drank. After that, he took
the bottle of ointment and spread it on the places where the
Dakwa had gashed and scraped him.

He felt better by the moment. Picking up the robe Lamar had
lent him, he put it on. More strongly he walked out and to the
place where he had gone in to fight the Dakwa.

The water was calm now, and clearer. He could even make
out what was prisoned down there at the root of the oak; you
could see it if you knew what you were looking for. It was still
there. It would stay there.

Midway through the afternoon, Lamar tied up at the dock
again. He came with heavy steps to the cabin door, loaded down
with a huge can of kerosene and a gunnysack crammed with
provisions. Cobbett was inside, wearing the GOLDEN GLOVES
robe, busy at the stove.

"Welcome back," he greeted Lamar over his shoulder. "I've
been fixing a pot of beans for supper. I've put in a few smoked
spare ribs you had, and some ketchup and sliced onions, and a
sprinkle of garlic salt I happened to bring with me."

Lamar dropped his burden and stared. "What are you a-doing
in my bathrobe again? Did you manage to get chopped up the
way you did last night, you damned fool?"

"A little, but not as badly chopped up as something else."

"What are you blathering about? Listen, though. In town, I
found out that these resort folks can be made to drain out their
lake. If I bring the proper kind of lawsuit in court—"

"Don't do it," said Cobbett emphatically. "Without the water
in there, something ugly will come in sight. Right at the foot of
the steep drop behind the garden."

"The Dakwa?" quavered Lamar. "You trying to say you killed
it?"

"Not exactly. I have a theory that it can't be killed. But I went
in all doped over with your sacred Cherokee ointment and
smoked up with cedar, and I was able to stand it off. Finally, I
spiked it to the roots of the tree down there."

Lamar crinkled his face. He was beginning to believe, to be
aware of implications.

"What about when it comes up again?" he asked.

"I doubt if it can come up until the oak rots away," said
Cobbett. "That will take years. Meanwhile, we can study the

matter of how to cope with it. I'd like to talk to your friend, that Cherokee medicine man. He might figure how to build on the Indian knowledge we already have.''

"We might do something with dynamite,'' Lamar began to suggest. "The way some people blow fish up.''

Cobbett shook his head. "The Dakwa might not be affected. And a charge let off would break up that tree, tear down some of the bank, even wreck your cabin.''

"We can get scientists,'' said Lamar, gesturing eagerly. "I know some marine scientists, a couple of fellows who could go down there with diving gear.''

"No,'' said Cobbett, turning from the stove. "You don't want them to have bad dreams all their lives, do you?''

The Kings of the Sea
by
Sterling E. Lanier

Although he has published novels—most notably the well received Hiero's Journey, *its sequel* The Unforsaken Hiero, *and* Menace Under Marswood—*Sterling E. Lanier is probably best known in the fantasy and science fiction fields for his sequence of stories describing the odd adventures of Brigadier Donald Ffellowes, the bulk of which have been collected in* The Peculiar Exploits of Brigadier Ffellowes. *Unusually well crafted examples of that curious sub-genre known as the "club story" or "bar story," Lanier's Ffellowes stories are erudite, intelligent, witty, fast-paced—and often just plain scary.*

    That's certainly true of the story that follows, a bloodcurdler that may make you leery about even going to the shore, let alone in the water . . .

*   *   *

I don't remember how magic came into the conversation at the club, but it had, somehow.

"Magic means rather different things to different people. To me . . ." Brigadier Donald Ffellowes, late of Her Majesty's forces, had suddenly begun talking. He generally sat, ruddy, very British and rather tired-looking, on the edge of any circle. Occasionally he would add a date, a name, or simply nod, if he felt like backing up someone else's story. His own stories came at odd intervals and to many of us, frankly verged on the incredible, if not downright impossible. A retired artilleryman, Ffellowes now lived in New York, but his service had been all over the world, and in almost every branch of military life, including what seemed to be police or espionage work. That's really all there is to be said about either his stories or him, except that once he started one, no one ever interrupted him.

"I was attached to the embassy in Berlin in '38, and I went to Sweden for a vacation. Very quiet and sunny, because it was summer, and I stayed in Smaaland, on the coast, at a little inn.

146

For a bachelor who wanted a rest, it was ideal, swimming every day, good food, and no newspapers, parades, crises or Nazis.

"I had a letter from a Swedish pal I knew in Berlin to a Swedish nobleman, a local landowner, a sort of squire in those parts. I was so absolutely happy and relaxed I quite forgot about going to see the man until the second week of my vacation, and when I did, I found he wasn't at home in any case.

"He owned a largish, old house about three miles from the inn, also on the coast road, and I decided to cycle over one day after lunch. The inn had a bike. It was a bright, still afternoon, and I wore my bathing trunks under my clothes, thinking I might get a swim either at the house or on the way back.

"I found the place easy enough, a huge, dark-timbered house with peaked roofs, which would look very odd over here, and even at home. But it looked fine there, surrounded by enormous old pine trees, on a low bluff over the sea. There was a lovely lawn, close cut, spread under the trees. A big lorry—you'd say a moving van—was at the door, and two men were carrying stuff out as I arrived. A middle-aged woman, rather smartly dressed, was directing the movers, with her back to me so that I had a minute or two to see what they were moving. One of them had just manhandled a largish black chair, rather archaic in appearance, into the lorry and then had started to lift a long, carved wooden chest, with a padlock on it, in after the chair. The second man, who must have been the boss mover, was arguing with the lady. I didn't speak too much Swedish, although I'm fair at German, but the two items I saw lifted into the van were apparently the cause of the argument, and I got the gist of it, you know.

"'But, Madame,' the mover kept on saying, 'are you sure these pieces should be *destroyed*? They look very old.'

"'You have been paid,' she kept saying, in a stilted way. 'Now get rid of it any way you like. Only take it away, now, at once.'

"Then she turned and saw me, and, believe it or not, blushed bright red. The blush went away quickly, though, and she asked me pretty sharply what I wanted.

"I answered in English, that I had a letter to Baron Nyderstrom. She switched to English, which she spoke pretty well, and appeared a bit less nervous. I showed her the letter, which was a simple note of introduction, and she read it and actually smiled at me. She wasn't a bad-looking woman—about 45-48, somewhere in there, anyway—but she was dressed to the nines, and her hair was dyed an odd shade of metallic brown. Also, she had a really hard mouth and eyes.

" 'I'm so sorry,' she said, 'but the baron, who is my nephew, is away for a week and a half. I know he would have been glad to entertain an English officer friend of Mr.'—here she looked at the letter—'of Mr. Sorendson, but I'm afraid he is not around, while as you see, I am occupied. Perhaps another time?' She smiled brightly, and also rather nastily, I thought. 'Be off with you,' but polite.

"Well, really there was nothing to do except bow, and I got back on my bike and went wheeling off down the driveway.

"Halfway down the drive, I heard the lorry start, and I had just reached the road when it passed me, turning left, away from the direction of the inn, while I turned to the right.

"At that point something quite appalling happened. Just as the van left the drive, and also—as I later discovered—the estate's property line, something, a great weight, seemed to start settling over my shoulders, while I was conscious of a terrible cold, a cold which almost numbed me and took my wind away.

"I fell off the bike and half stood, half knelt over it, staring back after the dust of the lorry and completely unable to move. I remember the letters on the license and on the back of the van, which was painted a dark red. They said, *Solvaag and Mechius, Stockholm.*

"I wasn't scared, mind you, because it was all too quick. I stood staring down the straight dusty road in the hot sun, conscious only of a terrible weight and the freezing cold, the weight pressing me down and the icy cold numbing me. It was as if time had stopped. And I felt utterly depressed, too, sick and, well, *hopeless.*

"Suddenly, the cold and the pressure stopped. They were just gone, as if they had never been, and I was warm, in fact, covered with sweat, and feeling like a fool there in the sunlight. Also, the birds started singing among the birches and pines by the road, although actually, I suppose they had been all along. I don't think the whole business took over a minute, but it seemed like hours.

"Well, I picked up the bike, which had scraped my shins, and started to walk along, pushing it. I could think quite coherently, and I decided I had had either a mild coronary or a stroke. I seemed to remember that you felt cold if you had a stroke. Also, I was really dripping with sweat by now and felt all swimmy; you'd say dizzy. After about five minutes, I got on the bike and began to pedal, slowly and carefully, back to my inn, deciding to have a doctor check me out at once.

"I had only gone about a third of a mile, numbed still by shock—after all I was only twenty-five, pretty young to have a heart attack or a stroke, either—when I noticed a little cove, an arm of the Baltic, on my right, which came almost up to the road, with tiny blue waves lapping at a small beach. I hadn't noticed it on the way to the baron's house, looking the other way, I guess, but now it looked like heaven. I was soaked with sweat, exhausted by my experience, and now had a headache. That cool sea water looked really marvelous, and as I said earlier, I had my trunks on under my clothes. There was even a towel in the bag strapped to the bike.

"I undressed behind a large pine tree ten feet from the road, and then stepped into the water. I could see white sand for about a dozen feet out, and then it appeared to get deeper quickly. I sat down in the shallow water, with just my neck sticking out, and began to feel human again. Even the headache receded into the background. There was no sound but the breeze soughing in the trees and the chirping of a few birds, plus the splash of little waves on the shore behind me. I felt at peace with everything and shut my eyes, half sitting, half floating in the water. The sun on my head was warm.

"I don't know what made me open my eyes, but I must have felt something watching, some presence. I looked straight out to sea, the entrance of the little cove, as I opened them, and stared into a face which was looking at me from the surface of the water about eight feet away, right where it began to get deeper."

No one in the room had moved or spoken once the story had started, and since Ffellowes had not stopped speaking since he began, the silence as he paused now was oppressive, even the muted sound of traffic outside seeming far off and unreal.

He looked around at us, then lit a cigarette and continued steadily.

"It was about two feet long, as near as I could tell, with two huge, oval eyes of a shade of amber yellow, set at the corners of its head. The skin looked both white and vaguely shimmery; there were no ears or nose that I could see, and there was a big, wide, flat mouth, opened a little, with blunt, shiny, rounded teeth. But what struck me most was the rage in the eyes. The whole impression of the face was vaguely—only vaguely, mind you—serpentine, snakelike, except for those eyes. They were mad, furious, raging, and not like an animal's at all, but like a man's. I could see no neck. The face 'sat' on the water, so to speak.

"I had only a split second to take all this in, mind you, but I was conscious at once that whatever this was, it was livid at *me* personally, not just at people. I suppose it sounds crazy, but I *knew* this right off.

"I hadn't even moved, hadn't had a chance, when something flickered under the head, and a grip like a steel cable clamped onto my hip. I dug my heels in the sand and grabbed down, pushing as hard as I could, but I couldn't shake that grip. As I looked down, I saw what had hold of me and damn near fainted, because it was a hand. It was double the size of mine, dead white, and had only two fingers and a thumb, with no nails, but it was a hand. Behind it was a boneless-looking white arm like a giant snake or an eel, stretching away back toward the head, which still lay on the surface of the water. At the same time I felt the air as cold, almost freezing, as if a private iceberg was following me again, although not to the point of making me numb. Oddly enough, the cold didn't seem to be *in* the water, though I can't explain this very well.

"I pulled back hard, but I might as well have pulled at a tree trunk for all the good it did. Very steadily the pressure on my hip was increasing, and I knew that in a minute I was going to be pulled out to that head. I was kicking and fighting, splashing the water and clawing at that hand, but in the most utter silence. The hand and arm felt just like rubber, but I could feel great muscles move under the hard skin.

"Suddenly I began to scream. I knew my foothold on the bottom sand was slipping and I was being pulled loose so that I'd be floating in a second. I don't remember what I screamed, probably just yelling with no words. I knew for a certainty that I would be dead in thirty seconds, you see." He paused, then resumed.

"My vision began to blur, and I seemed to be slipping, mentally, not physically, into a blind, cold world of darkness. But still I fought, and just as I began to be pulled loose from my footing, I heard two sounds. One was something like a machine gun, but ringing through it I heard a human voice shouting and, I thought, shouting one long word. The shout was very strong, ringing and resonant, so resonant that it pierced through the strange mental fog I was in, but the word was in no language I knew. Then I blacked out, and that was that.

"When I opened my eyes, I was in a spasm of choking. I was lying face down on the little beach, my face turned sideways on my crossed arms, and was being given artificial respiration. I vomited up more water and then managed to choke out a word or two, probably obscene. There was a deep chuckle, and the person who had been helping me turned me over, so that I could see him. He pulled me up to a sitting position and put a tweed-clad arm around my shoulders, giving me some support while I recovered my senses.

"Even kneeling as he was, when I turned to look at him, I could see he was a very tall man, in fact, a giant. He was wearing a brown tweed suit with knickerbockers, heavy wool knee socks and massive buckled shoes. His face was extraordinary. He was what's called an ash-blond, almost white-haired, and his face was very long, with high cheekbones, and also very white, with no hint of color in the cheeks. His eyes were green and very narrow, almost Chinese looking, and terribly piercing. Not a man you would ever forget if you once got a look at him. He looked about thirty-five, and was actually thirty, I later found out.

"I was so struck by his appearance, even though he was smiling gently, that I almost forgot what had happened to me. Suddenly I remembered though, and gave a convulsive start and tried to get up. As I did so, I turned to look at the water, and there was the cove, calm and serene, with no trace of that thing, or anything else.

"My new acquaintance tightened his grip on my shoulders and pulled me down to a sitting position, speaking as he did so.

" 'Be calm, my friend. You have been through a bad time, but it is gone now. You are safe.'

"The minute I heard his voice, I knew it was he who had shouted as I was being pulled under. The same timbre was in

his speech now, so that every word rang like a bell, with a
concealed purring under the words.

"I noticed more about him now. His clothes were soaked to
the waist, and on one powerful hand he wore an immense ring
set with a green seal stone, a crest. Obviously he had pulled me
out of the water, and equally obviously, he was no ordinary
person.

" 'What was it,' I gasped finally, 'and how did you get me
loose from it?'

"His answer was surprising. 'Did you get a good look at it?'
He spoke in pure, unaccented 'British' English, I might add.

" 'I did,' I said with feeling. 'It was the most frightful, bloody
thing I ever saw, and people ought to be warned about this coast!
When I get to a phone, every paper in Sweden *and* abroad will
hear about it. They ought to fish this area with dynamite!'

"His answer was a deep sigh. Then he spoke. 'Face-to-face,
you have seen one of Jormungandir's Children,' he said, 'and
that is more than I or any of my family have done for generations.' He turned to face me directly and continued, 'And I must
add, my friend, that if you tell a living soul of what you have
seen, I will unhesitatingly pronounce you a liar or a lunatic.
Further, I will say I found you alone, having a seeming fit in
this little bay, and saved you from what appeared to me to be a
vigorous attempt at suicide.'

"Having given me this belly-punch, he lapsed into a brooding
silence, staring out over the blue water, while I was struck dumb
by what I had heard. I began to feel I had been saved from a
deadly sea monster only to be captured by an apparent madman.

"Then he turned back to me, smiling again. 'I am called
Baron Nyderstrom,' he said, 'and my house is just a bit down
the road. Suppose we go and have a drink, change our clothes
and have a bit of a chat.'

"I could only stammer, 'But your aunt said you were away,
away for more than a week. I came to see you because I have a
letter to you.' I fumbled in my bathing suit, and then lurched
over to my clothes under the trees. I finally found the letter, but
when I gave it to him, he stuck it in his pocket. 'In fact I was
just coming from your house when I decided to have a swim
here. I'd had a sick spell as I was leaving your gate, and I thought
the cool water would help.'

" 'As you were leaving my gate?' he said sharply, helping me to get into my clothes. 'What do you mean "a sick spell," and what was that about my aunt?'

"As he assisted me, I saw for the first time a small, blue sports car, of a type unfamiliar to me, parked on the road at the head of the beach. It was in this, then, my rescuer had appeared. Half carrying, half leading me up the gentle slope, he continued his questioning, while I tried to answer him as best I could. I had just mentioned the lorry and the furniture as he got me into the left-hand bucket seat, having detailed in snatches my fainting and belief that I had had a mild stroke or heart spasm, when he got really stirred up.

"He levered his great body, and he must have been six foot five, behind the wheel like lightning, and we shot off in a screech of gears and spitting of gravel. The staccato exhaust told me why I thought I had heard a machine gun while fighting that incredible thing in the water.

"Well, we tore back up the road, into and up his driveway, and without a word, he slammed on the brakes and rushed into the house as if all the demons of hell were at his heels. I was left sitting stupefied in the car. I was not only physically exhausted and sick, but baffled and beginning again to be terrified. As I looked around the pleasant green lawn, the tall trees and the rest of the sunny landscape, do you know I wondered if through some error in dimensions, I had fallen out of my own proper space and landed in a world of monsters and lunatics!

"It could only have been a moment when the immense figure of my host appeared in the doorway. On his fascinating face was an expression which I can only describe as being mingled half sorrow, half anger. Without a word, he strode down his front steps and over to the car where, reaching in, he picked me up in his arms as easily as if I had been a doll instead of 175 pounds of British subaltern.

"He carried me up the steps and as he walked, I could hear him murmuring to himself in Swedish. It sounded to me like gibberish, with several phrases I could just make out being repeated over and over. 'What could they do, what else could they do! She would not be warned. What else could they do?'

"We passed through a vast dark hall, with great beams high overhead, until we came to the back of the house, and into a large sunlit room, overlooking the sea, which could only be the library or study. There were endless shelves of books, a huge desk, several chairs, and a long, low padded window seat on which the baron laid me down gently.

"Going over to a closet in the corner, he got out a bottle of aquavit and two glasses, and handed me a full one, taking a more modest portion for himself. When I had downed it—and I never needed a drink more—he pulled up a straight-backed chair and set it down next to my head. Seating himself, he asked my name in the most serious way possible, and when I gave it, he looked out of the window a moment.

" 'My friend,' he said finally, 'I am the last of the Nyderstroms. I mean that quite literally. Several rooms away, the woman you met earlier today is dead, as dead as you yourself would be, had I not appeared on the road, and from the same, or at least a similar cause. The only difference is that she brought this fate on herself, while you, a stranger, were almost killed by accident, and simply because you were present at the wrong time.' He paused and then continued with the oddest sentence, although, God knows, I was baffled already. 'You see,' he said, 'I am a kind of game warden and some of my charges are loose.'

"With that, he told me to lie quiet and started to leave the room. Remembering something, however, he came back and asked if I could remember the name of the firm which owned the mover's lorry I had seen. Fortunately I could, for as I told you earlier, it was seared on my brain by the strange attack I had suffered while watching it go up the road. When I gave it to him, he told me again not to move and left the room for another, from which I could hear him faintly using a telephone. He was gone a long time, perhaps half an hour, and by the time he came back, I was standing looking at his books. Despite the series of shocks I had gone through, I now felt fairly strong, but it was more than that. This strange man, despite his odd threat, had saved my life, and I was sure that I was safe from *him* at least. Also, he was obviously enmeshed in both sorrow and some danger, and I felt strongly moved to try and give him a hand.

"As he came back into the room, he looked hard at me, and I think he read what I was thinking, because he smiled, displaying a fine set of teeth.

"So—once again you are yourself. If your nerves are strong, I wish you to look on my late aunt. The police have been summoned and I need your help.'

"Just like that! A dead woman in the house and he needed my help!

"Well, if he was going to get rid of me, why call the police? Anyway, I felt safe as I told you, and you'd have to see the man, as I did, to know why.

"At any rate, we went down the great hall to another room, much smaller, and then through that again until we found ourselves in a little sewing room, full of women's stuff and small bits of fancy furniture. There in the middle of the room lay the lady whom I had seen earlier telling the movers to go away. She certainly appeared limp, but I knelt and felt her wrist because she was lying face down. Sure enough, no pulse at all and quite cold. But when I started to turn her over, a huge hand clamped on my shoulder and the baron spoke. 'I don't advise it,' he said warningly. 'Her face isn't fit to look at. She was frightened to death, you see.'

"I simply told him I had to, and he just shrugged his shoulders and stepped back. I got my hands under one shoulder and started to turn the lady, but my God, as the profile came into view, I dropped her and stood up like a shot. From the little I saw, her mouth was drawn back like an animal's, showing every tooth, and her eye was wide open and glaring in a ghastly manner. That was enough for me.

"Baron Nyderstrom led me from the room and back into the library, where we each had another aquavit in silence.

"I started to speak, but he held up his hand in a kind of command, and started talking.

" 'I shall tell the police that I passed you bathing on the beach, stopped to chat, and then brought you back for a drink. We found my aunt dead of heart failure and called the police. Now sir, I like you, but if you will not attest to this same story, I shall have to repeat what I told you I would say at the beach, and I am well known in these parts. Also, the servants are away on holiday, and I think you can see that it would look ugly for you.'

"I don't like threats, and it must have showed, because although it would have looked bad as all hell, still I wasn't going to be a party to any murders, no matter how well planned. I told him so, bluntly, and he looked sad and reflective, but not particularly worried.

" 'Very well,' he said at length, 'I can't really blame you, because you are in a very odd position.' His striking head turned toward the window in brief thought, and then he turned back to face me directly and spoke.

" 'I will make a bargain with you. Attest my statement to the police, and then let me have the rest of the day to talk to you. If, at the end of the day, I have not satisfied you about my aunt's death, you have my word, solemnly given, that I will go to the police station and attest *your* story, the fact that I have been lying and anything else you choose to say.'

"His words were delivered with great gravity, and it never for one instant occurred to me to doubt them. I can't give you any stronger statement to show you how the man impressed me. I agreed straightaway.

"In about ten minutes the police arrived, and an ambulance came with them. They were efficient enough, and very quick, but there was one thing that showed through the whole of the proceedings, and it was that the Baron Nyderstrom was *some-body*! All he did was state that his aunt had died of a heart attack and that was that! I don't mean the police were serfs, or crooks either for that matter. But there was an attitude of deference very far removed from servility or politeness. I doubt if royalty gets any more nowadays, even in England. When he had told me earlier that his name was 'known in these parts,' it was obviously the understatement of the decade.

"Well, the police took the body away in the ambulance, and the baron made arrangements for a funeral parlor and a church with local people over the telephone. All this took a while, and it must have been 4:30 when we were alone again.

"We went back into the library. I should mention that he had gotten some cold meat, bread and beer from a back pantry, just after the police left, and so now we sat down and made ourselves some sandwiches. I was ravenous, but he ate quite lightly for a man of his size, in fact only about a third of what I did.

"When I felt full, I poured another glass of an excellent beer, lit a cigarette, sat back and waited. With this man, there was no need of unnecessary speech.

"He was sitting behind his big desk facing me, and once again that singularly attractive smile broke through.

" 'You are waiting for your story, my friend, if I may call you so. You shall have it, but I ask your word as a man of honor that it not be for repetition.' He paused briefly. 'I know it is yet a further condition, but if you do not give it, there is no recourse except the police station and jail for me. If you do, you will hear a story and perhaps—perhaps, I say, because I make no promises—see and hear something which no man has seen or heard for many, many centuries, save only for my family and not many of them. What do you say?'

"I never hesitated for a second. I said 'yes,' and I should add that I've never regretted it. No, never."

Ffellowes' thoughts seemed far away, as he paused and stared out into the murky New York night, dimly lit by shrouded street lamps, and the fog lights on passing cars. No one spoke, and no sound broke the silence of the room but a muffled cough. He continued.

"Nyderstrom next asked me if I knew anything about Norse mythology. Now this question threw me for an absolute loss. What did a dangerous animal and an awful death have to do with Norse mythology, to say nothing of a possible murder?

"However, I answered I'd read of Odin, Thor, and a few other gods as a child in school, the Valkyries, of course, and that was about it.

" 'Odin, Thor, the Valkyries, and a few others?' My host smiled, 'You must understand that they are rather late Norse and even late German adaptions of something much older. Much, much older, something with its roots in the dawn of the world.

" 'Listen,' he went on, speaking quietly but firmly, 'and when I have finished we will wait for that movers' truck to return. I was able to intercept it, and what it took, because of that very foolish woman, must be returned.'

"He paused as if at a loss how to begin, and then went on. His bell-like voice remained muted, but perfectly audible, while he detailed one of the damnedest stories I've ever heard. If I hadn't been through what I had that day, and if he hadn't been what he was, I could have thought I was listening to the Grand Master of all the lunatics I've ever met.

" 'Long ago,' he said, 'my family came from inner Asia. They were some of the people the later comers called *Aesir*, the gods of Valhalla, but there were not gods, only a race of wandering conquerors. They settled here, on this spot, despite warnings from the few local inhabitants, a small, dark shore-dwelling folk. This house is built on the foundations of a fortress, a very old one, dating at the very least back to the second century B.C.

It was destroyed later in the wars of the sixteenth century, but that is modern history.

" 'At any rate, my remote ancestors began soon to lose people. Women bathing, boys fishing, even full-grown warriors out hunting, they would vanish and never return. Children had to be guarded and so did the livestock, which had a way of disappearing also, although that of course was preferable to the children.

" 'Finally, for no trace of the mysterious marauders could be found, the chief of my family decided to move away. He had prayed to his gods and searched zealously, but the reign of silent, stealthy terror never ceased, and no human or other foe could be found.

" 'But before he gave up, the chief had an idea. He sent presents and a summons to the shaman, the local priest, not of our own people, but of the few, furtive, little shore folk, the strand people, who had been there when we came. We despised and avoided them, but we had never harmed them. And the bent little shaman came and answered the chief's questions.

" 'What he said amounted to this. We, that is my people, had settled on the land made sacred in the remote past to Jormungandir. Now Jormungandir in the standard Norse sagas and myths is the great, world-circling sea serpent, the son of the renegade Aesir Loki and a giantess. He is a monster who on the day of Ragnarok will arise to assault Asgard. But actually, these myths are based on something quite, quite different. The ancient Jormungandir was a god of the sea all right, but he was here before any Norsemen, and he had children, who were semi-mortal and very, very dangerous. All the Asgard business was invented later, by people who did not remember the reality, which was both unpleasant and a literal, living menace to ancient men.

" 'My ancestor, the first of our race to rule here, asked what he could do to abate the menace. Nothing, said the shaman, except go away. Unless, if the chief were brave enough, he, the shaman, could summon the Children of the God, and the chief could ask *them* how *they* felt!

" 'Well, my people were anything but Christians in those days, and they had some rather nasty gods of their own. Also, the old chief, my ancestor, was on his mettle, and he liked the land he and his tribe had settled. So—he agreed, and although his counselors tried to prevent him, he went alone at night to the shore with the old shaman of the shore people. And what is more, he returned.

" 'From that day to this we have always lived here on this stretch of shore. There is a vault below the deepest cellar where certain things are kept and a ceremony through which the eldest son of the house of Nyderstrom must pass. I will not tell you more about it save to say that it involves an oath, one we have never broken, and that the other parties to the oath would not be good for men to see. You should know, for you have seen one!'

"I had sat spellbound while this rigmarole went on, and some of the disbelief must have showed in my eyes, because he spoke rather sharply all at once.

" 'What do you think the Watcher in the Sea was, the "animal" that seized you? If it had been anyone else in that car but myself—!'

"I nodded, because after recalling my experience on my swim, I was less ready to dismiss his story, and I had been in danger of forgetting my adventure. I also apologized and he went on talking.

" 'The woman you spoke to was my father's much younger sister, a vain and arrogant woman of no brainpower at all. She lived a life in what is now thought of as society, in Stockholm, on a generous allowance from me, and I have never liked her. Somewhere, perhaps as a child, she learned more than she should about the family secret, which is ordinarily never revealed to our women.

" 'She wished me to marry and tried ceaselessly to entrap me with female idiots of good family whom she had selected.

" 'It is true that I must someday marry, but my aunt irritated me beyond measure, and I finally ordered her out of the house and told her that her allowance would cease if she did not stop troubling me. She was always using the place for house parties for her vapid friends, until I put a stop to it.

" 'I knew when I saw her body what she had done. She must have found out that the servants were away and that I would be gone for the day. She sent men from Stockholm. The local folk would not obey such an order from her, in my absence. She must have had duplicate keys, and she went in and down and had moved what she should never have seen, let alone touched.

It was sacrilege, no less, and of a very real and dangerous kind. The fool thought the things she took held me to the house, I imagine.

" 'You see,' he went on, with more passion in his voice than I had previously heard. '*They* are not responsible. They do not see things as we do. They regarded the moving of those things as the breaking of a trust, and they struck back. You appeared, because of the time element, to have some connection, and they struck at you. You do see what I mean, don't you?'

"His green eyes fixed themselves on me in an open appeal. He actually wanted sympathy for what, if his words were true, must be the damnedest set of beings this side of madness. And even odder, you know, he had got it. I had begun to make a twisted sense of what he said, and on that quiet evening in the big shadowed room, I seemed to feel an ancient and undying wrong, moreover one which badly needed putting right.

"He seemed to sense this and went on, more quietly.

" 'You know, I still need your help. Your silence later, but more immediate help now. Soon that lorry will be here and the things it took must be restored.

" 'I am not now sure if I can heal the breach. It will depend on the Others. If they believe me, all will go as before. If not— well, it was my family who kept the trust, but also who broke it. I will be in great danger, not only to my body but also to my soul. Their power is not all of the body.

" 'We have never known,' he went on softly, 'why they love this strip of coast. It is not used so far as we know, for any of their purposes, and they are subject to our emotions or desires in any case. But they do, and so the trust is honored.'

"He looked at his watch and murmured 'six o'clock.' He got up and went to the telephone, but as his hand met the receiver, we both heard something.

"It was a distant noise, a curious sound, as if, far away somewhere, a wet piece of cloth were being dragged over stone. In the great silent house, the sound could not be localized, but it seemed to me to come from deep below us, perhaps in a cellar. It made my hair stiffen.

" 'Hah,' he muttered. 'They are stirring. I wonder—'

"As he spoke, we both became conscious of another noise, one which had been growing upon us for some moments unaware, that of a powerful motor engine. Our minds must have worked together for as the engine noise grew, our eyes met and we both burst into simultaneous gasps of relief. It could only be the furniture van, returning at last.

"We both ran to the entrance. The hush of evening lay over the estate, and shadows were long and dark, but the twin lights turning into the drive cast a welcome luminance over the entrance.

"The big lorry parked again in front of the main entrance, and the two workmen I had seen earlier got out. I could not really understand the rapid gunfire Swedish, but I gathered the baron was explaining that his aunt had made a mistake. At one point both men looked appalled, and I gathered that Nyderstrom had told them of his aunt's death. [He told me later that he had conveyed the impression that she was unsound mentally: it would help quiet gossip when they saw a report of the death.]

"All four of us went around to the rear of the van, and the two men opened the doors. Under the baron's direction they carried out and deposited on the gravel the two pieces of furniture I had seen earlier. One was the curious chair. It did not look terribly heavy, but it had a box bottom, solid sides instead of legs and no arm rests. Carved on the oval-topped head was a hand grasping a sort of trident, and when I looked closely, I got a real jolt. The hand had only two fingers and a thumb, all without nails, and I suddenly felt in my bones the reality of my host's story.

"The other piece was the small, plain, rectangular chest, a bit like a large toy chest, with short legs ending in feet like a duck's. I mean three-toed and *webbed*, not the conventional 'duck foot' of the antique dealers.

"Both the chair and the chest were made of a dark wood, so dark it looked oily, and they had certainly not been made yesterday.

"Nyderstrom had the two men put the two pieces in the front hall and then paid them. They climbed back into their cab, so far as I could make out, apologizing continuously for any trouble they might have caused. We waved from the porch and then watched the lights sweep down the drive and fade into the night. It was fully dark now, and I suddenly felt a sense of plain old-fashioned fright as we stood in silence on the dark porch.

" 'Come,' said the baron, suddenly breaking the silence, 'we must hurry. I assume you will help?'

" 'Certainly,' I said. I felt I had to, you see, and had no lingering doubts at all. I'm afraid that if he'd suggested murdering someone, by this time I'd have agreed cheerfully. There was a compelling, hypnotic power about him. Rasputin was supposed to have had it and Hitler also, although I saw *him* plenty, and never felt it. At any rate, I just couldn't feel that anything this man wanted was wrong.

"We manhandled the chair and the chest into the back of the house, stopping at last in a back hall in front of a huge oaken door, which appeared to be set in a stone wall. Since the house was made of wood, this stone must have been part of the original building, the ancient fort, I guess, that he'd mentioned earlier.

"There were three locks on the door, a giant old padlock, a smaller new one and a very modern-looking combination. Nyderstrom fished out two keys, one of them huge, and turned them. Then, with his back to me, he worked the combination. The old house was utterly silent, and there was almost an atmospheric hush, the kind you get when a bad thunderstorm is going to break. Everything seemed to be waiting, waiting for something to happen.

"There was a click and Nyderstrom flung the great door open. The first thing I noticed was that it was lined with steel on the other, inner side, and the second, that it opened on a broad flight of shallow steps leading down on a curve out of sight into darkness. The third impression was not visual at all. A wave of odor, strong but not unpleasant, of tide pools, seaweed and salt air poured out of the opening. And there were several large patches of water on the highest steps, large enough to reflect the light.

"Nyderstrom closed the door again gently, not securing it, and turned to me. He pointed, and I now saw on one wall of the corridor to the left of the door, about head height, a steel box, also with a combination lock. A heavy cable led from it down to the floor. Still in silence, he adjusted the combination and opened the box. Inside was a knife switch, with a red handle. He left the box open and spoke, solemnly and slowly.

" 'I am going down to a confrontation. You must stay right here, with the door open a little, watching the steps. I may be half an hour, but at most three quarters. If I come up *alone*, let me out. If I come up *not* alone, slam the door, turn the lock and throw that switch. Also if anything *else* comes up, do so. This whole house, under my direction, and at my coming of age, was extensively mined and you will have exactly two and a half minutes to get as far as possible from it. Remember, at *most*, three quarters of an hour. At the end of that time, even if nothing has happened, you will throw that switch and run. . . !'

"I could only nod. There seemed to be nothing to say, really.

"He seemed to relax a little, patted me on the shoulders and turned to unlock the strange chest. Over his shoulder he talked to me as he took things out. 'You are going to see one thing at any rate, a true Sea King in full regalia. Something, my friend, no one has seen who is not a member of my family since the late Bronze Age.'

"He stood up and began to undress quickly, until he stood absolutely naked. I have never seen a more wonderful figure of a man, pallid as an ivory statue, but huge and splendidly formed. On his head, from out of the stuff in the chest, he had set a narrow coronet, only a band in the back, but rising to a flanged peak in front. Mounted in the front peak was a plaque on which the three-fingered hand and trident were outlined in purple gems. The thing was solid gold. Nyderstrom then stooped and pulled on a curious, short kilt, made of some scaly hide, like a lizard's and colored an odd green-gold. Finally, he took in his right hand a short, curved, gold rod, ending in a blunt, stylized trident.

"We looked at each other a moment and then he smiled. 'My ancestors were very successful Vikings,' he said, still smiling. 'You see, they always could call on *help*.'

"With that, he swung the door open and went marching down the steps. I half shut it behind him and settled down to watch and listen.

"The sound of his footsteps receded into the distance, but I could still hear them in the utter silence for a long time. His family vault, which I was sure connected somehow with the sea, was a long way down. I crouched, tense, wondering if I would ever see him again. The whole business was utterly mad, and I believed every word of it. I still do.

"The steps finally faded into silence. I checked my watch and found ten minutes had gone by.

"Suddenly, as if out of an indefinite distance, I heard his voice. I recognized it instantly, for it was a long quavering call, sonorous and bell-like, very similar to what I had heard when he rescued me in the afternoon. The sound came from far down in the earth, echoing faintly up the dank stairs and died into silence. Then it came again, and then it died, yet again.

"My heart seemed to stop. I knew that this brave man was summoning something no man had a right to see and calling a council in which no one with human blood in his veins should sit.

"Silence, utter and complete, followed. I could hear nothing, save for an occasional faint drop of water falling somewhere out of my range of vision.

"I glanced at my watch. Twenty-one minutes had gone by. The minutes seemed to crawl endlessly, meaninglessly. I felt alone and in a strange dream, unable to move, frozen, an atom caught in a mesh beyond my comprehension.

"Then far away, I heard it, a faint sound. It was faint but regular, and increasing in volume, measured and remorseless. It was a tread, and it was coming up the stair in my direction.

"I glanced at my watch, thirty-four minutes. It could be my friend, still within his self-appointed limits of time. The step came nearer, nearer still. It was, so far as my straining ear could judge, a single step. It progressed further, and suddenly into the circle of light stepped Nyderstrom.

"He was alone and as he came up he waved in greeting. He was dripping wet and the light gleamed on his shining body. I threw the door wide and he stepped through.

"As his head emerged into the light, I stepped back, almost involuntarily. There was a look of exhaltation and wonder on it, such as I have never seen on a human face. The strange green eyes flashed, and there was a faint flush on the high cheekbones. He looked like a man who has seen a vision of Paradise.

"He walked rather wearily, but firmly, over to the switch box, which he closed and locked. Then he turned to me, still with that blaze of radiance on his face.

" 'All is well, my friend. They are again at peace with men. They have accepted me and the story of what has happened. All will be well now, with my house, and with me.'

"I stared at him hard, but he said no more and began to divest himself of his incredible regalia. He had one more thing to say, and I can hear it still as if it were yesterday, spoken almost as an afterthought.

" 'They say the blood of the guardians is getting too thin again. But that also is settled. I have seen my bride.' "

Grumblefritz

An Open Letter to
Readers Living in Manhattan

by

Marvin Kaye

Here's a funny, poignant story about a mild-tempered, yellow-eyed monster with an Irish brogue who waits patiently in the nocturnal wastelands of New York City for the lost dreams of our youth . . .

An assistant professor of creative writing at New York University, Marvin Kaye's interests include magic, mystery, the theater, Sherlock Holmes, and the investigation of the supernatural. His books include Masters of Solitude, Wintermind, *and* A Cold Blue Light, *all written in collaboration with Parke Godwin,* The Incredible Umbrella, The Amorous Umbrella, *and, as editor, the anthologies* Devils and Demons, Fiends and Creatures, *and* Ghosts. *His most recent books are the anthology* Masterpieces of Terror and the Supernatural *and the mystery novel* Bullets for Macbeth.

*   *   *

Dear Fellow Gothamites,

Forgive me for interrupting your leisurely perusal of improbable literature. I do not do so lightly, but the situation is desperate. We New Yorkers are in danger of losing one of our most precious natural resources.

I refer to the sea serpent who lives next to the Statue of Liberty. His name is Grumblefritz. He's my friend.

You will appreciate, I hope, that I approach this topic with diffidence. On several occasions, I have exchanged heated words with family members on the subject of my acquaintanceship with Grumblefritz. So you may readily imagine how much more difficult it is for me to broach the subject to total strangers. But in the face of imminent crisis, I am forced to set aside my customary reticence.

* * *

165

I first met Grumblefritz one night while I was flying over Manhattan. [I was not in an airplane. I was just flying.]

There was a bright, clear moon in the sky. It shone through the shades of my bedroom on the twelfth floor of my apartment building, not far from the Hudson River. It was shortly past midnight, but I wasn't tired, so I rose gracefully to the ceiling, floated to the southwest window [it's much easier to flow through than the one facing due south], and glided gently forth above 85th Street.

There was a light mist in the air that felt refreshingly cool upon my astral cheeks.

For a while, I lolled lazily over the West Side, then, wishing a bit of exercise, shot due west, veered south and followed the silver line of the river as it flowed down toward The Battery. I showed off a little, I confess, looping-the-loop over and around the World Trade Center. At length, I swooped out past the Hudson basin and into Upper Bay where the Statue of Liberty glowed like some great green troll haunting the depths.

My energy began to flag. Thinking of the invitation carved upon Dame Liberty, I determined to employ her as a resting-place. So I wafted down and lit on her torch. [No pun intended.]

The evening dew, combined with the water-mist, dampened my hair and skin, but not my spirits. I delighted in the orange glow illuminating the sky above my island home: a magic nimbus that vaguely recalled earlier times when my ambitions were not blunted by the dull tread of the years.

It must have been that ghost-scent of muted goals that tickled my friend's palate, for that is when the back of my neck bristled. My scalp started tingling. A riot of goose-pimples prickled the skin of my legs and arms.

Something was watching me, I was sure of it. Yet I couldn't imagine what. I am practically invisible when I indulge in nocturnal aviation.

I glanced about but saw nothing. I squinted my eyes half-shut, thinking perhaps some fellow traveler, hopefully a feminine itinerant, hovered nearby . . .

And then a gentle breeze that smelled like a mixture of cotton candy and cinnamon teardrops tousled my hair. I

craned my head up and got my first glimpse of Grumblefritz. Or, to be precise [for it is only by attention to minutiae
that I may hope to gain credence], I spied a single portion
of Grumblefritz.

One yellow eye.

I gawked. The mammoth orb blinked once, then crinkled
down at me with an air of weary benevolence.

"Welcome, wee morsel," said a deep, mellow voice.
"What brings you here, to the Isle of Grumblefritz?" The
musical tone was reminiscent of the clear lilting English
spoken in Dublin.

However, I was not reassured by "morsel," so I floated
some distance away before replying.

As I tread air, I studied the newcomer. Though he was
tall and suggested great hidden bulk, his skin wrinkled sadly,
as from undernourishment. Half his reptilian body remained concealed beneath the waves of the bay, but his
crimson-crested head blinked benignly down from a height
some twenty stories above the topmost flametip of the Statue
of Liberty.

"Greetings, O Surprising Entity," said he. "I am Grumblefritz, and this is my domain. You are the only dream I've
seen these many months, and you seem a mite insubstantial.
How did you come here? Did a wayward spell waft you to
Grumblefritz?"

"Your Mighty Serpentship," quoth I, "permit me to correct you. I am no wispy dream, merely a disembodied
dreamer."

He sighed so deeply that his emerald scales rattled and
clanked against one another. "Ah, I should have guessed
as much. Few dreams remain, and those there are must be
coaxed forth."

Although the serpent's body, were it fully revealed, must
be huger than a megalosaurian, he seemed the mildest of
creatures. I found his rueful smile oddly appealing. Therefore, I drew nearer.

"O puissant water-sprite," saith I, "what use make you
of dreams?"

"Sweet stripling," he smiled bleakly, "I do not deign to

dine on people, fish, or fowl. Grumblefritz eatteth nothing coarser than granulated dreams.''

"But in that case, and considering where we are, don't you get awfully hungry?"

"You better believe it!" Grumblefritz snorted.

He and I soon became fast friends. We spent the better part of the night sharing our loneliness and commiserating on the way the world ignores its artists and sea serpents. Before I flew home, I vowed to search out some goodies for him to eat.

But I did not reckon on the difficulty of the assignment. In the past few weeks, I have expended colossal stores of energy trying to fish up palatable dreams for Grumblefritz to grow fat on. But he is the fussiest of connoisseurs.

For instance, I brought him a few hopes skimmed off the surface of the Hudson in my neighborhood, but he complained they were too green. So I waited down by the base of Battery Park, thinking to garner the riper wishes as they flowed into the bay, yet when I brought some to Grumblefritz, he haughtily turned up his nose. "You picked those where the waters of the Hudson merge with the East River. Pfui! They are tainted with those slivery *cauchemars* that wriggle their way down from Yorkville!"

I've plucked daydreams from Wall Street, but Grumblefritz says they are too stale. I flew north to the Harlem River, but he worries the spicing might inflame his gall bladder. Once I even zoomed all the way out to Far Rockaway because Grumblefritz sensed there was a teenager there with a Cindarella wish.

He was right. A fifteen-year-old with acne stared at her mirror and squinted away the wens. I sneaked up behind her and tried to steal her dream, but she fought desperately to keep it. So I relinquished my hold and waited till she was asleep. Only by then, her dream had changed into something a bit slimy, like those crawly fantasies on Eighth Avenue that Grumblefritz says he'll die before eating.

* * *

"Look," I protested one night, "I can't bear to see you waste away like this! It's not much, but I am going to make a sacrifice to you of my one remaining dream!"

He wrinkled his upper lip suspiciously. "Wee one," the sea serpent addressed me, "I hope you are not referring to that tawdry hope of yours that someday you will shout SHA-ZAM! and immediately be lightning-blasted into becoming Captain Marvel?"

Hanging my head, I admitted it was so.

"I appreciate the gesture," Grumblefritz said, "but you can keep that dream. I can't swallow anything but Prime, and that isn't even Grade A."

I'm really worried about my friend. It's almost impossible to find anything he'll condescend to eat, and meanwhile, he grows thinner and thinner. Last night, in desperation he muttered something about moving to Philadelphia or perhaps Washington, but we both know that Delaware River water will rot his scales [he's half-dragon on his mother's side], while anything he finds in the Potomac will just be empty calories.

"The real trouble," he moaned weakly, "is that I am used to dining on Big Dreams, my tiny traveler! Collective Dreams! Not these safe and selfish little reveries that no one—not even the dreamers themselves—truly prize."

I patted Grumblefritz, trying to comfort him, but at last, his protracted fast turned him delirious. "I remember!" said he, rolling his great head from side to side on the stones of Liberty Island, "How well I remember when Broadway attracted the brightest of dreams! In those days, ah, what feasts! Such delicacies! Ambrosial!"

And he fainted from hunger.

O my friends and fellow New Yorkers! Think about it! Do *you* recall the Great Dreams of our youth? Well, if it hadn't been for Grumblefritz's appetite, we would all still be slogging through tons of discarded ambitions and tarnished talents and tired-out potentials.

Now that dreams are scarce, we *must* do something! Out of sheer nostalgia, or gratitude, if you will, can't we New

Yorkers make a single concerted effort and strive to produce *one last Great Dream* so Grumblefritz will not starve?

 S.O.S., my friends! S.O.S. !
 Save Our Sea Serpent!

Hopefully,
M.N. Kaye

The Devil of Malkirk

by

Charles Sheffield

One of the best contemporary "hard science" writers, British-born Charles Sheffield is a theoretical physicist who has worked on the American space program, and is currently chief scientist of the Earth Satellite Corporation. Sheffield is also the only person who has ever served as president of both the American Astronautical Society and the Science Fiction Writers of America. His books include the best-selling nonfiction title Earthwatch, *and the novels* Sight of Proteus, The Web Between the Worlds, Hidden Variables, My Brother's Keeper, The McAndrew Chronicles, Between the Strokes of Night, The Nimrod Hunt, *and* Trader's World. *His most recent novel is* Proteus Unbound. *Sheffield lives with his family in Bethesda, Maryland.*

For all his expertise in the space sciences, Sheffield shows an odd fondness for writing about the past, and has produced an excellent series of historical fantasies detailing the curious adventures of Erasmus Darwin, the scientist grandfather of Charles Darwin; these stories have been collected in Erasmus Magister. *In the story that follows, perhaps the best of the Erasmus Darwin tales, Sheffield creates a meticulously researched and brilliantly detailed vision of eighteenth-century British society, and takes us along to the remotest reaches of the Scottish Highlands to unravel a spooky and unusual mystery . . .*

* * *

The spring evening was warm and still, and the sound of conversation carried far along the path from the open window of the house. It was enough to make the man walking the gravel surface hesitate, then turn his steps onto the lawn. He walked silently across the well-trimmed grass to the bay window, stooped, and peered through a gap in the curtains. A few moments more, and he returned to the path and entered the open door of the house.

Ignoring the servant waiting there, he turned left and went at once into the dining room. He looked steadily around him, while the conversation at the long table gradually died down.

"Dr. Darwin?" His voice was gruff and formal.

The eight men seated at dinner were silent for a moment, assessing the stranger. He was tall and gaunt, with a dark, sallow complexion. Long years of intense sunlight had stamped a permanent frown across his brow, and a slight, continuous trembling of his hands spoke of other legacies of foreign disease. He returned the stares in silence.

After a few seconds one of the seated men pushed his chair back from the table.

"I am Erasmus—Darwin." The slight hesitation as he pronounced his name suggested a stammer more than any kind of contrived pause. "Who are you, and what is your business here?"

The speaker had risen to his feet as he spoke. He stepped forward and was revealed as grossly overweight, with heavy limbs and a fat, pock-marked face. He stood motionless, calmly awaiting the intruder's reply.

"Jacob Pole, at your service," said the stranger. Despite the warmth of the April evening he was wearing a grey scarf of knitted wool, which he tightened now around his neck. "Colonel Jacob Pole of Litchfield. You and I are far afield tonight, Dr. Darwin, but we are neighbors. My house is no more than two miles from yours. As for my business, it is not of my choosing and I fear it may be a bad one. I am here to ask your urgent assistance on a medical matter at Bailey's Farm, not half a mile from this house."

There was a chorus of protesting voices from the table. A thin-faced man who wore no wig stood up and stepped closer.

"Colonel Pole, this is my house. I will forgive your entry to it uninvited and unannounced, since we understand that medical urgencies must banish formalities. But you interrupt more than a dinner among friends. I am Matthew Boulton, and tonight the Lunar Society meets here on serious matters. Mr. Priestley is visiting from Calne to tell of his latest researches on the new air. He is well begun, but by no means finished. Can your business wait an hour?"

Jacob Pole stood up straighter than ever. "If Disease could be made to wait, I would do the same. As it is . . ." He turned to Darwin again. "I am no more than a messenger here, one who happened to be dining with Will Bailey. I have come at the request of Dr. Monkton, to ask your immediate assistance."

There was another outcry from those still seated at the table.
"Monkton! Monkton asking for assistance? Never heard of
such a thing."

"Forget it, 'Rasmus! Sit back down and try this rhubarb pie."

"If it's Monkton," said a soberly dressed man on the right-
hand side of the table, "then the patient is as good as dead. He's
no doctor, he's an executioner. Come on, Colonel Pole, take a
glass of claret and sit down with us. We meet too infrequently
to relish a disturbance."

Erasmus Darwin waved him to silence. "Steady, Josiah. I
know your views of Dr. Monkton." He turned full-face to Pole,
to show a countenance where the front teeth had long been lost
from the full mouth. The jaw was jowly and in need of a razor.
Only the eyes belied the impression of coarseness and past disease. They were grey and patient, with a look of deep sagacity
and profound power of observation.

"Forgive our jests," he said. "This is an old issue here. Dr.
Monkton has not been one to ask my advice on disease, no
matter what the circumstance. What does he want now?"

The outcry came again. "He's a pompous old windbag."

"Killer Monkton—don't let him lay a finger on you."

"I wouldn't let him touch you, not if you want to live."

Pole had been staring furiously about him while the men at
the table mocked Monkton's medical skills. He ignored the glass
held out towards him, and a scar across the left side of his forehead was showing a flush of red.

"I might share your opinion of Dr. Monkton," he said curtly.
"However, I would extend those views to all doctors. They kill
far more than they cure. As for you gentlemen, and Dr. Darwin
here, if you all prefer your eating and drinking to the saving of
life, I cannot change those priorities."

He turned to glare at Darwin. "My message is simple. I will
give it and leave. Dr. Monkton asks me to say three things: that
he has a man at Bailey's Farm who is critically ill; that already
the *facies* of death are showing; and that he would like *you*"—
he leaned forward to make it a matter between him and Darwin
alone—"to come and see that patient. If you will not do it, I
will go back and inform Dr. Monkton of it."

"No." Darwin sighed. "Colonel Pole, our rudeness to you
was unforgivable, but there was a reason for it. These meetings
of the Society are the high point of our month, and animal spirits

sometimes drive us to exceed the proprieties. Give me a moment to call for my greatcoat, and we will be on our way. My friends have told you their opinions of Dr. Monkton, and I must confess I am eager to see his patient. In my years of practice between here and Litchfield, Dr. Monkton and I have crossed paths many times—but never has he sought my advice on a medical matter. We are of very different schools, for both diagnosis and treatment.''

He turned back to the group, silent now that their high spirits were damped. ''Gentlemen, I am sorry to miss both the discussion and the companionship, but work calls.'' He moved to Pole's side. ''Let us go. The last of the light is gone but the moon should be up. We will manage well without a lantern. If Death will not wait, then nor must we.''

The road that led to Bailey's Farm was flanked by twin lines of hedgerow. It had been an early spring, and the moonlit white of flowering hawthorn set parallel lines to mark the road ahead. The two men walked side by side, Darwin glancing across from time to time at the other's gloomy profile.

''You appear to have no great regard for the medical profession,'' he said at last. ''Though you bear marks of illness yourself.''

Jacob Pole shrugged his shoulders and did not speak.

''But yet you are a friend of Dr. Monkton?'' continued Darwin.

Pole turned a frowning face towards him. ''I most certainly am *not*. As I told you, I am no more than a messenger for him, one who happened to be at the farm.'' He hesitated. ''If you press the point—as you seem determined to do—I will admit that I am no friend to any doctor. Men put more blind faith in witless surgeons than they do in the Lord Himself.''

''And with more reason,'' said Darwin softly.

Pole did not seem to hear. ''Blind faith,'' he went on. ''And against all logic. When you pay a man money to cut off your arm, it's no surprise that he tells you an arm must come off to save your life. In twenty years of service to the country, I am appalled when I think how many limbs have come off for no reason more than a doctor's whim.''

''And on that score, Colonel Pole,'' said Darwin tartly, ''your twenty years of service must also have told you that it would take a thousand of the worst doctors to match the limb-lopping effects of even the least energetic of generals. Look to the ills of your own profession.''

There was an angry silence, and both men paced faster along the moon-lit road.

The farm stood well back, a hundred yards from the main highway to Litchfield. The path to it was a gloomy avenue of tall elms, and by the time they were halfway along it, they could see a tall figure standing in the doorway and peering out towards them. As they came closer, he leaned back inside to pick up a lantern and strode to meet them.

''Dr. Darwin, I fear you are none too soon.'' The speaker's voice was full and resonant, like that of a singer or a practiced clergyman, but there was no warmth or welcome in it.

Darwin nodded. ''Colonel Pole tells me that the situation looks grave. I have my medical chest with me back at Matthew Boulton's house. If there are drugs or dressings needed, Dr. Monkton, they can be brought here in a few minutes.''

''I think it may already be too late for that.'' They had reached the door, and Monkton paused there. He was broad-shouldered, with a long neck and a red, bony face. His expression was dignified and severe. ''By the time Colonel Pole left here, the man was already sunk to unconsciousness. Earlier this evening there was delirium, and utterances that were peculiar indeed. I have no great hopes for him.''

''He is one of Bailey's farm workers?''

''He is not. He is a stranger, taken ill on the road near here. The woman with him came for help to the farm. Fortunately I was already here, attending to Father Bailey's rheumatics.'' He shrugged. ''That is a hopeless case, of course, in a man of his age.''

''Mm. Perhaps.'' Darwin sounded unconvinced, but he did not press it. ''But it was curiously opportune that you were here. So tell me, Dr. Monkton, just what is this stranger's condition?''

''Desperate. You will see it for yourself,'' he went on at Darwin's audible grunt of dissatisfaction. ''He lies on a cot at the back of the scullery.''

''Alone? Surely not?''

''No. His companion is with him. I explained to her that his condition is grave, and she seemed to comprehend well enough for one of her station.'' He set the lantern on a side table in the entrance and took a great pinch of snuff from a decorated ivory box. "Neither one of them showed much sign of learning. They are poor workers from the North, on their way to London to seek employment. She seemed more afraid of me than worried about her man's condition."

"So I ask again, what is that condition?"' Darwin's voice showed his exasperation. "It would be better for you to give me your assessment out of their hearing—though I gather that he is hearing little enough."

"He hears nothing, not if lightning were to strike this house. His condition, in summary: the eyes deep-set in the head, closed, the whites only showing in the ball; the countenance, dull and grey; skin, rough and dry to the touch; before he became delirious he complained that he was feeling bilious."

"There was vomiting?"

"No, but he spoke of the feeling. And of pain in the chest. His muscle tone was poor and I detected weakened irritability."

Darwin grunted skeptically, causing Monkton to look at him in a condescending way.

"Perhaps you are unfamiliar with von Haller's work on this, Dr. Darwin? I personally find it to be most convincing. At any rate, soon after I came to him, the delirium began."

"And what of his pulse?" Darwin's face showed his concentration. "And was there fever?"

Monkton hesitated for a moment, as though unsure what to answer.

"There was no fever," he said at last. "And I do not think that the pulse was elevated in rate."

"Huh." Darwin pursed his full lips. "No fever, no rapid pulse—and yet delirium." He turned to the other man. "Colonel Pole, did you also see this?"

"I did indeed." Pole nodded vigorously. "Look here, I know it may be the custom of the medical profession to talk about symptoms until the patient is past saving—but don't you think you should see the man for yourself, while he's alive?"

"I do." Darwin smiled, unperturbed by the other's gruff manner. "But first I wanted all the facts I can get. Facts are important, Colonel, the fulcrum of diagnosis. Would you prefer me to rush in and operate, another arm or leg gone? Or discuss the man's impending death in the presence of his wife or daughter? That is not a physician's role, the addition of new misery beyond disease itself. But lead the way, Dr. Monkton, I am ready now to see your patient.''

Jacob Pole frowned as he followed the other two men back through the interior of the old farmhouse. His expression showed mingled irritation and respect. ''You sawbones are all the same,'' he muttered. ''You have an answer for everything except a man's illness.''

The inside of the farmhouse was dimly lit. A single oil lamp stood in the middle of the long and chilly corridor that led to the scullery and kitchen. The floor was uneven stone flags, and the high shelves carried preserved and wrinkled apples, their acid smell pleasant and surprising.

Monkton opened the door to the scullery, stepped inside, and grunted at the darkness there.

''This is a nuisance. I told her to stay here with him, but she has gone off somewhere and allowed the lamp to go out. Colonel Pole, would you bring the lantern from the corridor?''

While Pole went back for it, Darwin stood motionless in the doorway, sniffing the air in the dark room. When there was light Monkton looked around and gave a cry of astonishment.

''Why, he's not here. He was lying on that cot in the corner.''

''Maybe he died, and they moved him?'' suggested Pole.

''No, they wouldn't do that,'' said Monkton, but for the first time his voice was uncertain. ''Surely they would not move him without my permission?''

''Looks as though they did though,'' said Pole. ''We can settle that easily enough.''

He threw back his head. ''Willy, where are you?'' The shout echoed through the whole house. After a few seconds there was an answering cry from upstairs.

''What's wrong, Jacob? Do you need help there?''

''No. Has anybody been down here from upstairs, Willy? While I was gone, I mean.''

''No. I didn't want to risk the sickness.''

''That sounds right,'' grunted Pole. ''That's brave old Willy, hiding upstairs with his pipe and flagon.''

''Has anyone downstairs been using tobacco?'' asked Darwin quietly.

''What?'' Pole stared at him. ''Tobacco?''

''Use your nose, man. Sniff the air in here.'' Darwin was prowling forward. ''There's been a pipe alight here in the past quarter of an hour. Do you smell it now? I somehow doubt that it was the man's wife that was smoking it.''

He walked forward to the cot itself and laid a plump hand flat upon it. "Quite cold. So here we are, but we find no dead man, and no dying man. Dr. Monkton, in your opinion how long did the stranger have to live?''

"Not long.'' Monkton cleared his throat uncomfortably. "Not more than an hour or two, I would judge.''

"Within an hour of final sacrament, and then gone,'' grunted Darwin. He shook his head and sat on the edge of the cot. "So now what? I don't think we'll find him easily, and we've all three sacrificed an evening to this already. If you are willing to waste a few more minutes, I'd much like to hear what the patient said when he became delirious. What do you say, gentlemen? May we discuss it?''

Pole and Monkton looked at each other.

"If you wish, although I am very doubtful that it—'' began the physician, his rich voice raised a good half octave.

"All right,'' interrupted Pole. "Let's do it. But I don't propose to debate this here, in the scullery. Let's go upstairs. I'm sure Will Bailey can find us a comfortable place, and a glass as well if you want it—perhaps he can even find you an acceptable substitute for that rhubarb pie.'' He turned to the other physician. "As you know, Dr. Monkton, when you were tending to the man, I did little more than watch. With your leave, maybe I should say what I saw, and you can correct me as you see fit. Agreed?''

"Well, now, I don't know. I'm not at all sure that I am willing to—''

"Splendid.'' Jacob Pole picked up the lamp and started back along the corridor, leaving the others the choice of following or being left behind in darkness.

"Colonel Pole!'' Monkton lost his dignity and scuttled after him, leaving Darwin, smiling to himself, to bring up the rear. "Slower there, Colonel. D'you want to see a broken leg in the dark here?''

"No. With two doctors to attend it, a broken leg would more than likely prove fatal.'' But Pole slowed his steps and turned so that the lamp threw its beam back along the corridor. "What an evening. Will Bailey and I had just nicely settled in for a pipe of Virginia and a talk about old times—we were together at Pondicherry, and at the capture of Manila—when word came up from downstairs that Dr. Monkton needed another pair of hands to help.''

"Why not Will Bailey?" asked Darwin from behind him. "It is his house."

"Aye, but Willy had shipped a pint or two of porter, and I've been running dry for the past five years. I left him there to nod, and I came down." Pole sniffed. "I'm no physician—you may have guessed that already—but when I saw our man back there in the scullery, I could tell he was halfway to the hereafter. He was mumbling to himself, mumbling and muttering. It took me a few minutes to get the hang of his accent—Scots, and thick enough to cut. And he was all the time shivering and shaking, and muttering, muttering. . . ."

The woman had been standing by the side of the cot, holding the man's right hand in both of hers. As the hoarse voice grew louder and more distinct, she leaned towards him.

"John, no. Don't talk that way." Her voice was frightened, and for a brief moment the man's eyes seemed to flicker in their sunk pits, as though about to open. She looked nervously at Jacob Pole and at Dr. Monkton, who was preparing a poultice of kaolin and pressed herbs.

"His mind's not there. He—he doesna' know whut he's sayin. Hush, Johnnie, an' lie quiet."

"Inland from Handa Island, there by the Minch," said the man suddenly, as though answering some unspoken question. "Aye, inside the loch. That's where ye'll find it."

"Sh. Johnnie, now quiet ye." She squeezed his hand gently, an attractive dark-haired woman bowed down with worry and work. "Try and sleep, John, ye need rest."

The unshaven jaw was moving again, its dark bristles emphasizing the pale lips and waxen cheeks. Again the eyelids fluttered.

"Two hundred years," he said in a creaking voice. "Two hundred years it lay there, an' niver a mon suspected whut was in it. One o' auld King Philip's ships, an' crammed. Aye, an' not one to ken it 'til a month back, wi' all the guid gold."

Jacob Pole started forward, his thin face started. The woman saw him move and shook her head.

"Sir, pay him no mind. He's not wi' us, he's ramblin' in the head."

"Move back, then, and give me room," said Monkton. His manner was brisk. "And if you, sir"—he nodded at Pole—"will hold his shoulders while I apply this to his chest. And you, my good woman, go off to the kitchen and bring more hot water. Perhaps this will give him ease."

"I canna' leave him now. The woman's voice was anguished. "There's no sayin' whut he'll come out with. He might—" Her voice trailed off under the doctor's glare, and she picked up the big brass bowl and reluctantly crept out. Jacob Pole took the man firmly by the shoulders, leaning forward to assure his grip.

"Inland from Handa Island," said the man after a few seconds. His breath caught and rattled in his throat, but there seemed to be a tone of a confidence shared. "Aye, ye have it to rights, a wee bit north of Malkirk, at the entrance there of Loch Malkirk. A rare find. But we'll need equipment to take it, 'tis twenty feet down, an' bullion weighs heavy. An' there's the Devil to worrit about. Need help. . . ."

His voice faded and he groaned as the hot poultice was applied to his bare chest. His hands twitched, flew feebly upwards towards his throat, and then flopped back to his sides.

"Hold him," said Monkton. "there's a new fit coming."

"I have him." Pole's voice was quiet and he was leaning close to the man, watching the pallid lips. "Easy, Johnnie."

The dark head was turning to and fro on the folded blanket, grunting with some inner turmoil. The thin hands began to clench and unclench.

"Go south for it." The words were little more than a whisper. "That's it, have to go south. Ye know the position here in the Highlands, but we'll have to have weapons. Ye canna' fight the Devil wi' just dirks an' muskets, ye need a regular bombard. I've seen it—bigger than leviathan, taller than Foinaven, an' strong as Fingal. Five men killed, an' three more crippled, an' nothin' to show for it."

"It's coming," said Monkton suddenly. "He's stiffening in the limbs."

The breath was coming harder in the taut throat. "Go get the weapons . . . wi'out that we'll lose more o' the clansmen. Weapons, put by Loch Malkirk, an' raise the bullion . . . canna' fight the Devil . . . wi' just dirks. Aye, I'll do it . . . south, then. Need weapons . . . bigger than leviathan. . . .''

As the voice faded, his thin hands moved up to clasp Pole's restraining hands, and Pole winced as black fingernails dug deep into his wrists.

"Hold tight," said Monkton. "It's the final spasm."

But even as he spoke, the stranger's muscles began to lose their tension. The thin hands slid down to the chest, and the harsh breathing eased. Jacob Pole stood looking down at the still face.

"Has he—gone?"

"No." Monkton looked puzzled. "He still breathes, and it somehow seems to have eased. I—I thought . . . Well, he's quiet now. Would you go and find the woman, and see where that hot water has got to? I would also like to cup him."

Pole was peering at the man's face. "He seems a lot better. He's not shaking the way he was. What will you do next?"

"Well, the cupping, he certainly needs to be bled." Monkton coughed. "Then I think another plaster, of mustard, Burgundy pitch, and pigeon dung. And perhaps an enema of antimony and rock salt, and possibly scared bitters."

"Sweet Christ." Pole shook his head and wiped his nose on his sleeve. "Not for me. I'd rather be costive for a week. I'll go fetch his woman."

"And that was it?" Darwin was seated comfortably in front of the empty fireplace, a dish of dried plums and figs on his lap. Jacob Pole stood by the window, looking moodily out into the night and glancing occasionally at Will Bailey. The farmer was slumped back in an armchair, snoring and snorting and now and then jerking back for a few moments of consciousness.

"That's as I recall it—and I listened hard." Pole shrugged. "I don't know what happened after I left the room, of course, but Dr. Monkton says the man was peaceful and unconscious until he too left. The woman stayed."

Darwin picked up a fig and frowned at it. "I have no desire to further lower your opinion of my profession, but now that he is gone I must say that Dr. Monkton's powers of observation are not impressive to me. You looked at that man's face, you say. And as a soldier you have seen men die?"

"Aye. And women and children, sad to say." Pole looked at him morosely. "What's that to do with it?"

Darwin sighed. "Nothing, it seems—according to you and my colleague, Dr. Monkton. Think, sir, think of that room you were in. Think of the *smell* of it."

"The tobacco? You already remarked on that, and I recall no other."

"Exactly. So ask yourself of the smell that was *not* there. A man lies dying, eh? He displays the classic Hippocratic facies of death, as Dr. Monkton described it—displays them so exactly that it is as though they were copied from a text. So. But where was the smell of mortal disease? You know that smell?"

Pole turned suddenly. "There was none. Damme, I knew there was something odd about that room. I know that smell all too well—sweet, like the charnel house. Now why the blazes didn't Dr. Monkton remark it? He must encounter it all the time."

Darwin shrugged his heavy shoulders and chewed on another wrinkled plum. "Dr. Monkton has gone beyond the point in his profession where his reputation calls for exact observation. It comes to all of us at last. 'Man, proud man, drest in a little brief authority, most ignorant of what he's most assured.' Aye, there's some of that in all of us, you and me, too. But let us go, if you will, a little further. The man gripped your wrists and you held his shoulders. There was delirium, you have told me that, in his voice. But what was the *feel* of him?"

Pole paced back and forth along the room, his skinny frame stooped in concentration. He finally stopped and glared at Will Bailey. "Pity you've no potion to stop him snoring. I can't hear myself think. A man can't fix his mind around anything with that noise. Let's see now, what was the feel of him."

He held his hands out before him. "I held him *so*, and he gripped at my wrists *thus*. Dirty hands, with long black nails."

"And their warmth? Carry your mind back to them."

"No, not hot. He wasn't fevered, not at all. But not cold, either. But. . . ." Pole paused and bit his lip. "Something else. The Dutch have my guts, his hands were *soft*. Black and dirty, but not rough, the way you'd expect for a farmer or a tinker. His hands didn't match his clothes at all."

"I conjectured it so." Darwin spat a plum stone into the empty fireplace. "Will you allow me to carry one step further?"

"More yet? Damme, to my mind we've enough mystery already. What now?"

"You have seen the world in your army service. You have been aboard a fighting ship and know its usual cargo. Did anything strike you as strange about our dying friend's story?"

"The ship, one of King Philip's galleons, sunk off the coast of Scotland two hundred years ago." Pole licked at his chapped lips, and a new light filled his eyes. "With a load of bullion on board it."

"Exactly. A wreck in Loch Malkirk, we deduce, and bearing gold. Now, Colonel Pole, have you ever been involved in a search for treasure?"

Before Pole could answer there was a noise like a hissing wood fire from the other armchair. It was Will Bailey, awake again and shaking with laughter.

"Ever been involved in a hunt for treasure, Jacob! There's a good one for me to tell yer wife." He went into another fit of merriment. "Should I tell the doctor, Jacob?"

He turned to Darwin. "There was never a man born under the sun who followed treasure harder. He had me at it, too—diving for pearls off Sarawak, and trawling for old silver off the Bermudas' reefs." He lay back, croaking with laughter. "Tell 'im, Jacob, you tell 'im all about it."

Pole peered at him in the dim light. "Will Bailey, you're a shapeless mass of pox-ridden pig's muck," he said mildly. "Tell him about yourself, instead of talking about me. Who ate the poultice off the black dog's back, eh? Who married the chimney sweep, and who hanged the monkey?"

"So you have found treasure before?" interjected Darwin, and Pole turned his attention back to the doctor.

"Not a shilling's worth, though I've sought it hard enough, along with fat Will there. I've searched, aye, and I've even hunted bullion out on the Main, in sunk Spanish galleons; but I've never found enough to pay an hour's rent on a Turkish privy. What of it, then?"

"Consider our wrecked galleon, resting for two hundred years off the coast of Scotland. How would it have got there? Spanish galleons were not in the habit of sailing the Scottish coast—still less at a time when England and Spain were at war."

"The Armada!" said Bailey. "He's saying yon ship must have been part of the Spanish Armada, come to invade England."

"The Armada indeed. Defeated by Drake and the English fleet, afraid to face a straight journey home to Cadiz through the English Channel, eh? Driven to try for a run the long way, around the north coast of Scotland, with a creep down past Ireland. Many of the galleons tried that."

Pole nodded. "It fits. But—"

"Aye, speak your but." Darwin's eyes were alight with pleasure. "What is your but?"

"But a ship of the Armada had no reason to carry bullion. If anything, she'd have been stripped of valuables in case she went down in battle."

"Exactly!" Darwin slapped his fat thigh. "Yet against all logic we find sunk bullion in Loch Malkirk. One more factor, then I'll await your comment: you and I both live fifteen miles from here, and I at least am an infrequent visitor; yet I was called on to help Dr. Monkton—who has never before called me in for advice or comment on anything. *Ergo*, someone knew my whereabouts tonight, and someone persuaded Monkton to send for me. *Who?* Who asked you to fetch me from Matthew Boulton's house?"

Pole frowned. "Why, *he* did." He pointed at Will Bailey.

"Nay, but the woman told me you and Monkton asked for that." Bailey looked baffled. "Only she didn't know the way and had to get on back in there with her man. That's when I asked you to do it—I thought you knew all about it."

Darwin was nodding in satisfaction. "Now we have the whole thing. And observe, at every turn we come back to the two strangers—long since disappeared, and I will wager we see no more of them."

"But what the devil's been going on?" said Pole. He scratched at his jaw and wiped his nose again on his sleeve. "A dying man, Spanish bullion, a leviathan in Loch Malkirk—how did we get into the middle of all this? I come here for a bite of free dinner and a quiet smoke with Willy, and before I know it I'm running over the countryside as confused as Lazarus' widow."

"What is *really* going on?" Darwin rubbed at his grey wig. "As to that, at the moment I could offer no more than rank conjecture. We lack tangible evidence. But for what it is worth, Colonel, I believe that you were involved largely accidently. My instincts tell me that I was the primary target, and someone aimed their shafts at my curiosity or my cupidity."

"The bullion?" Pole's eyes sparkled. "Aye, that's where they tickled me, too. If you go, I'd like a chance to join you. I've done it before, and I know some of the difficulties. Rely on me."

Darwin shook his head. The plate of fruit had been emptied, and there was a dreamy look on his coarse features. "It is not the treasure. That can be yours, Colonel—if it proves to exist. No, sir, there's sweeter bait for me, something I can scent but not yet see. The Devil, and one thing more, must wait for us in Malkirk."

The pile in the courtyard of the stage inn had been growing steadily. An hour before, three leather bags had been delivered, then a square oak chest and a canvas-wrapped package. The coachman sat close to the wall of the inn, warming his boots at a little brazier and shielding his back against the unseasonably cold May wind. He was drinking from a tankard of small beer and looking doubtfully from the swelling heap of luggage to the roof of the coach.

Finally he looked over his shoulder, measured the angle of the sun with an experienced eye, and rose to his feet. As he did so, there was a clatter of horses' hooves.

Two light pony traps came into view, approaching from opposite directions. They met by the big coach. Two passengers climbed down from them, looked first at the pile of luggage on the ground, then at the laden traps, and finally at each other. The brooding coachman was ignored completely.

The fat man shook his head.

"This is ridiculous, Colonel. When we agreed to share a coach for this enterprise it was with the understanding that I would take my medical chest and equipment with me. They are bulky, but I do not care to travel without them, for even a few miles from home. However, it did not occur to me that you would then choose to bring with you all your household possessions." He waved a brawny arm at the other trap. "We are *visiting* Scotland, not removing ourselves to it permanently."

The tall, scrawny man had moved to his light carriage and was struggling to take down from it a massive wooden box. Despite his best effort he was unable to lift it clear, and after a moment he gave up, grunted, and turned to face the other. He shook his head.

"A few miles from home is one thing, Dr. Darwin. Loch

Malkirk is another. We will be far in the Highlands, beyond real civilization. I know that it has been thirty years since the Great Rebellion, but I'm told the land is not quiet. It still seethes with revolt. We will need weapons—if not for the natives, then for the Devil.''

Darwin had checked that his medical chest was safely aboard the coach. Now he came across to grasp one side of the box on the other trap, and between them they lowered it to the ground.

''You are quite mistaken,'' he said. ''The Highlands are unhappy but they are peaceful. Dr. Johnson fared well enough there, only three years ago. You will not need your weapons, though there is no denying that the people there hold loyal to Prince Charles Edward—''

''—the Young Pretender,'' grunted Pole. ''The upstart blackguard who—''

''—who has what many would accept as a *legitimate* claim to the throne of Scotland, if not of England.'' Darwin was peering curiously into the wooden box, as Pole carefully raised the lid. ''His loss in '46 was a disaster, but the clans are loyal in spite of his exile. Colonel Pole''—he had at last caught a glimpse of the inside of the box—''weapons are one thing, but I trust you are not proposing to take *that* with you to Malkirk.''

''Certainly am.'' Jacob Pole crouched by the box and lovingly stroked the shining metal. ''You'll never see a prettier cannon than Little Bess. Brassbound, iron sheath on the bore, and fires a two-inch ball with black powder. Show me a devil or a leviathan in Loch Malkirk, and I'll show you something that's a good deal more docile when he's had one of these up his weasand.'' He held up a ball, lofting it an inch or two in the palm of his hand. ''And if the natives run wild, I'm sure it will do the same for them.''

Darwin reached to open the lid wider. ''Musket and shot, too. Where do you imagine that we are traveling, to the Moon? You know the Highlanders are forbidden to carry weapons, and we have little enough room for *rational* appurtenances. The ragmatical collection you propose is too much.''

''No more than your medical chests are too much.'' Pole straightened up. ''I'll discard if you will, but not otherwise.''

''Impossible. I have already winnowed to a minimum.''

''And so have I.''

The coachman stood up slowly and carried his empty tankard

back into the inn. Once inside he went over to the keg, placed his tankard next to it, and jerked his head back towards the door.

"Listen to that," he said gloomily. "Easy money, I thought it'd be, wi' just the two passengers. Now they're at each other before they've set foot in the coach, and I've contracted to carry them as far as Durham. Here, Alan, pour me another one in there before I go, and make it a big 'un.''

The journey north was turning back the calendar, day by day and year by year. Beyond Durham the spring was noticeably less advanced, with the open apple blossom of Nottingham regressing by the time they reached Northumberland to tight pink buds a week away from bloom. The weather added to the effect with a return to the raw, biting cold of February, chilling fingers and toes through the thickest clothing. At Otterburn they had changed coaches to an open dray that left them exposed to the gusts of a hard northeaster, and beyond Stirling the centuries themselves peeled away from the rugged land. The roads were unmetaled, mere stony scratches along the slopes of the mountains, and the mean houses of turf and rubble were dwarfed by the looming peaks.

At first Darwin had tried to write. He made notes in the thick volume of his Commonplace Book, balancing it on his knee. Worsening roads and persistent rain conspired to defeat him, and at last he gave up. He sat facing forward in the body of the dray, unshaven, swaddled in blankets and covered by a sheet of grey canvas with a hole cut in it for his head.

"Wild country, Colonel Pole." He gestured forward as they drove northwest along Loch Shin. "We are a long way from Litchfield. Look at that group."

He nodded ahead at a small band of laborers plodding along the side of the track. Jacob Pole made a snorting noise that could have as well come from the horse. He was smoking a stubby pipe with a bowl like a cupped hand, and a jar of hot coals stood on the seat behind him.

"What of 'em?" he said. His pipe was newly charged with black tobacco scraped straight from the block, and he blew out a great cloud of blue-grey smoke. "I see nothing worth talking about. They're just dreary peasants."

"Ah, but they are pure *Celt*," said Darwin cheerfully. "Observe the shape of their heads, and the brachycephalic cranium.

We'll see more of them as we go further north. It's been the way of it for three thousand years, the losers in the fight for good lands are pushed north and west. Scots and Celts and Picts, driven and crowded to the northern hills.''

Jacob Pole peered at the group suspiciously as he tamped his pipe. ''They may look like losers to you, but they look like tough fodder to me. Big and fierce. As for your idea that they don't carry weapons, take a look at those scythes and sickles, and then define a weapon for me.'' He patted his pocket under his leather cloak. ''Ball and powder is what you need for savages. Mark my words, we'll be glad of these before we're done in Malkirk.''

''I am not persuaded. The Rebellion was over thirty years ago.''

''Aye, on the surface. But I've never yet heard of treasure being captured easy; there's always blood and trouble comes with it. It draws in violence, as sure as cow dung draws flies.''

''I see. So you are suggesting that we should turn back?'' Darwin's tone was sly.

''Did I say that?'' Pole blew out an indignant cloud of smoke. ''Never. We're almost there. If we can find boat and boatman, I'll be looking for that galleon before today's done, Devil or no Devil. I've never seen one in this world, and I hope I'll not see one in the next. But with your ideas on religion, I'm surprised you believe in devils at all.''

''Devils?'' Darwin's voice was quiet and reflective. ''Certainly I am a believer in them, as much as the Pope himself; but I think he and I might disagree on the shapes they bear in the world. We should get our chance to find out soon enough.'' He lifted a brawny arm from under the canvas. ''That has to be Malkirk, down the hill there. We have made better time from Lairg than I anticipated.''

Jacob Pole scowled ahead. ''And a miserable-looking place it is, if that's all there is to it. But look close down there—maybe we're not the only visitors to those God-forsaken regions.''

Half a mile in front of them two light carriages blocked the path that led through the middle of the village. The ill-clad cluster of people gathered around them turned as Pole drove the dray steadily forward and halted twenty yards from the nearer carriage.

He and Darwin stepped down, stretching joints stiffened by

the long journey. As they did so, three men came forward through the crowd. Darwin looked at them in surprise for a moment before nodding a greeting.

"I am Erasmus Darwin, and this is Colonel Jacob Pole. You received my message, I take it? We sent word ahead that we desire accommodation for a few days here in Malkirk."

He looked intently from one to the other. They formed a curiously ill-matched trio. The tallest of them was lean and dark, even thinner than Jacob Pole, and the possessor of bright, dark eyes, that snapped from one scene to the next without ever remaining still. He had long-fingered hands, red cheeks that framed a hooked nose and a big chin, and he was dressed in a red tunic and green breeches covered by a patchwork cloak of blues and greys. His neighbor was of middle height and conventionally dressed—but his skin was coal-black and his prominent cheekbones wore deep patterns of old scars.

The third member stood slightly apart from the others. He was short and strongly built, with massive bare arms. His face was half-hidden behind a massive growth of greying beard, and he seemed to crackle with excess energy. He had nodded vigorously as soon as Darwin asked about the message.

"Aye, aye, we got your message right enough. But I thought it came for these gentlemen." He jerked his head to the others at his side. "There was no word with it, ye see, saying who was comin', only a need for beds for two. But ye say ye're the Darwin as sent the note to me?"

"I am." Darwin looked rueful. "I should have said more with that message. It never occurred to me there might be two arrivals here in one day. Can you find more room for us?"

The broad man shrugged. "I'll find ye a bed—but it will be one for the both of ye, I'll warn ye of that."

Jacob Pole stole a quick look at Darwin's bulky form.

"A good-sized bed," said the man, catching the glance. "In a middlin' size room. An' clean, too, and that has Malcolm Maclaren's own word on it." He thumped at his thick chest. "An' that's good through the whole Hielands."

While Maclaren was speaking, the tall cloaked man had been sizing up Pole and Darwin, his look darting intensely from one to the other absorbing every detail of their appearance.

"Our arrival has caused problems—not expected, we must solve." His voice was deep, with a clipped, jerky delivery and

a strong touch of a foreign accent. "Apologies. Let me intro-
duce—I am Dr. Philip Theophrastus von Hohenheim. At your
service. This is my servant, Zumal. Yours to command."

The black man grinned, showing teeth that had been filed to
sharp points. Darwin raised his eyebrows and looked quizzically
at the tall stranger.

"I must congratulate you. You are looking remarkably well,
Dr. Paracelsus von Hohenheim, for one who must soon be approaching his three hundredth year."

After a moment's startled pause the tall man laughed, showing
even yellow teeth. Jacob Pole and Malcolm Maclaren looked on
uncomprehendingly as Hohenheim reached out, took Darwin's
hand, and shook it hard.

"Your knowledge is impressive, Dr. Darwin. Few people
know my name these days—fewer yet can place my date of birth
so accurately. To make precise—I was born 1491, one year before Columbus of Genoa found the Americas." He bowed. "You
also know my work?"

As Hohenheim was speaking, Darwin had frowned in sudden
puzzlement and stood for a few moments in deep thought. Finally he nodded.

"In my youth, sir, your words impressed me more than any
others. If I may quote you: 'I admonish you not to reject the
method of experiment, but according as your power permits, to
follow it without prejudice. For every experiment is like a
weapon which must be used according to its own peculiar
power.' Great words, Dr. Hohenheim." He looked at the other
man coolly. "Throughout my career as a physician, I have tried
to adhere to that precept. Perhaps you recall what you wrote
immediately after that advice?"

Instead of replying, Hohenheim lifted his left hand clear of
his cloak and waved it rapidly in a circle, the extended fingers
pointing towards Jacob Pole. As he completed the circle, he
flicked his thumb swiftly across the palm of his hand and casually plucked a small green flask from the air close to Pole's head.
While the villagers behind him gasped, he rolled the flask into
the palm of his hand.

"Here." He held it out to Jacob Pole. "Your eyes tell it—
fluxes and fevers. Drink this. Condition will be improved, much
improved. I guarantee. Also—more liquids, less strong drink.
Better for you." He turned to Darwin. "And you, Doctor. Med-

icine has come a long way—great advances since I had to flee *charlatans* of Basel. Let me offer you advice, also. Barley water, liquorice, sweet almond, in the morning. White wine and anise—not too much—at night. To fortify mind and body.''

Darwin nodded. He looked subdued. "I thank you for your thoughtful words. Perhaps I will seek to follow them. The ingredients, with the exception of wine, are already in my medical chest.''

"Solution." Hohenheim snapped the fingers of his left hand in the air again, and again he held a flask. "White wine. To serve until other supply is at hand.''

The villagers murmured in awe, and Hohenheim smiled. "Until tomorrow. I have other business now. Must be in Iverness tonight, meeting there was promised.''

"Ye'll never do it, man," burst out Malcolm Maclaren. "Why, it's a full day's ride or more, south of here.''

"I have methods." There was another quick smile, a bow towards Pole and Darwin, then Hohenheim had turned and was walking briskly away towards the west, where the sea showed less than a mile away. While Malcolm Maclaren and the villagers gazed after him in fascinated silence, Jacob Pole suddenly became aware of the flask that he was holding. He looked at it doubtfully.

"With your permission." Darwin reached out to take it. He removed the stopper, sniffed at it, and then placed it cautiously against his tongue.

"Here." Pole grabbed the flask back. "That's mine. You drink your own. Wasn't that amazing? I've seen a lot of doctors, but I've never seen one to match his speed for diagnosis—it's enough to make me change my mind about all pox-peddling physicians. Made you think, didn't it?''

"It did," said Darwin ironically. "It made me think most hard.''

"And the way he drew drugs from thin air, did you see that? The man's a marvel. What were you saying about him being three hundred years old? That sounds impossible.''

"For once we seem to be in agreement." Darwin looked at the flask he was holding. "As for his ability to conjure a prescription for me from the air itself, that surprises me less than you might think. It is a poor doctor who lacks access to all the ingredients for his own potions.''

"But you were impressed." Pole was looking pleased with himself. "Admit it, Doctor, you were impressed."

"I was—but not because of his drugs. That called for some powers of manipulation and manual dexterity, no more. But one of Hohenheim's acts impressed me mightily—and it was one performed without emphasis, as though it was so easy to be undeserving of comment."

Pole rubbed at his nose and took a tentative sip from his open flask. He pulled a sour face. "Pfaugh. Essence of badger turd. But all his acts seemed beyond me. What are you referring to?"

"One power of the original Paracelsus, Theophrastus von Hohenheim, was to know all about a man on first meeting. I would normally discount that idea as mere historical gossip. But recall, if you will, Hohenheim's first mode of address to me. He called me *Doctor Darwin*."

"That's who you are."

"Aye. Except that I introduced myself here simply as *Erasmus* Darwin. My message to Maclaren was signed only as Darwin. So how did Hohenheim know to call me doctor?"

"From the man who carried your message here?"

"He knew me only as Mister Darwin."

"Maybe Hohenheim saw your medical chest."

"It is quite covered by the canvas—invisible to all."

"All right." Pole shrugged. "Damme, he must have heard of you before. You're a well-known doctor."

"Perhaps." Darwin's tone was grudging. "I like to believe that I have a growing reputation, and it calls for effort for any man to be skeptical of his own fame. Even so. . . ."

He turned to Malcolm Maclaren, who was still watching Hohenheim and Zumal as they walked towards the sea. Darwin tugged gently at his leather jacket.

"Mr. Maclaren. Did you talk of my message to Dr. Hohenheim before we arrived?"

"Eh? Your message?" Maclaren rubbed a thick-nailed hand across his brow. "I was just startin' to mention something on it when the pair of ye arrived here. But did ye ever see a doctor like that. Did ye ever?"

Darwin tugged again at his jacket. "Did Hohenheim seem to be familiar with my name?"

"He did not." Maclaren turned to stare at Darwin and shook his jacket free. "He said he'd never before heard of ye."

"Indeed." Darwin stepped back and placed his ample rear on the step of the dray. He gazed for several minutes towards the dark mass of Foinaven in the northeast, and he did not move until Pole came bustling up to him.

"Unless you're of a mind to sit there all day in the rain, let's go along with Mr. Maclaren and see where we'll be housed. D'ye hear me?"

Darwin looked at him vacantly, his eyes innocent and almost childlike.

"Come on, wake up." Pole pointed at the blank-walled cottages, rough stone walls stuffed with sods of turf. "I hope it will be something better than this. Let's take a look at the bed, and hope we won't be sleeping sailor-style, two shifts in one bunk. And I'll wager my share of the bullion to a gnat's snuffbox that there's bugs in the bed, no matter what Malcolm Maclaren says. Well, no matter. I'll take those over Kuzestan scorpions if it comes to a nip or two on the bum. Let's away."

West of Malkirk the fall of the land to the sea was steep. The village had grown on a broad lip, the only level place between mountains and the rocky shore. Its stone houses ran in a ragged line north-south, straddling the rutted and broken road. Jacob Pole allowed the old horse to pick its own path as the dray followed Malcolm Maclaren. He was looking off to the left, to a line of breakers that marked the shore.

"A fierce prospect," remarked Darwin. He had followed the direction of Pole's looks. "And no shore for a shipwreck. See the second line of breakers out there, and the rocks of the reef. It is hard to imagine a ship holding together for one month after a wreck here, still less for two centuries."

"My thought exactly," said Pole gruffly. "Mr. Maclaren?"

"Aye, sir?" The stocky Highlander halted and turned at Pole's call, his frizzy mop of hair wild under the old bonnet.

"Is the whole coastline like this—I mean, rocky and reef-bound?"

"It is, sir, exceptin' only Loch Malkirk, a mile on from here. Ye can put a boat in there easy enough, if ye've a mind to do it. An' there's another wee bit landing south of here that some of the men use." He remained standing, arms across his chest. "Why'd ye be askin'? Will ye be wantin' a boat, same as Dr. Hohenheim?"

"Hohenheim wants a boat?" began Pole, but Darwin silenced him with a look and a hand laid on his arm.

"Not now," he said, as soon as Maclaren had turned to walk again along the path. "You already said it, the lure of gold will attract trouble. We could have guessed it. We are not the only ones who have heard word of a galleon."

"Aye. But *Hohenheim* . . ." Jacob Pole sank into an unquiet silence.

They were approaching the north end of the village, where three larger houses stood facing each other across a level sward. Maclaren waved his hand at the one nearest the shore, where a grey-haired woman stood at the door.

"I wish ye could have had a place in that, but Dr. Hohenheim has one room, and his servant, that heathen blackamoor, has the other. But we can gi' ye a room that's near as good in here." He turned to the middle and biggest house, and the woman started over to join them.

"Jeanie. Two gentlemen needs a room." He went into a quick gabble of Gaelic, then looked apologetically at Pole and Darwin. "I'm sorry, but she hasna' the English. I've told her the place has to be clean for ye, an' that ye'll be here for a few days at least. Anythin' else ye'll need while ye are here in Malkirk? Best if I tell her now."

"I think not," said Darwin. But he swung lightly to the ground from the seat of the dray and began to walk quickly across to the black-shuttered third house. He had seen the repeated looks that Malcolm Maclaren and the woman had cast in that direction.

"I don't suppose there is any chance of rooms in here?" he said, not slowing his pace at all. "It will be some inconvenience, sharing a room, and if there were a place in this house, even for one of us—"

"No, sir!" Maclaren's voice was high and urgent. "Not in that house, sir. There's no room there."

He came after Darwin, who had reached the half-open door and was peering inside.

"Ye see, there's no place for ye." Maclaren had moved around and blocked the entrance with a thick arm. "I mean, there's no furniture there, no way that ye could stay there, you or the colonel."

Darwin was looking carefully around the large stone-floored

room, with its massive single bed and empty fireplace. He frowned.

"That is a pity. It has no furnishings, true enough, but the bed is of ample size. Could you perhaps bring some other furniture over from another house, and make it—"

"No, sir." Maclaren pushed the door to firmly and began to shepherd Darwin back towards the other house. "Ye see, sir, that's my brother's house. He's been away inland these past two month, an' the house needs a cleanin' before he comes back. We expect him in a day or two—but ye see, that house isna' mine to offer ye. Come on this way, an' we'll make you comfortable, I swear it."

He went across to the dray, ripped away the canvas with a jerk, grunted, and lifted the box containing Little Bess clear with one colossal heave. The other two men watched in amazement as he braced his legs, then staggered off towards the center house with his burden.

Pole raised his eyebrows. "I won't argue the point with *him*. It took two of us to lift that. But what's over there he's so worried about? Weapons maybe? Did you see guns or claymores?"

"There was a bed in there—nothing else." Darwin's intrigued tone was at odds with his words.

"You are sure?" Pole had caught the inflection in the other man's voice. "Nothing mysterious there?"

"I saw nothing mysterious." Darwin's voice was puzzled. He went over to the dray and took one of his bags down from it. His expression was thoughtful, his heavy head hunched forward on his shoulders. "You see, Colonel Pole, that is one of the curiosities of the English language. I saw nothing, and it was mysterious. A room two months empty and neglected, and I saw nothing there—no dust, no cobwebs, no mold. Less than I would expect to see in a house that had been cleaned three days ago. The room was *polished*." He rubbed his chin.

"But what does that mean?"

Darwin shrugged. "Aye, that's the question." He looked at the dirty grey smoke rising from the house in front of them. "Well, we will find out in due course. Meanwhile, unless my nose is playing me tricks, there's venison cooking inside. A good dish of collops would sit well after our long journey. Come on, Colonel, I feel we have more than earned an adequate dinner."

He went in, through a door scarcely wide enough to permit

passage of his broad frame. Jacob Pole stared after him and scratched his head.

"Now what the devil was all *that* about? Him and his mysterious nothings. That's like a sawbones, to conceal more than they tell. I'll still bet there's weapons in that place, hidden away somewhere. I saw their looks."

He picked up a small case and followed into the house's dark interior, where he could now hear the rattle of plates and cups.

Jacob Pole awoke just before true dawn, at the first cock crow. He climbed out of bed, slipped on his boots, and picked up the greatcoat that lay on the chest of drawers. Despite his misgivings, the bed had been adequately large and reasonably clean. He looked to the other side of it. Darwin lay on his back, a great mound under the covers. He was snoring softly, his mouth open half an inch. Pole picked up his pipe and tobacco and went through to the other room to sit by the embers of the peat fire.

He had spent a restless night. Ever since dinner his thoughts had been all on the galleon, and he had been unable to get it out of his mind. Hohenheim was after the bullion, that was clear enough. Maclaren had made no secret of the galleon's presence, but it was also clear from the way that he shrugged the subject away with a move of his great shoulders that he knew nothing of anything valuable aboard it. He had seemed amazed that anyone, still less two parties, should be interested in it at all. The Devil, too, had been casually shrugged off.

Yes, surely it was there—had been there as long as anyone in the village could remember.

Its dimensions?

He had pondered for a while at Darwin's question. As large as a whale, some said—others said much larger. It lived near the galleon, but it was peaceful enough. It would merely be a man's fancy to say that the creature *guarded* anything in the loch.

The three men had played a curious game of three-way tag for a couple of hours. Pole had wanted to talk only of the galleon, while neither Darwin nor Maclaren seemed particularly interested. Darwin had concentrated his attention on the Devil, but again Maclaren had given only brief and uninformative answers to the questions. He had his own interests. He pushed Darwin to talk of English medicine, of new drugs and surgical procedures, of hopeless cases and miracle cures. He wanted to know if Hohenheim could do all the things that he hinted at—make the blind see, save the living, even raise the dead. When Darwin spoke Maclaren leaned forward unblinking, stroking his full beard and scratching in an irritated way at his breeches' legs, as though resenting the absence of the kilt.

Pole shook his head. It had been a long, unsatisfying evening, no doubt about it.

He picked up a glowing lump of peat, applied it to his pipe, and sucked in his first morning mouthful of smoke. He sighed with satisfaction and went at once into a violent and lengthy fit of coughing. Eyes streaming, he finally had to stagger across and take a few gulps from the water jug before he could breathe again and stand there wheezing by the window.

"You missed your true vocation, Colonel," said a voice behind him. "If you were always available to wake the village, the cockerel would soon be out of work."

Darwin stood at the door in his stockinged feet. He was blinking and scratching his paunch with one hand, while the other held his nightcap on his head.

Pole glared at him and took another swig from the water jug. Then he looked out of the window next to him, stiffened, and snorted.

"Aye, and it's just as well that one of us gets up in the morning. Look across there. A light in that house, and that means Hohenheim is up already—and I'll wager he'll be on his way to Loch Malkirk while we're still scratching around here. He's ahead of us already, and with his powers I wouldn't put anything past him. We have to get moving ourselves, and over to the loch as soon as we can."

"But you heard Hohenheim last night, announcing his intention to be in Inverness. What makes you think that he is still in Malkirk?" Darwin nodded to the grey-haired woman, who had silently appeared to tend the fire and set a black cauldron of water on it. "He is probably not even here."

"He is, though." Pole nodded his head again towards the window. The door of the other house had opened, and two figures were emerging. It was too dark to make out their clothing, but there was no mistaking the tall, thin build, backed by a shorter form that seemed to be a part of the darkness itself.

"Hohenheim, and his blackamoor." Pole's voice held a gloomy satisfaction. "As I feared, and as I told you, we come to seek bullion, and we find we are obliged to compete with a man who can see the future, travel fast as the wind to any place that he chooses, and conjure powerful nostrums from thin air. That makes me feel most uneasy. By the way, did you take the draught that he provided for you?''

''I did not,'' said Darwin curtly. He sat down at the table and pulled a deep dish towards him. ''I found one bowl of Malcolm Maclaren's lemon punch more than enough strange drink for me last night. My stomach still sits uneasy. Come, Colonel, sit down and curb your impatience. If we are to head for Loch Malkirk, we should not do so until we have food in us. The good woman is already making porridge, and I think there will be more herring and bowls of frothed milk. If we are to embark on rough water, at least let us do so well-bottomed.''

Pole sat down bad-temperedly, glared at his offending pipe, and pecked half-heartedly at porridge, oatcake, and smoked fish. He watched while Darwin devoured all those along with goat's whey, a dish of tongue and ham, and a cup of chocolate. But it went rapidly, and in five minutes the plates were clear. Pole rose at once to his feet.

''One moment more,'' said Darwin. He went across to the woman, who had watched him eating with obvious approval. He pointed at a plate of oatcakes. She nodded, and he gave her an English shilling. As he loaded the cakes into a pocket of his coat, Jacob Pole nodded grudgingly.

''Aye, you're probably right to hold me there, Doctor. There'll likely be little hospitality for us at the loch.''

Darwin raised his eyebrows at the sudden truce, then turned again to the woman. He pointed at the rising sun, then followed its path across the sky with his arm. He halted when he had reached a little past the vertical, and pointed at the cauldron and the haunch of dried beef hanging by the wall. The woman nodded, spoke a harsh-sounding sentence, laughed, and came forward to pat Darwin's ample stomach admiringly.

Darwin coughed. He had caught Pole's gleeful look.

''Come on. At least dinner is assured when we return.''

''Aye. And more than that, from the look of it.'' Pole's voice was dry.

The path to Loch Malkirk was just as Maclaren had described it, running first seaward, then cutting back inland over a steep incline. The ground was still wet and slippery with a heavy dew that hung sparkling points of sunlight over the heather and dwarf juniper. By the time they had traveled fifty yards their boots and lower breeches were soaked. When the loch was visible beyond the brow of the hill, they could see the mist that still hung over the surface of the water.

Darwin paused at the top of the rise and laid his hand on Pole's arm. "One second, Colonel, before we head down. We could not find a better place than this to take a general view of how the land lies."

"More than that," said Pole softly. "We'll have a chance to see what Hohenheim is doing without him knowing it. See, he's down there, off to the left."

The shape of the loch was like a long wine bottle, with the neck facing to the northwest. An island off-shore stood like a cork, to leave narrow straits through which the tides raced in and out. Once in past the neck of the bottle, the water ran deeper and the shore plunged steeply into the loch. Hohenheim and Zumal stood at the head of the narrows, looking to the water.

Darwin squinted across at the other side, estimating angles and widths. He sucked his lips in over his gums. "What do you think, Colonel?"

"Eh? Think about what?"

"The depth, out in the middle there." Darwin followed Pole's gaze to where Hohenheim and his servant had moved to a small coble and were preparing to launch it. "Aye, it seems they may be answering my question for me soon enough—that's a sounding line they're loading with the paddles. Steep sides and hard rock. It would not surprise me to find that the loch sounds to a thousand feet. There's depth sufficient to cover a galleon ten times over."

"Or hide a devil as big as you choose." Pole wriggled in irritation, and Darwin patted him on the arm.

"Hold your water, Colonel. Our friends there will not be raising any treasure ship today; they lack equipment. With luck, they will do some of your work for you. Do not overestimate Hohenheim."

"You saw that he has great powers."

"Did I? I am less sure. Observe, he uses a boat, so at least he cannot walk upon the waters."

Their voices had been dropped to whispers, and while they spoke, Zumal had pushed the boat off, Hohenheim sitting in the bow. He was in the same motley clothes, quite at ease and hold-ing the sounding line in his lap. At his command Zumal paddled twenty yards off-shore, then checked their forward motion. Hoh-enheim stood up, swung his right arm backward and forward a couple of times, and released the line. Darwin muttered to him-self and leaned in concentration.

"What's wrong?" Pole had noticed Darwin's move from the corner of his eye.

"Nothing. Only a suspicion that Hohenheim . . . ."

Darwin's voice trailed off as the weighted line unwound end-lessly into the calm waters of the loch. Soon Hohenheim had paid out all that he held, still without touching bottom. He spoke to Zumal, gathered in the line, and sat quietly as the coble moved slowly off towards the mouth of the loch. He tried the line again, and as they moved farther, the depth decreased until it was less than twenty feet in the neck at the entrance.

Hohenheim nodded and said something to his companion. They both had all their attention on the line. It was Jacob Pole, looking back along the length of the inlet, who noticed the swirl-ing ripple spreading across its surface. It showed as a line of crosscurrent, superimposing itself on the pattern of wavelets that was now growing in response to the morning sea-breeze. The forward edge of the moving ripple was running steadily towards the coble at the seaward end of the loch. Pole gripped Darwin's arm hard.

"See it there. Along the loch."

The ripple was still moving. Now its bow was less than fifty yards from where Hohenheim was reeling in his line. As the spreading wave came closer, there seemed to be a hint of lighter grey moving beneath the surface. The wave moved closer to the boat, thirty yards, then twenty. Pole's grip had unconsciously tightened on Darwin's arm until his knuckles showed white. At last, where the bed of the loch became sharply shallower, the moving wavefront veered away to the left. Another moment and it was gone. All that remained were spreading ripples, lifting the coble gently as the light craft was caught in their swell.

Hohenheim looked round as he felt the motion of the boat, but there was nothing to be seen. After a moment he turned his attention back to the line.

Pole released his hold on Darwin.

"The Devil," he said softly. "We've seen the Devil."

Darwin's eyes were glittering. "Aye, and it's a Devil indeed. But what in the name of Linnaeus is it? That's a real test for your systems taxonomical. It is not a whale, or it would surface and sound for its breathing. It is not a great eel—not unless all our ideas on size are in preposterous error. And it cannot be fish or flesh in any bestiary I can construct."

"Be damned with the name we give it." The shaking in Pole's hand was more pronounced, from excitement and alarm. "It was *big*, to make a wave that size—and fast. You scoffed at me when I brought Little Bess, but I was right. We'll need protection when we're on the loch. I'll have to carry it here and set it up to train where we need—forget the muskets, they'll be no better than a peashooter with that monster."

"I am not sure that the cannon will serve any useful purpose. But, meanwhile, we have a duty." Darwin started heavily down the hill towards the loch side.

"Here, what are you up to?" Pole hesitated, then bent to pick up his pipe and spyglass from the heather as Hohenheim and his servant turned to face the sudden sounds from the hillside.

"To give fair warning," called Darwin over his shoulder. Then he was down by the water's edge, waving at the two in the boat and calling them to look behind them.

Hohenheim turned, scanned the loch's calm surface, then spoke quietly to Zumal. The black man paddled the coble in close to the loch side, running it to within a few feet of Darwin.

"I see no monster," Hohenheim was saying as Jacob Pole hurried up to them. "Nor did Zumal—and we were near, on water. Not spying in secret from shade of heather."

"There is a creature in the loch," said Darwin flatly. "Big, and possibly dangerous. I called to you for your own protection."

"Ah." Hohenheim put his finger to his nose and looked at Darwin with dark, suspicious eyes. "Very kind. You did not want to drive us from loch, eh? If so, you need better story—much better."

He looked at Darwin slyly. "So we are here for same purpose as each other. You would argue with that? I think not."

"If you mean a sunken galleon, for my part I would certainly argue." As he spoke, Darwin continued to scan the surface of the loch, seeking any sign of a new disturbance there. "I came here for quite different reasons."

"But I didn't," said Pole. "Aye, I'll admit it—why not? It drew me here, three hundred miles, that galleon, just as it drew you. How did you hear of it?"

Hohenheim pulled his tattered cloak around him and stretched to his full height. "I have methods, secret methods. Accept that I heard, and do not question."

"All right, if that's what you want, but I would like to suggest an alliance. What do you say? There's a ship out yonder, and Dr. Darwin spoke the truth, there is something out in the loch that needs to be watched for. The people of Malkirk set no value on the galleon, but we do. What do you say? Work together, we and you, and we'd have the work done in half the time. Equal shares, you and us."

Pole stopped for breath. All his words had rushed out in one burst, while Hohenheim had listened, his black eyebrows arched. Now he laughed aloud and shook his head.

"Never, my good Colonel. Never. If we were equal, then maybe. Maybe I would listen. But we are not equal. I am ahead of you—in everything. In knowledge, skills, tools. Do it, my friend, try and beat me. I have power you lack, eh? Knowledge you lack, eh? Equipment, you ask about? Yesterday I was in Inverness, buying tools for seeing loch. Tonight it comes, tomorrow we use. Here, see for self."

He snapped his fingers a few inches from Jacob Pole's chin. As usual his gesture seemed exaggerated, larger than life, and when he opened his hand he was holding a square of brown paper.

"Here is list. Read, see for self—you will need every item on it. And you will be forced to buy in Inverness, two days away for you. By time you ready to begin, we will be finished and away from here."

Pole's sallow face had flushed at the tone in Hohenheim's voice. He shook off Darwin's hand and stepped within inches of the tall doctor.

"Hohenheim, last night you impressed me mightily. And you did us both a favor giving us those potions. This morning Dr. Darwin did his best to return that favor, warning you of a danger out on the loch. Instead of thanking him you insult us, saying we made up a monster to keep you away. Well, go ahead, ignore the warning. But don't look for help from me if you get in trouble. And as for the galleon, we'll work without you." He stepped back. "Come on, Dr. Darwin, I see no reason to stay here longer."

He turned and began to stride back up the hillside. Hohenheim looked after him and waved one hand in a contemptuous gesture of dismissal. His laugh followed Pole up the hill, while Darwin stood silent, staring hard at the other's lean face and body. His face was an intent mask of thought and dawning conviction.

"Dr. Hohenheim," he said at last. "You have mocked a well-meant and sincere warning; you have refused Colonel Pole's honest offer of cooperation; and you have dismissed my word when I told you I did not come to Malkirk for the galleon. Very well, that is your option. Let me say only this, then I will leave you to ponder it. The danger in the loch is real, I affirm again—more real than I would have believed an hour ago, more real than the treasure that you are so intent on seeking. But beyond that, *Doctor* Hohenheim, I think I know what you are and how you came here. Bear that in mind, the next time you seek to astonish Malcolm Maclaren and his simple villagers with your magic flights to Inverness, or your panaceas drawn from the air."

He snapped his fingers—clumsily, with none of Hohenheim's panache—turned, and began to stump after Jacob Pole up the hilly path that led to Malkirk. Hohenheim's jeering laugh sped his progress as he went.

"He's still there, with another crowd around him. Now he's taken a big knitting needle from one of the women. I wonder what he's going to do with it? I could give him a suggestion or two."

Jacob Pole stood upright, turning from the window where he had stooped to look at the open area between the houses.

"Here, Doctor, come over and look at this."

Darwin sighed, closed his Commonplace Book in which he was carefully recording observations of the local flora, and stood up.

"And with what new mystery are we now being regaled?" He looked out onto the dusk of a fine evening. On the green in front of them, Hohenheim had taken the knitting needle and waved it twice in a flashing circle. He grasped the blunt end in both hands, directed the bone point at his heart, and pushed inwards. The needle went into his chest slowly, an inch, then another, until it was buried more than half its length. He released his hold, and as the villagers around him gasped, a bead of crimson blood oozed out along the white bone and dripped onto his tunic.

Hohenheim let the needle remain for a few seconds, a white spike of bone deep in his chest. Then he slowly withdrew it, holding it cupped in his palms. When it was fully clear, he ran the length between fingers and thumb, spun it in a flashing circle, and handed it to be passed among the villagers. They touched it gingerly. As it went from hand to hand, he took a small round box from his cloak, dug out a nailful of black salve on his index finger, and rubbed it into the round hole in his shirt. He was smiling.

"What is that drug?" Pole had his nose flattened against the dirty glass. "To save him from a wound like that—I've never known anything like it."

"I think I have," said Darwin drily, and went back to his seat. But Jacob Pole was no longer listening. He went to the door and out, to join the group watching Hohenheim. The latter nodded as he appeared.

"Good evening again, Colonel." His voice was friendly, as though the morning incident had never happened. "We'll have no sea monsters, eh? But you come at right time. Now I will show antidote, cure for all poisons. So far, I have used only for crowned heads of Europe. Great secret of high value." He glanced towards the house. "A pity that Dr. Darwin is not here, he might learn much—or maybe not."

He reached into the tall cabinet by his side and took out a slim container of oily fluid. The pitch stopper came out easily, and he sniffed at it for a moment.

"Very good. Here is phial, see? Now, pass it round, one to another. Smell it—but not taste it. Deadly poison. If you want, replace with other poison—makes no difference to my antidote. I have made this extract from yew leaves. Colonel, you take it."

Pole sniffed carefully at the bottle. "It's terrible."

"Pass on to next man."

The villager next to Pole handled the bottle delicately, as though it might explode. It went from hand to hand, some sniffing, others content to look; and at last came back to Hohenheim.

"Good. Now watch close." He reached again into the cabinet beside him and took out a neatly made cage of iron spokes around a wooden frame. A grey rat ran from side to side within, nervously rearing up against the narrow bars and sniffing hungrily at the air. Hohenheim held the cage high for a few seconds, so that the villagers could observe the rat closely. He set the cage on the ground, poured a drop or two of liquid from the phial onto a fragment of oat bread, and slipped it deftly between the bars.

The rat paused for a few moments, while the circle of villagers held their breath. At last the rat sidled forward, sniffed the bread, and devoured it.

He put his left hand to his right wrist and began to count in a clear, deep voice. At thirty, the rat hesitated its movements around the floor of the cage, and reared up against the bars. Ten more beats, and it slipped to its belly, paws scrabbling against the wood.

Hohenheim did not wait to complete the count. He lifted the phial to his lips and tossed the contents down his throat. As the villagers muttered to themselves, he inverted the bottle, allowing a few last drops of viscous liquid to fall to the grass.

"Now—and quickly—the antidote."

He pulled a flask of green liquid from his cloak, drained it, and carefully replaced the stopper. Amid the excited hubbub of the watching group, talking to each other in Gaelic about what they had witnessed, Hohenheim turned to Malcolm Maclaren. He was quite calm and relaxed, with no trace of nervousness about the poison.

"There is a limited amount of this antidote. If any have desperate need—or want for future use—I can make arrangement. Normally I do not sell, but here where doctors few I will make special case. You tell them, eh? While you do it"—he was looking at the southern road in the gathering dusk, nodding knowingly—"I think I have business to attend. See? I bought yesterday in Inverness, now it comes. If you will help unload, I can use tomorrow."

He pointed to the laden cart coming towards them, drawn easily down the hill by two dusty horses. "Those are my supplies for work here." He turned to Jacob Pole." As I told you, we are well advanced in plans. We have located the wreck, we have equipment to look at it. Maybe you and Dr. Darwin stop wasting your time here, would like to make arrangements to go home to south? Galleon will be done before you begin to look, eh? So good night, Colonel, and sleep well.''

He nodded to Pole, bowed again to the circle of villagers, and strolled away towards the arriving cart. It was heavily laden with boxes and packages, and most of the villagers followed him, openly inquisitive. Jacob Pole stood, biting at a fingernail and staring angrily after Hohenheim.

''Arrogant pox-hound!'' he said to Zumal, who alone still stood by him. The black man ignored him. He was busy. He turned the dead rat out of the cage, replaced everything back in the tall cabinet, and carefully closed it. Placing it on a low trolley, he pushed it to the house and went inside. While Pole still stood there undecided, Malcolm Maclaren came back along the path towards him. The stocky Scotsman was looking worried, biting his lip and frowning.

''Colonel, I'm not wantin' to trouble ye now, but is Dr. Darwin inside an' available for a word?''

''He is inside.'' Pole still sounded angry. ''But if you can keep him to one word, you're a better man than I am.''

He led the way to the house. Darwin was sitting in the same chair, still at work on his notes. A bottle of Athole brose stood untouched by his side, and he had been forced to light the oil lamp, but otherwise everything was exactly as Pole had left it. Darwin looked up and nodded calmly to Maclaren.

''Another display of medical thaumaturgy, I have no doubt. What was the latest wonder? *Ex Hohenheim semper aliquid novi,* if you will permit me to paraphrase Pliny.'' His tone was cheerful as he laid down his pen and closed the book. ''Well, Malcolm Maclaren, what can I do for you?''

The Scot fidgeted uneasily for a few seconds, his dark face working under the full growth of beard.

''I did not come to talk to ye of Hohenheim,'' he said at last. ''No, nor of your galleon that ye seek to raise. I'm askin' help. Ye may recall I spoke to ye about my brother, away inland these past two month. We had word come in today, rare bad news. He took an accident, out on the mountains. A fall.''

Darwin puffed out his cheeks but did not speak. Malcolm Maclaren rubbed his big hands together, struggling for the right words.

''A bad fall,'' he said finally. ''An' we hear of injury to his

head. They're bringin' him on back here, an' I'm expectin' him
tomorrow, before nightfall. I was thinkin' . . . ." He paused,
then the words came in one rush. "I was wonderin' if ye might
be willin' to do some kind of examination of him and see if
there's any treatment that would help him to regain his health
and strength—we have plenty money, that's no problem, an' we'll
pay your usual fee an' more, if I have to."

"Aha," said Darwin, so softly that Jacob Pole had trouble
catching his words. "At last I think we see it." He stood up.
"Fee is not an issue, Malcolm Maclaren. I will examine him
gladly and give you my best opinion as to his condition. But I
wonder a little that you are not consulting Dr. Hohenheim. He
is the one who has been displaying prodigies of medical skill to
the people of your village. Whereas I have done nothing here to
show power as a physician."

Maclaren gloomily shook his grizzled head. "Don't say that.
I've had argument enough this very day on that subject, from
man and woman both. I saw what he can do. Yet there's some-
thin' I canna' put a name to, that makes me . . . ."

His voice trailed off and he and Darwin stood eye to eye for
a long moment, until Darwin nodded.

"You're an observing man, Malcolm Maclaren, and a shrewd
one. Those are rare qualities. If your evaluation of Dr. Hohenheim is not one that you can readily place on logical foundations,
that is not necessarily sufficient reason to mistrust it. Like the
animals, humans communicate on many levels more basic than
words."

He turned to Jacob Pole. "You heard the request, and I am
sure you see the problem it creates for me. I promised to help
you with your equipment. But if I am also to be here, awaiting
the arrival of Maclaren's brother, I will be unable to do it. I
know you will not wish to wait another day—"

"And there's no reason for that," said Maclaren gruffly. "If
it's another pair of hands ye need, I've twenty men ready to
serve—even if I have to break heads to persuade them of it.
When do ye need that help?"

"Tomorrow afternoon will do well enough." Jacob Pole
sensed that Maclaren was in his most cooperative mood. "I'll
want help to carry something to the loch. On that score, you
know all about the Devil there. But have you ever seen it yourself, and is it dangerous?"

''Aye, I've seen it, but never close, and never more than a shape in the water. Others here have seen it better. But I've never heard word of harm that came to any man that left the beast to live in its own way.'' Maclaren sat down, lifting his head to look at the others. ''We've had trouble in these parts, plenty of it, but it was not from the beast in the loch. Men have lost their lives, these past years in the Highlands—an' their heritances. But it was not the Devil's doin' that left the women lonely an' took all of us down close to beggary. For that ye have to look closer to your own kind. Aye, but I'm runnin' loose an' sayin' more than I ought to say.''

He shook his head, stood up, and abruptly left the room. Pole, following him to the door, could at first see no sign of him in the dusk. Then he made out a squat, dark figure striding rapidly across to the house with the black shutters. For the first time since they arrived, a light was showing in the window there.

It was a problem, and one that he could have anticipated. Jacob Pole crouched by the box that held Little Bess, grumbled to himself, and frowned at the late afternoon sunlight that was turning the peaks to the east into soft purple.

Darwin had been adamant, and Maclaren had agreed with him. The villagers could help carry the box, but they must not see the cannon inside. With weapons forbidden since the Disarming Act, a Highlander risked fines and transportation if he so much as assisted in knowingly carrying arms. The responsibility for handling Little Bess at the loch had to remain with Jacob Pole alone.

Very well; but how in damnation was he supposed to manhandle two hundredweight of cannon so that it pointed correctly to cover the loch? He was no Malcolm Maclaren, barrel chest and bulging muscles.

Grunting and swearing, Pole lifted the one pound balls out of the box and laid them on the canvas next to the bags of black powder. Thank God the weather was fine, so nothing would get wet [but better hurry, and be done before the dew fell]. With powder and shot removed, the box and cannon was just light enough to be dragged around to face the right direction. But now the sides of the box made it impossible either to prime or fire. And the cannon was too heavy to lift clear. Pole sighed and took the iron lever that he had used to pry open the top of the container. He began to remove the sides, one by one. It was a slow and tedious job, and by the time that the last pin had been loosed and the wooden frame laid to the ground, dusk was already well on its way.

At that point, he hesitated. He had intended to fire one test round, to make sure that range and angle were correct. But perhaps that should wait for the morning, when the light would be better and the travel of the ball more easily seen. After a few moments of thought, he loaded a bag of black powder and a ball, and placed the fuze all ready. Then he went across to a square of covering canvas, well away from the powder, and took out tobacco, pipe, flint and tinder. He sat down. His pipe was already charged, and the flint in his hand, when he looked down the hill to the surface of Loch Malkirk. He had been too absorbed in his own work to pay any attention there. Now he realized that two figures were busy by the loch's edge.

Hohenheim and Zumal were wheeling a handcart full of boxes and packages. At the flat-bottomed coble they halted and began to transfer cartons. As the breeze dropped, Hohenheim's words carried clearly up from the quiet water. Pole, crouched there in his brown cloak, was indistinguishable from the rocks and the heather.

He repressed his instinctive reaction, to call a greeting. As they finished loading and moved off-shore, he sat, pipe still unlit, and watched closely.

"Steady now, forward until I give the word." That was Hohenheim, leaning far forward in the boat's bow. With the sun almost on the horizon, the shadow of the boat was like a long, dark spear across the calm surface of the loch. Hohenheim was leaning over into the shadow, so that it was impossible for Jacob Pole to see what he was doing.

"Back-paddle, and slow us—*now*." The coble was stationary on the calm surface. The man in the bow reached down over the front of the boat, pulled up a loop of line from the water, and tied it to a ring in front of him.

"Looks good. I see no drift at all since yesterday." Hohenheim turned and nodded to Zumal. "Get ready now, and I will prepare the rest."

The black man laid down the paddle and began to strip off his clothes. The setting sun was turning the surface of the loch into a single glassy glare in Jacob Pole's eyes, and Zumal was no more than a dark silhouette against the dazzling water. Pole raised a hand to shield his eyes and tried to get a closer look at Hohenheim's activities.

The scene suddenly changed. As he watched, the even surface of the loch seemed to tear, to split along a dark central line, and to divide into two bright segments. Pole realized that he was seeing the effects of a moving ripple, a bow wave that tilted the water surface so that the sunlight no longer reflected directly to his eyes. Something big was moving along the loch. He dropped his pipe unheeded to the heather, and his heart began to beat faster.

The coble was close to the seaward end of the loch, where the shallow water lay. The moving wave was still more than a quarter of a mile away in the central deep. But it was moving steadily along towards the boat. Pole watched in fascination as it came within about forty yards, to where the bed of the loch began to rise. Then the wave veered left and turned back along the shore. The two men in the coble were too busy to notice. Hohenheim had now taken a small barrel from the bottom of the boat, removed its top, and was adjusting something inside it. He said a few soft words to Zumal, naked now in the stern, and laughed. Behind them the ripples still spread across the sweep of water.

"Ready?"

Pole heard the single word from Hohenheim as the sun finally dipped below the western horizon and everything took on the deeper tones of true twilight. Zumal's nod was barely visible in the gloom.

"As soon as I lower it, follow it down. It lasts only a short while, so act quickly."

Pole watched the flash of flint and metal that followed the last words. It sparked three times, then there was the glow of tinder. Hohenheim was holding a smoldering wad of cotton over the open end of the barrel.

"*Now.*"

A dazzling white light was shining from the barrel's mouth. Hohenheim lifted it out and dropped it over the side. The flare sank at once to the bottom, but instead of being extinguished by the water it seemed to burn brighter than ever, with a blue-white flame.

The bottom of the loch was suddenly visible as a rugged, shiny floor of rock and sand. Close to the coble, just a few feet from the underwater flare, Jacob Pole could see the outline of a long ship's hulk. As he crouched by his cannon, almost too excited to breathe, he saw the naked form of Zumal slip over the side of the coble, swim to the float, and move hand-over-hand down to the anchor that had marked the wreck.

Shielding his eyes from the direct light, Pole peered at the shape of the hulk. After a few seconds he could make out details through the unfamiliar pattern of light and shadow on the bed of the loch. He gasped as he realized what he was seeing.

In the village, the fading light had been the signal for some new activity. Darwin could sense the bustle of movement through the walls of the house, and there was a constant clatter of footsteps in and out of the kitchen.

It was one of the few signs of a rising tension. After Jacob Pole left, Maclaren had dropped in every half hour, trying to appear casual, and spoken a few distracted words to Darwin before hurrying out again. At five o'clock Maclaren had made a final visit and departed with the woman who did the cooking, leaving Darwin to dine as best he might on cold goose, oat bread, chicken fricassee, and bread pudding, and to order his thoughts however he chose.

When Maclaren finally appeared again, he looked like a different person. His lowland garb was gone, and in its place were brogues, knee-length knitted socks, the kilt, and a black waistcoat with gold-thread buttons.

"Aye, I know," he said at Darwin's inquiring look. " 'Tis against the law yet to wear Highland dress. But I'll do no less to welcome my brother home, whatever the law says. An' there's talk of a change of the rule in a year or two, so what's the harm? Surely a man ought to be allowed to dress any which way he chooses. But would ye be all ready, then?"

Darwin nodded. He stood, picked up the well-worn medical chest that had been his companion on a thousand night journeys, and followed Maclaren outside into the warm spring night. The Highlander led the way at a stately pace to the stone house with the black shutters. In spite of the darkness, Darwin had the feeling that many eyes followed their progress from the shadows.

At the door Maclaren halted. "Dr. Darwin, I'm not one to

want to deceive myself. It's a bad wound, that I know, and I'm a man that respects the truth. I'm not after lookin' for ill news, but will ye gi' me the word, that ye'll tell me honest if it's good news or bad?''

The light was spilling out into the quiet night. Darwin turned to look steadily into the other man's worried eyes.

"Unless there is good reason to do it, to save life or lessen suffering, it is my belief that a full and honest diagnosis is always best. You have my word. No matter where the truth may take us tonight, I will provide it as I see it. And in return I ask that what I say should not create ill-feeling to me and to Colonel Pole.''

"Ye have that word, an' it's my life that stands behind it.''

Maclaren pushed the door wide open and they went on in.

The room had not changed, but now lamps had been placed in eight or nine places around it. Everything was well-lit and spotlessly clean. There were lamps on each side of the big bed, where a man lay covered to the chest by a tartan blanket.

Darwin stepped forward. For many seconds he was motionless, scrutinizing the man's chalk-white face and loose posture.

"What is his age?''

"Fifty-five.'' Maclaren's voice was a whisper.

Darwin stepped forward and turned the blanket back to the thighs. When he rolled back an eyelid under his thumb, the man did not move. He opened the mouth, studying the decaying teeth, and grunted to himself thoughtfully.

"Here. Help me turn him to his side.'' Darwin's voice was neutral, giving no clue as to his thoughts. With Maclaren's help they moved the man to his right side, revealing the red cicatrice that ran all the way from the crown of his head down to above the left temple. Darwin bent close and moved his hand gently along it, feeling the shape of the bone beneath the scar. The wound was indented, a deep cleft in the skull, and no hair grew above it.

Darwin sucked in a deep breath. "Aye, a sore wound indeed. One cleavage, straight from the sphenoid wing to the top of the calvaria. It is a wonder to see any man living after such an injury.''

He pulled the blanket back farther, to show the legs and feet covered in a white and gold robe. Then he was a long while silent, scowling down at the patient. He sniffed the man's breath,

examined nose and ears, and finally lifted the arms and legs to
palpate the joints and muscles. The palms of the hands and the
short, well-trimmed nails came in for their own brief examination, and he felt the condition of the sinews in wrists and ankles.

"Lift him to a sitting position," he said at last. "And let me
see his back."

The skin over the ribs was white and unmarked, free of all
sores and blemishes. Darwin nodded, looked again at the white
of the eye that showed beneath the lid, and sighed.

"You can let him lie back again. And you can tell some man
or woman that I have never in my life seen an injured person
better cared for. He has been fed, washed, exercised, and lovingly looked after. But his condition . . ."

"Tell me, Doctor." Maclaren's look was resolute. "Do not
disguise it."

"I will not, though my medical opinion will bring bitter news
for you. His wound will prove mortal, and his condition cannot
be improved. It can only worsen, and you must not expect any
waking from unconsciousness."

Maclaren clenched his teeth, and the muscles stood out along
his jaw. "Thank you, Doctor," he said in a whisper. "An' the
end, how far away will it be?"

"I can answer that only if you will give me some information.
How long has he been unconscious? It is apparent that this is
not a recent wound, with the degree of healing that it now ex-
hibits."

"Aye, ye speak true there." Maclaren's face was grim. "Near
three year, it has been. He was hurt in the summer of '73, and
not wakened after that. We've tended him since then."

"I am sorry to end your hopes." Darwin drew the sheet back
over the man on the bed. "He will die within the year. You
brought me a long way for this, Malcolm Maclaren. Your devotion deserves a better reward."

Maclaren looked swiftly to the door, then back again. "What
do ye mean, Doctor?"

Darwin waved his arm to door and window. "Let them all
come in, if you wish. They are as worried as you are, and it
serves no purpose to have them hide and listen outside."

"Ye think . . . ." Maclaren hesitated.

"Come on, man, and do it." Darwin leaned again to look at
the figure on the bed. "If you worry still about my state of

knowledge and discretion, I could offer you a tale. It is a story of loyalty and desperation. Of a man, who might be this very man here''—he touched the smooth brow of the unconscious patient— ''returned after many years to his home land. There was an accident. Let us put it that way, although a sword or axe could leave just such a wound. After the accident the man was lovingly cared for, and the doctors of these parts did all they could, but there was no progress in his condition. At last, despite daily exercise of muscles and the best food that could be found, he began to weaken, to show signs of worsening. More expert advice and medical attention seemed to be the only hope. But how to obtain it, without revealing all and risking the wrath of a still-vengeful government?''

''Aye, how indeed?'' said Maclaren. He sighed and walked over to the door. A few words of Gaelic, and a file of somber men and women into the room. Each went to the bed, knelt there for a moment, then moved back to stand by the wall. When all had entered, Maclaren spoke to them again, a longer speech this time. While Darwin watched, the faces in front of him seemed to fold and crumple as all hope drained from them.

''I have told them,'' said Maclaren, as he turned back to the bed.

Darwin nodded. ''I saw it.''

''They are brave folk. They will bear it bravely, whatever I tell them. But to ye I have told nothin', not one word, an' yet ye seem to know all. How can that be?'' Maclaren's voice was husky but he held his head up high. ''How can ye know this, as well as I know it? Are ye what Hohenheim has claimed to be, a man who can divine all by magical methods?''

''I would never claim what I believe impossible for any man.'' Darwin had moved forward again to the bed and was gently turning the head of the unconscious man. ''I proceed by much simpler methods, ones available to all. Let me, if you will, continue with my tale. This man needed help, if help could be found, from other physicians. It would be futile of me to plead excessive modesty and to deny that in the past few years my reputation as a court of last resort for difficult medical cases has spread throughout England—aye, and through Europe, too, if my friends are to be believed. Let us suppose it is true, and that my name was known here. Perhaps I could help, or at least tell the worst. But the idea of a direct approach, with a patient who was perhaps an outlaw and an exile—not to add that he is one of royal blood—why, that would be unthinkable. A subterfuge of some kind was necessary, one that would allow an examination without revealing too much. And if the patient could not easily be carried for a long distance, the presence of the physician in the Highlands must somehow be assured.''

He paused and looked up at Maclaren. ''Who was it worked out the details of the plan?''

Maclaren was sitting on the stone floor, his chin resting on his cupped hands. ''It was I,'' he said softly. ''An' God knows, it came from desperation, not from choosin'. But I still do not see how ye could know any of this.''

''I was suspicious before I left Litchfield. You followed the first rule of successful deception: build upon what is real, and invent as little as you must. But you went too far, with a double lure, of great treasure and of a fantastic animal. The beast in Loch Malkirk would have been sufficient to bring me here without further embroidery, but you could not have known that. So there was added the galleon and the priceless treasure, all to be revealed to me by the words of a dying man.''

Maclaren smiled ruefully. ''It worked. Ye came here, an' that was a surprise to me. So where was the error in it?''

''Your plan went astray not in outline, but in detail. You had hired good actors, that was necessary, and they were well-grounded in their roles—enough to convince Dr. Monkton. You had also told them to beware my examination, I surmise, since I would surely see through the deception. But Colonel Pole was there, and he was an accurate reporter. How could a tinker have the hands of a gentleman, or a delirious man suffer no fever?''

''We were not careful enough in choosin'—but still ye came, an' I don't see why ye did.''

''The mystery that you had never intended brought me, more than treasure or Devil. Before we left Litchfield, I was asking myself, what would make anyone try to draw me here, three hundred miles from home? That curiosity was *my* motive, but what could *their* motive be? From the moment that we set out I was vastly curious, and when I arrived here my perplexity was increased. For here was Hohenheim, and I could not readily see how he fitted the situation at all.''

Maclaren glanced around him at the circle of grieving faces. He shrugged. ''Dr. Darwin, I said that I will tell ye true, an' I will. But I swear by the man who lies there helpless before us—an' I know no higher oath than mine to Prince Charles Edward—I cannot tell why Hohenheim came. He was no part of my thoughts or plans, an' his arrival surprised me totally. I am sorry to disappoint ye.''

"You do not," said Darwin. He had a satisfied look on his face. "What you have just told me fleshes out the picture, and I can tell you the answer myself. As to how Hohenheim knew at once that I was a doctor, upon my arrival, that is easy. *You* had told him, by referring without thinking to a 'Doctor Darwin' who was coming to Malkirk. Hohenheim thought of me that way from the time you did it—but when he first spoke, that knowledge perturbed me mightily. As for the rest, Hohenheim has been the unintentional confusion factor, the place where your plan suffered an accidental complication. Look back to the instrument by which your scheme was carried out—the hired players—and you will see the rest. Hohenheim—''

The boom of a cannon sounded through the quiet night, shockingly loud and near. Darwin and Maclaren looked at each other in confusion. There was a rush to the door of the house as the echo carried back from the eastern hills.

It was not a Spanish galleon. Jacob Pole was sure of it, sure as soon as he saw the ship's lines by the light of the flare. Everything stood out clearly in that white and penetrating light, and even the crusting of silt and the deep corrosion of iron parts were not enough concealment. A man without naval experience might be fooled, because there were similarities enough to cause confusion; but Pole saw through those and was stunned by the knowledge. He was looking at a coastal cargo ship, high in the stern with three masts, and he had seen many like it in English and Irish waters. It was not—could not be—the galleon they were seeking. And Hohenheim and Zumal did not know it!

Pole squatted by Little Bess and frowned down at the scene below. Zumal was down on the wreck's listing deck, prising at the forward hatch with a long iron bar. It was slowly opening and releasing a cloud of fine silt that fogged the water. Outside that cloud, the bed of the loch showed as a dazzling confusion of white sand and black rock. Above, Hohenheim was busy in the coble, lowering other tools and preparing a second underwater flare.

They did not know enough about ships to realize that this was not a wreck likely to bear treasure of any kind. But if they had discovered and were exploring the wrong ship, so much the better. The galleon must be somewhere else in the loch.

Pole nodded to himself and looked back along the length of the inlet. If he had to search for another wreck, there could be no better time for it than now, when the floor of the loch was so brightly lit. The powerful light made every detail in the water visible for scores of yards. He could see schools of fish, flashing here and there in panic from the alien glare in the water. Away from the loch's entrance the whole underwater panorama was a frenzy of darting silver shapes. And a great shadow moved swiftly among them, scattering them wildly from its path.

The light allowed Jacob Pole to see what had been hidden from them the previous day. The Devil was speeding along, the crest of its back a couple of yards below the surface as it moved away from Zumal and the bright flare. Pole could see a small head and a long neck leading a massive body and powerful tail. The back was grey, and as it rolled to make a turn, there was a flash of pink on its sides, and brief sight of a red underbelly. It was at least seventy feet from head to tip of tail, and its swift forward motion came from the powerful body and winglike side fins.

The creature was flying blindly along the loch, seeking escape from the light. Its frenzied rush set up a big wave and brought the beast closer to the surface as it neared the inland end of the loch. The surface was foaming under the power of the lashing tail. As the Devil turned, the flare back at the loch entrance began to fade. A moment more, and the bow wave was racing back along the loch, with the beast close enough to the surface for the smooth back to be revealed.

Hohenheim had the second flare ready, and Zumal was hanging on the side of the coble, taking breath before he dived again. They were both looking uncertainly along the water, not sure what was causing the sudden pattern of choppy waves.

Pole stood up and waved. "Hohenheim! Look out—you're in danger."

Without waiting to see the effects of his shout, he bent over the cannon. It took a second or two to line Little Bess to fire along the loch, and another second to strike the spark and apply the match at the breech. His hands were trembling with tension, and he could not control them.

The beast in the loch was less than fifty yards from the coble, and both men below were now aware of its rapid approach. Zumal cried out and tried to hoist himself into the coble, while Hohenheim left the second flare to burn in the bow while he took up the paddle and tried to move the boat away towards the safety of the shore. They were going too slowly. Pole glanced up and saw that the Devil's dash towards the sea would take it straight into the coble.

As he straightened to shout again, the cannon beside him roared and leapt backwards in recoil. He was surrounded by black smoke and could scarcely see where the ball went. The direction was good, but the timing a little too late. Instead of hitting the Devil's body, the ball grazed the long tail and spent its energy uselessly in the waters of the loch. The beast leapt forward even faster.

A second shot would take minutes to ready. Pole watched helplessly as the Devil surged frantically for the loch entrance.

The second flare was still alight. At the impact it flew high in the air. Fragments of the coble went with it, and Hohenheim's body spun away, the limbs loose and broken like a wrecked puppet. There was an agonized scream—Hohenheim or Zumal, Pole could not tell—and a crash of splintered wood. Then the Devil's broad back was standing six feet above the surface of the water as the beast thrashed and wriggled its way open through the shallows to the sea. It headed west and plunged into the deep water beyond the reefs.

Jacob Pole did not wait to chart the course of the Devil's departure. He was running down the hill, with the cannon's blast and the human scream of final agony still loud in his ears.

The surface of the loch was calm again. There was nothing to be seen but the bobbing light of the flare and shattered remnants of the coble.

At the sound of the cannon shot Malcolm Maclaren's face had turned white. He looked at the figure on the bed.

"If that is soldiers, an' him here. . . ."

Already four or five of the men had run silently from the room. Maclaren gestured to the women, and they moved to lift the unconscious man from the bed and wrap him in blankets.

Before they could reach him, Darwin stood in front of them, his hand raised.

"Hold this action, and your men, too. Maclaren, that came from the loch—from Colonel Pole. There may be trouble there, but it's no danger for you or for your Prince. If you want to send men anywhere, send them to the loch. That's where help is needed."

Logic had spoken to Maclaren faster than Darwin could. He had recalled the cannon that Pole had brought with him and carried to the loch. He shouted a command to the men outside, then moved swiftly over to the figure on the bed. There was new hopelessness in his expression, as though he was fully realizing for the first time the import of Darwin's pronouncement on the future.

He bent to kiss the unconscious man's hand, then looked up at Darwin.

"Ye are right about Colonel Pole, an' my men will be at the loch in minutes. An' if ye are right about this other, he canna' be revived—ever. It makes no difference now if he is living or dead; if he remains like this, it's over. Our fight's all over an' done." The despair in his voice was total. Darwin moved to his side and laid a gentle hand on his shoulder.

"Malcolm Maclaren, I am truly sorry. If it will ease your mind at all, be assured of this: Prince Charles Edward departed this world as a conscious, thinking human the moment that he took that injury. If you had found a way to transport me here to Scotland the very day that it happened, I could have done nothing for him."

"I hear ye." Maclaren rubbed a knuckle at his eyes. "The line is ended, an' now I must learn to bear it. But it comes hard, even though I've feared that word all these past three years. It is an end to all hope here."

"So help me to look to those who can still be assisted. Bring lamps, and let us go down to the loch." Darwin started for the door, then instinctively turned back to the bedside to pick up his medical case. Before he reached it, there was a shout and a commotion outside the house.

"Come on, Doctor," said Maclaren. "That's my men calling, something about Colonel Pole."

It took a few seconds to see anything after the bright lamps of the room. Darwin followed Maclaren and stood there blink-

ing, peering up the hill to where the group outside was pointing.
At last he could see a trio of Highlanders. In their midst and
supported by two of them was a stumbling and panting Jacob
Pole. He staggered up to Malcolm Maclaren and stood wheezing
in front of him.

"Talk to your blasted men—I can't get them to understand
plain English. Send 'em back to the loch."

"Why? Dr. Darwin was worried for your safety there, but
here ye are, safe an' well."

"Hohenheim and Zumal." Pole held his side and coughed.
"At the loch, but I couldn't help. Both dead, in the water."

Maclaren barked a quick order to three of the villagers, and
they left at a trot. While Pole leaned wearily on supporting arms,
Darwin stood motionless.

"Are you sure?" he said at last. "Remember, there have been
other examples where Hohenheim's actions were not what they
appeared to be."

"I'm sure. Sure as I stand here. I saw the boat smashed to
pieces with my own eyes. Saw Hohenheim broken, and both
their bodies." He bent forward, rubbing at his balding head with
a hand that still shook with fatigue. "The galleon they looked
at was the wrong ship. I saw it, there's an empty hold in an old
wreck, that's what they died for. The wrong ship. That's their
end."

"Aye, the end indeed," said Maclaren. He was watching as
a silent procession of women carried an unconscious body out
of the black-shuttered house and away towards the main village.
"An' a bitter end for all. Hohenheim came here of his own wish,
but it was no plan of mine that would make him die here." He
began to walk with head lowered after the women.

"Not quite the end, Malcolm Maclaren." Darwin's somber
tone halted the Scotsman. "There is one more duty for us tonight, and in some ways it is the most difficult and sorrowful of
all. Give me ten more minutes of your time, then follow your
lord."

"Nothing could be worse," said Maclaren. But he turned and
came back to where Darwin and Pole stood facing each other.
"What is left?"

"Hohenheim. He came here uninvited, and you asked why.
You did not seek to bring him, and I certainly did not. He has

been a mystery to all of us. Come with me, and we will resolve it now.''

Followed by Pole and Maclaren, he led the way across the turf to the house where Hohenheim and his servant had stayed. The door was closed, and no light showed within.

Darwin stepped forward and banged hard on the dark wood. When no answer came he gestured to Maclaren to bring the lamp that he was holding nearer, and opened the door. The three men paused on the threshold.

''Who is there?'' said a sleep-slurred voice from the darkness.

''Erasmus Darwin.'' He took the lamp from Maclaren, held it high, and walked forward to light up the interior.

''What do you want?'' The man in the bed rolled over, pushed back the cover, and sat up. Jacob Pole looked at him, gave a superstitious groan of fear, and stepped backwards.

The man in front of them was Hohenheim. The tunic and patchwork cloak hung over a chair, but there could be no mistaking the hooked nose, ruddy cheeks, and darting black eyes.

''It's impossible,'' said Pole. ''Less than ten minutes ago, I saw him dead. It can't be, I saw—''

''It is all too possible,'' said Darwin softly. ''And it is as I feared.''

He leaned towards the man in the bed, who was now more fully awake and beginning to scowl at the intruders. ''The deception is over. Hohenheim—for want of a true name I must continue to use your old one—we bring terrible news. There was an accident at the loch. Your brother is dead.''

The red cheeks paled, and the man stood up suddenly from the bed. ''You are lying. This is some trick, to try and trap me.''

Darwin shook his head sadly. ''It is no trick, and no trap. If I could find another way to say this, I would do so. Your brother and Zumal died tonight in Loch Malkirk.''

The man in front of him stood for a second, then gave a wild shout and rushed past them.

''Stop him,'' cried Darwin, as Hohenheim plunged out of the door and into the night.

''Is he dangerous?'' asked Maclaren.

''Only to himself. Send your men to follow and restrain him until we can reach him.''

Maclaren moved to the door and shouted orders to the startled group of villagers who were still waiting near the black-shuttered

house. Three of them set off up the hill in pursuit of Hohenheim's running figure. When Maclaren came back into the room,
Jacob Pole was slumped against the wall, his head bowed.

"Is he all right?" Maclaren said to Darwin.

"Give him time. He's overtired and he's had a great shock."

"I'm fine." Pole sighed. "But I've no idea what's going on
here. I never saw any brother, or any deception. Are you sure
you have an explanation for all this?"

"I believe that I do." Darwin walked around the room, studying the cases and boxes stacked against the walls. He finally
stopped at one of them and bent to open it.

"Why did these men come to Malkirk?" he said. "That is
easily answered. They came to seek treasure and the galleon.
But there is a better question: *How* did they come—how did they
know a galleon was in the loch? There is only one answer to
that. *They heard it from the actors hired to tempt me here.* And
is it not obvious that we have been dealing with stage players
here? You saw them and heard them. Think of the gestures, all
larger than life, and of the hands that drew materials from the
air. Their magic spoke to me strongly of the strolling magician,
the attraction at the fairs and festivals throughout the whole of
England."

"But how did you know their feats were not genuine?"

"Colonel, that would lie outside the compass of my beliefs.
It is much easier to believe in prestidigitation, in the cunning of
hand over eye. I reached that conclusion early, but I was faced
with one impossible problem. How could a man be here today,
and a few hours later be in Inverness? No stage magic or trickery
would permit that. Accept that a man cannot be in two places at
once, and you are driven to a simple conclusion: there must be
two men, able to pass as each other. Think of the value of that
for impossible stage tricks, and think how practice would perfect
the illusion. Two brothers, and Zumal as the link that would
travel between them to protect it."

"But you had no possible proof," protested Pole. "I mean,
a suspicion is one thing, but to jump from that to certainty—"

"Requires only that we use our eyes. You saw Hohenheim, at
the village. And the next day you saw him again, at the loch.
But in the village he favored his left hand, constantly—recall for
yourself his passes in the air, and his seizing from nowhere of
flasks and potions. Yet at the loch he had suddenly become *right-*

handed, for casting lines, for working the boat, for everything. We were seeing brothers, and like many twins they were one *dexter*, and one *sinister*."

Maclaren was nodding to himself. "I saw it, but I had not the wit to follow it. Now one of them is dead, and the other . . . ."

"Knows a grief that I find hard to imagine. We must seek him now and try to give him a reason for living. He should not be left alone tonight. With your permission, I will stay here, and when he is brought from the loch, I will talk to him—alone."

"Very well. I will go now and see if they have him safely." Maclaren walked quietly to the door.

"And here is your proof," said Darwin. He lifted from the open chest in front of him a long cloak. "See the hidden pockets and the tube that can be used to carry materials from them to the hands. No supernatural power; only skills of hand, and human greed."

Maclaren nodded. "I see it. An' when ye find the reason that makes him want to go on livin', ye can tell it to me."

He left, and Jacob Pole looked across at Darwin. "Does he mean that? Why would he think to stop living?"

"He has had a bad shock tonight. But for him I do not worry. Malcolm Maclaren is a brave man, and a strong one. When he recovers from his present sorrow, his life will begin again—better, I trust, than before."

Pole went across to the empty bed and sat down on it with a groan. "I'll be glad when tonight is over. I've had too much excitement for one day. Let tomorrow come, and I can go to the loch again and seek the *real* galleon." His eyes brightened. "If there's one thing to pull from this sorry mess, perhaps it will still be the bullion."

Darwin coughed. "I am afraid not. There is no treasure—no galleon. It was only a part of the tale that was used to draw us here."

"What!" Pole lifted his head. "Pox on it, are you telling me that after all our work we came three hundred miles for nothing? That there is no treasure?"

Darwin nodded. "There is no treasure. But we did not come for nothing." Now it was his eyes that showed a sparkle of excitement. "There is still the Devil. Tomorrow we will go again to the loch and learn the true nature of that animal. For that I would travel far more than three hundred miles. I want to study the beast thoroughly, and determine what—''

He paused. Something in Jacob Pole's unhappy look told him that the night's bad news was not yet complete.

FURTHER READING

FICTION

Aickman, Robert. "Niemandswasser," *Cold Hand in Mine*.

Baker, Carlos. "The Prevaricator," *The Talismans and Other Stories*.

Benson, A.C. "Out of the Sea," *The Thrill of Horror*.

Bloch, Robert. "Terror in Cut-Throat Cave," *Creature!*

Bradbury, Ray. "The Fog Horn," *The Stories of Ray Bradbury*.

Bradbury, Ray. "The Woman," *The Stories of Ray Bradbury*.

Brennan, Joseph Payne. "Slime," *Monsters, Monsters, Monsters*.

Buzzati, Dino. "The Colomber," *Restless Nights*.

Coburn, Anthony. "The Tale of the Fourth Stranger," *The Saturday Evening Post Stories*.

Cooper, Basil. "The Flabby Men," *And Afterward, the Dark*.

de Camp, L. Sprague. "Dead Man's Chest," *The Purple Pterodactyls*.

Drake, David. "Out of Africa," *From the Heart of Darkness*.

Engelhardt, Frederick. "The Draken," *Phoenix Feathers*.

Gallun, Raymond Z. "Davy Jones' Ambassador," *Earth Is the Strangest Planet*.

Greene, Sonia. "The Invisible Monster," *The Horror in the Museum and Other Revisions*.

Helfer, Harold. "Sea Serpent of Spoonville Beach," *The Bear Went Over the Mountain*.

Hoch, Edward D. "The Theft of the Silver Lake Serpent," *The Thefts of Nick Velvet*.

Hodgson, William Hope. "The Sea Horses," *Deep Waters*.

Hodgson, William Hope. "A Tropical Horror," *Creature!*

Hope-Simpson, Jacynth. "The Water Monster," *Monsters, Monsters, Monsters*.

Jenkins, William Fitzgerald. "De Profundis," *Far Boundaries*.

Kagan, Janet. "The Loch Moose Monster," *Isaac Asimov's Science Fiction Magazine*, March, 1989.

Kipling, Rudyard. "A Matter of Fact," *Kipling Stories*.

Mansfield, Katherine. "At the Bay," *The Art of the Novella*.

Masefield, John. "Port of Many Ships," *The Faber Books of Animal Stories*.

Miller, P. Schuyler. "The Thing on Outer Shoal," *Famous Monster Tales*.

Mitchison, Naomi. "The Sea Horse," *Modern Scottish Short Stories*.

Moravia, Alberto. "Back to the Sea," *The Existential Imagination*.

Outerson, William. "Fire in the Galley Stove," *Davy Jones' Haunted Locker*.

Reed, A.W. and Hames, Inez. "The Monster of Cakaudrove," *Monsters, Monsters, Monsters*.

Schmitz, James H. "Grandpa," *The Arbor House Treasury of Modern Science Fiction*.

Usher, Gray. "Ebb Tide," *The Graveyard Companion*.

Waldrop, Howard. "God's Hooks," *Bestiary!*

Walter, Elizabeth. "A Monstrous Tale," *Dead Woman and Other Haunting Experiences*.

Wyndham, John. "Phase Two," *Weirdies, Weirdies, Weirdies*.

NONFICTION

Baumann, Elwood D. *The Loch Ness Monster*.

Bendick, Jeanne. *The Mystery of the Loch Ness Monster*.

Canning, John. (ed.) *Fifty True Mysteries of the Sea*.

Clair, Colin. *Unnatural History: An Illustrated Bestiary*.

Cohen, Daniel. *The Encyclopedia of Monsters*.

Costello, Peter. *In Search of Lake Monsters*.

Costello, Peter. *The Magic Zoo: The Natural History of Fabulous Animals*.

Mackal, Roy P. *The Monster of Loch Ness*.

Morris, Rowana and Desmond. *Men and Snakes*.

Sweeney, James B. *Sea Monsters: A Collection of Eyewitness Accounts*.

Thompson, C.J.S. *The Mystery and Lore of Monsters*.

Welfare, Simon and Fairley, John. *Arthur C. Clarke's Mysterious World*.